Praise for

"Farcical, tongue-in-cheek, ~~and sometimes just plain silly,~~ *The Gentleman* pays homage to late Victorian melodrama and in its tone aspires to a P. G. Wodehouse–like insouciance. . . . [It] does provide consistent amusement for an idle evening. . . . On several occasions, Leo nearly approaches Wodehouse in the zing of his similes."
—*Washington Post*

"Wonderfully demented and comical . . . It's rather as if Tom Holt and Oscar Wilde got together and decided to do up a steampunk novelty. . . . Vain, self-centered, whiny, hyperbolic, Lionel is nonetheless a captivating raconteur, and reading this book, one falls fully under his hilarious tale-telling prowess. . . . This novel displays a kind of timeless quality that will ensure a long life for it. It might have appeared in the pages of *Punch*, circa 1886. Or on an augmented-reality tablet in the year 2086. Whenever you encounter it, you will be guaranteed a robust, riotous romp."
—*Locus*

"If you have a soft spot for whimsical Victorian pastiches . . . *The Gentleman* is your perfect end-of-summer read. . . . All in all a complete pleasure."
—*Vox*

"Leo has a whimsical gift. . . . His characters are rich with personality and eccentricity. . . . Leo brings [them] to life with charm, wit, and pomp, and he builds a fully realized—if not a little wacky—Victorian London teeming with adventure and mystery. . . . And yet, so much of the novel's great appeal comes from the hilariously realistic way in which it depicts the quirkiness of writers, the idiosyncratic relationships between them, and the painstaking work of their editors."
—*Electric Literature*

"A new favorite of mine is Forrest Leo's debut *The Gentleman*, a Victorian-era adventure if Lizzie Bennet were held hostage by David Lynch and Mel Brooks. Hilarious, devious, and totally entertaining, it's not one to miss."   —*Planet Jackson Hole*

"A fast-paced, comedic farce through hell . . . Fans of steampunk and Lemony Snicket will love this one."   —KQED.org

"[A] deliciously snarky story . . . I'm reminded of Glen David Gold's 'Carter Beats the Devil' and W. E. Bowman's classic parody *The Ascent of Rum Doodle*, although for my money, Leo's writing is even more hilarious."   —*Alaska Dispatch News*

"A lighthearted comedy of errors that never takes itself too seriously, *The Gentleman* is a delight."   —*BookRiot*

"This novel weaves together a brilliant sense of voice, a classic comedic touch that's as potent as it is gentle, and a group of characters that could just as easily exist in a *Monty Python's Flying Circus* sketch as they could in a P. G. Wodehouse novel. With his first book, Leo delivers us a story that's entertaining on about a dozen different levels, and he does it with a sense of joy that imbues his often self-serious narrator with a quality that makes every page lovable. . . . Endlessly brisk, charming, and most importantly, clever . . . [the] characters . . . seem both wholly original yet clearly carved out of the page of a thumping good potboiler. It's a marriage of old and new that's never tiring, and it makes for a delightful page-turner."   —*BookPage*

"With lively illustrations by Mahendra Singh . . . this debut Victorian steampunk novel is a fun romp with witty wordplay, a diverse array of quirky characters, and a surprisingly lovely ending."   —*Library Journal*

"Riotous . . . In his debut, Leo does an inspired job of parodying the conventions of Victorian fiction. Hilarious dialogue, a Pythonesque sense of the absurd, and comical complications worthy of Thorne Smith at his 'dev'lish' best round out the tale."   —*Publishers Weekly*

"A funny and charming romp, cheerfully wearing its influences—Wodehouse, Douglas Adams, Jack Pendarvis, Christopher Moore, and Monty Python—like arm garters. I thoroughly enjoyed this frothy, sweet story that reaffirms the romantic notions behind love and storytelling."
                              —Glen David Gold, author of *Carter Beats the Devil*

"An effervescent book with a cheerfully lunatic plot. Cavalier, funny, and totally engrossing. It's a delicious crumpet of a novel that will leave you wondering if Forrest Leo drinks tea with the devil."   —Sara Levine, author of *Treasure Island!!!*

"Let us all bow down before the nutty and delightful romp that is *The Gentleman*. An assured stylist tells a hilarious story with perfect pacing and aplomb: yes, please."
                              —Henry Alford, author of *Would It Kill You to Stop Doing That?: A Modern Guide to Manners*

"Simultaneously very strange and very familiar, *The Gentleman* has all the right echoes and influences—the 'scientific romance,' the postmodernist novel, the comedy of manners. It's witty and erudite, with great whiffs of Wells and Wilde and Wodehouse—all of it beautifully combined, with one of the best opening sentences I've read in years. Go on—open up!"
                              —Geoff Nicholson, author of *The Lost Art of Walking*

PENGUIN BOOKS

THE GENTLEMAN

Forrest Leo was born in 1990 on a homestead in remote Alaska, where he grew up without running water and took a dogsled to school. He holds a BFA in drama from New York University and has worked as a carpenter and a photographer, and in a cubicle.

www.forrestleo.com

The Gentleman

Being a Truthful Account Concerning the
Hazards of Love, Marriage, Duels, Poetry,
Inventors, Family, Anarchists, Airships,
Intercourse with the Devil, Ladies'
Undergarments, Painting from Life,
the History of Exploration, &c.

———◆———

Set Down by Mr Lionel Lupus Savage
& Edited with Objections by Mr Hubert
Lancaster, Esq, Containing Nothing Either
Allegorical or Metaphorical in Nature
& Never Deviating from the Truth.

FORREST LEO

PENGUIN PRESS

PENGUIN BOOKS

An imprint of Penguin Random House LLC
375 Hudson Street
New York, New York 10014
penguin.com

First published in the United States of America by Penguin Press,
an imprint of Penguin Random House LLC, 2016
Published in Penguin Books 2017

ISBN 9780399562631 (hardcover)
ISBN 9780399562655 (paperback)
ISBN 9780399562648 (ebook)

Printed in the United States of America
1   3   5   7   9   10   8   6   4   2

Designed by Amanda Dewey
Illustrations by Mahendra Singh

This is a work of fiction. Names, characters, places, and incidents
either are the product of the author's imagination or are used fictitiously,
and any resemblance to actual persons, living or dead, businesses,
companies, events, or locales is entirely coincidental.

To

Dad,

who'd have been proud,

and

Frank M. Robinson,

who taught me how

EDITOR'S NOTE.

I have been charged with editing these
pages and seeing them through to
publication, but I do not like the task.
I wish it on record that I think
it better they had been burned.

—Hubert Lancaster, Esq

In one great gulp I drank my tea and gazed

Upon the grim and gloomy world anew—

And gasped at how my griping eye had lied.

The rain still fell, the wind still blew, but now

I thought it grand! I love the rain!

Not rain nor cloud did cloud my eye—'twas thirst!

—Lionel Lupus Savage, from 'The Epiphany'*

---

*I have included this excerpt as epigraph because I believe it gives a sense of Mr Savage's poetic temperament for those unfamiliar with his work. It is taken from his first collection, *Pasquinades and Peregrinations*. I have not consulted him upon its inclusion.—HL.

The Gentleman

One

In Which I Find Myself
Destitute & Rectify Matters
in a Drastic Way.

My name is Lionel Savage, I am twenty-two years old, I am a poet, and I do not love my wife. I loved her once, not without cause—but I do not anymore. She is a vapid, timid, querulous creature, and I find after six months of married life that my position has become quite intolerable and I am resolved upon killing myself.

Here is how my plight came about.

Once upon a time about a year ago, I was very young and foolish, and Simmons informed me we hadn't any money left. (Simmons is our butler.)

'Simmons,' I had said, 'I would like to buy a boat so that I can sail the seven seas.'

I hadn't, I suppose, any real notion of actually sailing the seven seas—I am not an adventurous soul, and would relinquish my comfortable seat by the fire only with reluctance. But it seemed a romantic thing to own a boat in which one *could* sail the seven seas, should one suddenly discover he had a mind to.

But Simmons (whose hair is grey like a thunderhead) said with some remonstrance, 'I'm afraid you cannot afford a boat, sir.'

'I can't afford it? Nonsense, Simmons, a boat cannot cost much.'

'Even if it cost next to nothing, sir, you still could not afford it.'

My heart sank. 'Do you mean to tell me, Simmons, that we haven't any money left?'

'I'm afraid not, sir.'

'Where on earth has it gone?'

'I don't mean to be critical, sir, but you tend toward profligacy.'

'Nonsense, Simmons. I don't buy anything except books. You cannot possibly tell me I've squandered my fortune upon books.'

'Squander is not the word I would have used, sir. But it was the books that did it, I believe.'

Well, there it was. We were paupers. Such is the fate of the upper classes in this modern world. I didn't know what to do, and I dreaded telling Lizzie—she was in boarding school at the time, but even from a distance she can be quite fearsome. (Lizzie is my sister. She is sixteen.) Despite the popularity of my poetry, I was not making enough money at it to maintain our household at Pocklington Place. Another source of income was necessary.

I set out to find one. Being a gentleman,* the trades were quite out of the question. Commerce is not a gentlemanly pursuit and sounds wretched besides. I considered physic or law, but lawyers turn my stomach and physicians are scoundrels all. I decided it must be marriage.

Finding a suitable family to marry oneself off to might sound a bore, but turned out to be rather a lark. I sought out only families of enormous means, without bothering myself too much about social position. As such, I had a few truly unpleasant experiences—but no dull ones.

The Babingtons were every bit as eccentric as one reads in the papers and proved entirely unsuitable. (Not that I object to eccentricity; but it is not a quality one searches for in a wife.) Sir Francis Babington and I are old friends, he having once savaged† a collection of my poetry.

'Frank,' I said one evening, having contrived to run into him while taking a turn about the Park,‡ 'I suppose it's about time I came over for dinner.' (I abhor taking turns about the Park. I only do so when I have ulterior motives.)

'Looking for a wife, Savage?' said he.

---

*It is for the attentive reader to decide for himself whether Mr Savage is deserving of that epithet.—HL.

†I believe this is meant to be an unfortunate play upon my cousin's name. It is a literary offence typical of him.—HL.

‡My cousin refers naturally to Hyde Park. This (in case the reader has the misfortune to be on the Continent or in the Colonies) is the London park which people of fashion and breeding frequent.—HL.

'Certainly not,' I replied coldly. I was thrown off. I had not thought myself so transparent. I groped for a new subject but was not quick enough.

'Never fear, lad, you'll find no judgment here.' He was laughing. Sir Francis is a ruddy and a rotund man, and his laugh is well matched to his person. 'Been looking to unload Agnes for a while now, as a matter of fact. Helen and I ain't particular as far as who to, and you'll do just fine. Why don't you come round Tuesday evening?'

This sort of impropriety I would ordinarily celebrate, but not when auditioning fathers-in-law. I declined.

The Pembrokes I enjoyed greatly, but the prospect of a half-dozen sisters-in-law was untenable. (One sister is quite enough.) I made it as far as a dinner, which was proceeding reasonably well, when the littlest one (Mary? Martha?) decided to be Mr Hyde. She jumped up on the table, thumped her chest with her tiny fists, and heaved a roasted pheasant at my head. That was that.

The Hammersmiths could have been the ticket, but their daughter was, I believe, replaced at infancy with a horse.

I could carry on and mention the Wellingtons, Blooms, and Chapmans—but my native discretion forbids it. Suffice it to say that the field was quickly emptied of players, and my options began to run low.

At the end of the day, in fact, the only real possibility was the Lancasters. They were rich, they were respectable and respected, and their daughter was beautiful. I will say that, whatever else I may lament—Vivien is very beautiful. Her hair is beaten gold, her eyes are a meteorological blue, her figure is—well, you have heard about her figure. It was her beauty I fell in love with first.

The dinner at which we met was unremarkable. It was not a private affair, but something of a party. I had contrived to procure myself an invitation on the grounds of my literary fame, and it seemed most of the guests had done the same. Whitley Pendergast was there, of course, as was Mr Collier, Mr Blakeney, Mr Morley, and Lord and Lady Whicher. (Whitley Pendergast is my rival and sworn enemy, and a terrible poet besides. The rest are literary personages of some reputation and indifferent talent. Benjamin Blakeney's *Barry the Bard* I hope you have not read, and Edward Collier's *Penthesilea's Progress* I fear you have. I have forgotten what mangled offspring crawled from the pens of the others.) A few ministers of state rounded out the meal, but it would be in poor taste to mention them by name.*

I was seated between Pendergast and Vivien.

—But I have forgotten to finish setting the scene! Easton Arms, which is the Lancasters' place in town, is a large town house in Belgravia furnished in the best and most modern taste. They are a very modern family, though very old in name. The art on the walls was unremarkable not in execution but in choice. If you were to close your eyes and name the six artists respectable and cultured persons of no particular taste ought to have on their walls, then you will have a very

---

*I, too, was present. I dine often at Easton Arms. My father being brother to Lord Lancaster, I am Vivien's first cousin. As Mr Savage is my cousin's husband, he is thus by law my cousin also. It is for this reason I made bold to include an epigraph without obtaining his express permission. We harbour between us that particular and tenuous affection which marks the sobrinical bond.—HL.

good idea of what hung in Easton Arms.* I haven't a clue as to their names, as I do not keep up with such things. But you take my meaning.

Everything seemed gilt-edged. The mirrors, the frames of the paintings, the books on the shelves (I pulled several down and found the pages to be uncut)—even the curtains were trimmed with gold lace. The situation seemed promising. I prepared to be charming.

I had a passing acquaintance with Lord Lancaster, who has a restless mind trapped by the constraints of domesticity and a portly person, but I had never met his wife. She turned out to be much as you imagine her to be from the papers, only rather shorter and even more terrible.

The gentlemen of the party were enjoying cigars before dinner. I have no fondness for cigars, but I appreciate the ritual of girding up one's loins in the fellowship of one's own gender before mingling at table. Besides, Lord Lancaster's smoking room is notably fine. The walls are decorated with intriguing memorabilia sent home by his son—a dozen tribal masks from a dozen countries, bits of colourful native costume, a gleaming blunderbuss—and the fireplace is large and the armchairs luxurious.

We sprawled in that peculiarly insolent way of the male gentry, smoking expensive cigars and speaking of nothing in particular.

---

*I beg you to note that this is equivalent to declaring popular art bad art—which would I am afraid quite condemn the poetry of Mr Savage. In addition, it should be mentioned that the collection at Easton Arms has a national reputation for excellence.—HL.

Pendergast, a tragically short fellow with a peninsular nose, was attempting to be more pretentious than Collier, and was succeeding without too much effort. Every now and again he lobbed an insult my way, but I was not in the mood to test wits. I was too busy seducing Lancaster.

'Are you a political man, Mr Savage?'

'Not especially, my lord. I find that Politics and Art are rarely willing bedfellows; and when forced to it, Politics invariably takes Art's virtue without so much as a by-your-leave.'

He chuckled at that, but I did not. To never laugh at one's own wit is a thing I learned from Pendergast. (In a nearby armchair, Pendergast at that moment answered a question I did not hear with, 'Certainly not—I relegate such things to Mr Savage,' and laughed loudly.)

'Always wished I had time for art,' said Lancaster. 'Bought some paints, once, but Eleanor had 'em thrown out. Said it was an accident and blamed it on a maid, but you know how those things go. Probably for the best. Vivien, though—she inclines that way, you know.'

'Does she?' I murmured.

'Certainly,' said he. 'You and she ought to have a talk sometime. Think you'd get on famously.'

I was about to say something about how I should like that very much indeed, and to suggest future plans for such an acquaintance, when Lady Lancaster entered the room and curtly informed us that dinner was served and we were already late. I was nettled at the interruption. As it happened, though, I needn't have been—for when we took our places at the table I was upon Vivien's right.

Of all the literati at that salon, I was perhaps the most fa-mous. It was because of this, I am certain, that I was seated next to Vivien. Lady Lancaster has a fondness for fame. She does not court it herself, but courts those touched by it. (It is this, rather than any actual interest in the arts, which causes her to hold dinners like the one I am describing.) I was also perhaps the handsomest at the table. I mention it not out of vanity—I am not a vain man—but to emphasise the impor-tance the Lancasters attach to appearances, and also in case you have never seen a likeness of me. I am neither tall nor short, and very slender. I have very pale skin, very dark hair which is unruly, and very blue eyes—not a blue like Vivien's, but blue all the same. (The Lancaster blue is something akin to the sky at its bluest; the Savage blue is the sort of blue the sea turns when it is grey. If this does not make sense to you, you are not a poet.)*

I couldn't have known it at the time, but it was my good fortune that Vivien was approaching twenty-one and her mother felt it was past time she was married to someone in the public eye. Marriage is important to the Lancasters. It was and is a source of most acute pain to Lady Lancaster that her son is not yet domesticated. (He is at the moment in Siberia, I believe.)

I do a tolerable job of fitting into society.† I do not flaunt

---

*It appears I am no poet.—HL.
†This, too, is open for debate. Mr Savage at all times displays such deep contempt for society that one wonders at the grudge he nurses. Whence comes it? Is it innate or learned? Can it be cured? Such questions are beyond the scope of your humble editor.—HL.

my native eccentricity, nor do I endeavour to seem any more
mad than I am. The poetry published under my name displays
vision, refinement, learning, wit, and taste—but not insanity.
That I reserve for those offerings I distribute by secret means,
under noms de plume.* My fame, as I have said, is not insig-
nificant, and it was evident that Lady Lancaster, though drag-
onish in demeanour, was a dragon with a keen desire to
impress. (It need not be pointed out that a mercenary dragon
is far more dangerous than a work-a-day dragon.)

And so I was seated next to Vivien, and I do not believe it
was an accident. Pendergast was on my right, which was a
nuisance; but at the time I remember thinking it a small price
to pay to sit beside one so fair.

The dining room at Easton Arms is very grand. The table is
a mile or two long, and it was laid that evening with everything from venison to wild boar to caviar to quail eggs. There
were sauces which defied description and puddings which
boggled the mind. The serving trays were silver, but worked
with the requisite gold filigree. I was not alone among the
guests in my nervousness to take food from a platter worth
more than I had ever owned. We were spared, however, the
terror of actually holding one of those trays by the appearance of a flotilla of footmen who served us in frankly eerie
silence, controlled apparently by minute signals of Lady Lancaster's head.

The dinner began, and though I stole many glances at my

---

*These names include Horatio, Britannius Grammaticus, Iucundis Eremita, and
Charles Greenley.—HL.

fair neighbour, I found myself for the only time in my memory unable to begin a conversation. I spent the first course searching for a subject and feeling a coward. I could not, try as I might, speak to Vivien. I once made it so far as to venture a remark upon the weather, but Pendergast swooped in and intercepted it.

'I've been considering a poem about the rain, you know,' he said, as though my comment had been meant for him.

'I trust the rain is magnanimous enough to forgive whatever offence you might give it,' I replied.

'You wrote a rain poem once, didn't you, Savage?' called Blakeney from across the table.*

'I can't recall,' said I. 'I might have, but it's foggy in my memory.'

'Foggy!' exclaimed Lady Whicher rapturously. 'Did you hear, Henry? He said his rain poem was foggy!'

'A sloppy pun, Savage,' declared Pendergast.

'I'd have made a better, but I can't hear myself think over the noise of your cravat.'

'This cravat,' he replied pompously, 'was given me by a French countess who expressed an affinity for my verse.'

'One hears at the club that the cravat wasn't the only thing she gave you.' A scandalised murmur went round the table and it seemed I had scored a hit—but Pendergast was a stauncher opponent than that.

---

*See epigraph. It is for elucidation of this exchange as well as for other reasons that I elected to include it.—HL.

'No,' he said without missing a beat, 'she gave me also an annuity of two hundred pounds and a promise to bring out a uniform edition of my published works. I asked her to pay you the same compliment, but she said your output was too slim to bear the cost.'

'Did she?' I said, taking the bait. He was building to something, and it amused me to let him see it through.

'She did, and very bad manners I thought it, too. So I said, "But madam, surely the sparsity of Mr Savage's verse makes it the more precious, rather like ambergris?" To which she replied, "Much like ambergris, Mr Pendergast, I can only stomach Mr Savage's poetry after it has been refined in the fire."'

The table applauded his thrust, but I remained unruffled. I have always enjoyed sparring with Pendergast, and that night it was also a means to delay converse with the divinity on my left. Besides, the key to success in a battle of wits is to maintain one's equanimity at all times. While the company lauded his hit, I calmly considered a riposte. I had almost got one when Vivien spoke up.

'It is a pity, Mr Pendergast,' said she, in a voice which was low and husky and altogether glorious and in retrospect rather like a siren's, 'that much like Mr Savage's poetry, ambergris needs no fiery refinement.'

'Does it not?' cried Lady Whicher.

'Not a bit. Its value comes from its unaltered chemical makeup.'

'Ambergris or Mr Savage's poetry?' demanded Blakeney.

'Precisely!' I interposed, and just like that I was again on top. I attempted to thank my fair saviour, but the words transmuted by some reverse alchemy into an attack on Pendergast and his countess.

I will not bore you with the continuation of our match, as it proceeded through the duration of the second and most of the third course. I won in the end, but the victory was hollow to me—the entire episode was nothing but a cover to hide the fact that I could not speak to the woman beside me.

It was Vivien who at last broke the silence between us, and so I may say without hesitation that the fault for my current predicament lies squarely upon her shoulders. Had she not said anything I would not have been able to, and would have returned home to Pocklington Place that evening with a feeling of cowardice and self-reproach which would have lasted for a day or a week and then given way to my accustomed cheer.*

Instead, I left that evening with a wife.

I do not mean literally, of course—our courtship, while brief, was not *that* brief. But later when Simmons asked how the dinner had gone, I believe my words to him were, 'I have found a wife, and I haven't the least intention of letting her go.'

Bitterest of ironies! If I could return to that night in March and relive it, I should have eaten my foie gras with relish, taunted Pendergast with pleasure, and never spared a second glance at that awful creature on my left. Could I even return

---

*Like the unicorn, legends of my cousin's cheer persist only because they cannot be disproved.—HL.

as a spirit and whisper in my own corporeal ear, I should whisper with such urgency, 'Ignore her, sir! She will be your death!'

Well, but I cannot and I did not. Instead, when over the oysters she enquired, 'What are your thoughts on the matter, Mr Savage?' I turned and lost myself in those damned eyes and knew I was finished and did not mind a jot.

I will not here recount my wooing. It was, looking back, strangely joyous and brings me pain to recollect. There was throughout it a bizarre sense of burning happiness—a prickly feeling on the back of my neck, a pleasant tightness of the chest: something more than contentment, greater than the satisfaction of a match well made.

I thought it was the sensation of being in love. I have learned that it was not, it was the joy of the chase. I wonder now if I oughtn't have been a hunter. Perhaps I still could be one. I am certain that Simmons keeps an ancient musket somewhere, and I could steal a horse from my coachman and sally forth to murder foxes—or stow aboard an Arctic vessel and try my hand at clubbing seals, which cannot be difficult. But that is neither here nor there. I am a poet, I am a married man, and I am resolved upon my own immediate suicide—for I married for money instead of love, and when I did I discovered that I could no longer write.

Two

In Which My Sister Returns from School for Reasons Best Omitted, & I Am Forced to Deliver to Her a Previously Unmentioned Piece of Intelligence.

I sit trying to write. I cannot. I have written no poetry in my six months of marriage. I have written drivel, doggerel, detritus, but nothing worthy of Calliope's mantle.*

I sit at my desk in my study in my house which is called Pocklington Place which is in a nice part of London with

---

*The reader has undoubtedly noticed that Mr Savage presents this account in an affected present tense. I strongly petitioned him not to do so, but he was intransigent. A transcription follows of the brief missive he sent me regarding the choice: 'Hubert—there's method to my madness and madness to my method: glorious, rather inspired madness. By writing in the present tense I bring immediacy to the events. Which, obviously, is the reason present tense exists. If I did not write thus, the reader would instantly know that the whole thing turned out well, if I sounded merry, or ill, if I sounded melancholy, and the effect would be ruined. Now be a good chap and leave literature to the literary.—S.'—HL.

which you are almost certainly familiar and so I shall not name for I do not like callers. My desk is mahogany and very large. It once belonged to an earl, but he was a wretched poet and so he died and now it is mine.* That is called justice, and I would there were more of it in this world. My study is large, as it is also my library. My library used to be upstairs, but it became apparent that I should spend my life walking up and down the stairs between my library and my study unless drastic action were taken. So I called in an architect who called in several workmen who charged me a prodigious amount of money, and I bid them remove the floor of my library—though I might equally have said the ceiling of my study, for they were one and the same (the one being directly below the other). They did this, with much banging and sawing and hammering, and they put in several very tall sliding ladders so that I could reach my books, and a very grand spiral staircase made of wrought iron which leads to a sort of balcony ringing the room on what used to be the floor of the library and the ceiling of the study, and where there are a few armchairs. When the workmen left, I had the grand, two-storey study in which is the mahogany desk at which I now sit trying vainly to write.

If you have ever written, you will know that it is either an arduous business or a simple one, but rarely in between. For me it used to be the one but is now the other. (I trust that you know which I mean when.)

---

*It should be noted that despite Mr Savage's ambiguity the late earl was not his father. Mr Simmons purchased the desk at an estate sale on Mr Savage's behalf.—HL.

I rise. I tear my hair and gnash my teeth. I chew the sleeves of my smoking jacket, which is red velvet and threadbare and which once I believed to be lucky but do not any longer. The words will not come.

'Simmons!' I call.

I am pacing, which is a habit of mine when I am agitated.

'Simmons!' I yell again. 'Simmons, where are you? I am agitated!'

I pace my way to the door and wrench it open to call down the hallway, but he is standing there already. Which is a habit of his.

'I've decided to kill myself, Simmons.' I have been considering it for some months, but I have been putting it off because the weather has been fair. It is now foul, and still I cannot write, and it is time to do what must be done.

'Very good, sir,' says he. He is a good butler. 'Might one ask how?'

I am moderately taken aback. In all my months of contemplation the question has never occurred to me. It is a good one, I reflect. 'Don't know,' I say. 'Hadn't thought. I suppose I'll just shoot myself.'

Those who are not well acquainted with Simmons say that he has no expression in either his face or voice, but I have known him these very many years and know better—and right now he looks pained.

'Oh *sir*,' he says. 'Begging your pardon, but who do you imagine would have to clean up the brains or the heart fluid or what have you?'

'Who?' I ask, wondering if there is a special branch of the public works committee one calls in such instances.*

'Me,' he says. Apparently not.†

'I see. I'm sorry, Simmons. That was inconsiderate of me. I apologise.' Firearms, clearly, will not do.

'Think nothing of it, sir,' he rejoins handsomely. He truly is a paragon.

I am now confronted with the reality of my situation. Somehow it had never seemed so real before; but when faced with the notion of poor Simmons scrubbing my brains off the bookshelves, my mind protests. But I am no coward. I plunge forward. I ask him if he has any recommendations.

'Sir?'

'For the manner in which one might best take one's own life.' Simmons is at times amazingly quick to apprehend, and at others needs clarification. I wonder where his brain goes during the latter periods. I do not think of him as having an imagination, but I am perhaps wrong. It occurs to me that I have not in my life considered what happens inside other people's heads. I must write a poem about it someday.‡

'I see.' He is pensive for a moment, then says, 'I understand that drowning is, all things considered, not a bad way to go.'

I am disappointed in him, and tell him so. 'I'd have thought

---

*There is, and I have had to deal with them often.—HL.
†It is as well for Mr Savage that he has had no dealings with the Suicide Committee. Despite the morbid name, the Committee is peopled largely by unnervingly cheerful men of small stature who smile more than is necessary and laugh more than is polite. They disquiet me.—HL.
‡If this poem was ever written, I have not seen it. The reader will note that Mr Savage's trouble stems not from lack of ideas but from lack of follow-through.—HL.

better of you, Simmons. If I drown myself, my corpse is likely to float downriver and wash up on a foreign shore and frighten to death some poor Froggy* child building castles in the sand—and all because you had a frankly quite selfish aversion to a few minutes of brains clean-up. You ought to be ashamed of yourself.'

He looks suitably remorseful. 'I am, sir. Frightfully ashamed. What about gassing yourself?'

'Now you're thinking, old boy! I believe you're on the right track.' I am immensely cheered. It seems not only a quick and a clean method, but also a romantic one. To die from the newly installed gas jet would be tantamount to being literally killed by Progress, which is one of the more poetical thoughts I have had in some time.† I am about to tell him so when the doorbell rings. Simmons excuses himself and leaves the room.

Alone, I consider the gas lamp flaring overhead. I do not care for it and never have. Gas seems to me a most monstrous thing, impure, foul-smelling, and expensive. I have read of a young inventor in the North who makes the most marvellous contraptions powered entirely by steam, which seems to me a much better thing. Steam comes from water which comes from rain which comes from the sky. I like the sky, and I like rain. Gas, on the other hand, comes from I know not where, so I cannot know whether or not I like its progenitor. It occurs to me even now that it is truly the progeny of *humanity*, which makes me feel all the more justified in my distaste for it. It is

---

*I do not condone this form of racial epithet.—HL.
†See the third note on page 18.—HL.

reassuring when one realises that one's prejudices are not groundless.*

I hear Simmons open the door, and then the bottom drops from my stomach. An unmistakable voice squeals, 'Simmons!' and I hear luggage being dropped and even from here the sound of Simmons gasping for breath as Lizzie throws her arms around him.

For it is Lizzie. She enters my study in a whirlwind which proves it. My sister looks much as I do—her skin is pale, her hair is dark, her eyes are blue, and she is not a large person. I am biased, but I believe her to look quite well. She is dressed for travelling. Her cheeks are flushed with wind and happiness, her hair is tousled, and she hurls herself into me before I can rise. She smells of autumn and of Lizzie, which are my two favourite smells in the world. At any other time in my life I would be glad to see her.

'Hello, little sister,' I say as she crushes the air from my lungs. Though she be but little, she is fierce.

She at last releases me and stretches me at arm's length. She studies me and it makes me nervous. It has been the better part of a year since she set eyes on me, and I fear her opinion. I do not fear the opinions of many men, but I do fear hers.

---

*Firstly, this does not seem to me firm ground upon which to base a prejudice. Secondly, I believe that progress of any sort is good progress. Is that not the meaning of the word? To move forward? And is not moving forward good? I believe it must be. To retreat is not gentlemanly. Thirdly, on a scientific note, gas comes from coal. Coal comes from the earth, for which Mr Savage professes a fondness.—HL.

'You look *awful*, Nellie,' she says. 'What's happened to you?'

Simmons comes in before I can answer, straightening his tie and brushing a speck of dust from his immaculate uniform. 'Simmons,' Lizzie carries on imperiously, 'what have you let him do to himself? He looks like death. We may need to fetch a priest.' I wish Lizzie would not talk as though I am not present.

'Yes,' says Simmons. 'I am afraid he may not be constitutionally suited to—'

He is about to say 'marriage,' and it occurs to me in a moment of panic that I entirely failed to mention to Lizzie that I am no longer a bachelor. I tried to include it in several letters, but the words never quite materialised. It is as I said—now that I am married, I can no longer write. Lizzie would never forgive me if she knew that I married without her permission. I hurry to interrupt Simmons before he can say the awful word.

'Do you know,' I cut in, 'I met a priest this evening. I was walking home and he had tripped over a loose cobblestone and was cursing the Devil for putting it in his path, and I stopped and said to him, "Oh sir, for shame! Does not the poor Devil have enough to bear as it is? Besides which, you're a priest! And I'm a poet! Without the Devil we'd both of us be out of a job!" I thought myself distinctly clever. The priest, though—' And then something else occurs to me. I round on my sister and demand, 'Why are you not at school?'

Lizzie's eyes widen with a panic that is not, I believe, far removed from what I felt a moment before. I hope I was not so transparent. 'It's *so* good to see you both,' she babbles, 'but I must look a fright. Let me change and freshen up and I'll be all yours and then you can tell me what's happened to you.'

I glance at Simmons and see that she is an open book to him also. 'Lizzie,' I say sternly, 'what are you doing home?'

Her eyes flash about looking for some means of deliverance. She finds none and decides to makes a run for it. 'Got kicked out,' she blurts. 'Back in half a second!' And she dashes from the room.

I call after her, but to no avail. When Lizzie decides she is going to do something she is infrequently denied. 'This is your fault, Simmons,' I say.

'Very good, sir,' says he.

I am becoming flustered. I am not brittle by nature, but I do not like it when I have set my mind on something (for instance, suppertime suicide), and something else (for instance, my beloved little sister) comes along to upset my plans. Which is not to say that I am not happy to see Lizzie, because I am, though I do worry about her being home—it was a good school she was at (I had better not say which one), and I know her to be an excellent student, which means that for her to have been kicked out she would have had to do something truly—

'By the by, sir,' says Simmons, interrupting my thoughts, which is not necessarily a bad thing as I have a tendency to let them run wild, 'I anticipate a problem.'

I haven't the slightest idea what he is talking about, and tell him so.

'Her room, sir—' he begins, and my heart sinks. I had forgot about her room.

'NELLIE!' Lizzie shrieks from upstairs.

'Simmons,' I say, 'this dreadful day has gotten worse.'

Lizzie is a dainty person, but her feet as she storms down the stairs do not sound dainty. She bursts through the door in a towering fury.

'What have you done to my room?' she demands.

'Well, Lizzie,' I say in my most reasonable tone of voice, 'it's complicated.'

I pause to consider the best way to put matters, because they are indeed rather complicated. Before I can go on, she says, 'Where are my things?'

'In the attic.'

'And who,' she continues, as full of questions as ever, 'is living in my room?'

I cannot lie to my only relation upon this earth, but I am not yet ready to tell her the whole truth if it can be avoided. I quickly formulate a plan. I believe I may be able to gloss over some facts and change the subject. If I do so smoothly enough, she may not notice what it is I have said; and if I follow the revelation with a strong enough remonstrance then she may become distracted.

'My wife,' I say. 'Now, tell me immediately why you were kicked out of school.'

'Your WIFE?'

'The importance of a good education—'

But she is not to be thrown off the track, and interrupts me. 'You got MARRIED?'

I ignore her, less now for the sake of the defunct plan than because I am warming to my subject. 'Were you doing your work?' I demand. 'You weren't, were you? I never figured you for a laggard, Lizzie. Laziness—'

'I am not lazy! I got kicked out for a dalliance with the dean's son.* When did you get *married*?'

I match her fury. 'A *dalliance*? You had a DALLIANCE? You're *sixteen*!'

'Yes,' says this creature I no longer know, 'one wonders why I waited so long. WHY ARE YOU MARRIED?'

I find myself unhinged. To hear that one's sister is kicked out is a blow, but to find that she is kicked out for dallying with a tallywhacker is something that would break even the hardest man. 'I am married, Lizzie, because we ran out of money, and so to keep us clothed and keep our house and KEEP YOU IN SCHOOL, I sold myself to a rich woman, and now I can't write and can't even figure out how to take my own life in a way that isn't horribly inconvenient for those I leave behind me, and FOR GOD'S SAKE YOU HAD A *DALLI-ANCE*?'

Lizzie is perversely calmed by my anger, and becomes at once logical. 'Nellie,' she says sternly, 'I really think there were better financial alternatives than marriage.'

---

*I believe that I would here do well to venture a few words upon Miss Elizabeth Savage. She is made, in these pages, to seem to be of easy virtue and loose morals. This is not, I believe, actually the case. She is by no means conventional, and at times behaves in ways which, let it be understood, I hope that my daughters, if ever I have any, would not. But she does not do so from wilful deviance. There was a philosopher—whose name I cannot recall but who I much admired in my youth—who declared that he would taste any drink once. Miss Savage seems to live by that maxim. She pursues knowledge in a way not immoral, but amoral. She is an innocent who longs for experience, if the reader will pardon my allusion.—HL.

'Believe me, Lizzie, I wracked my brains and at the end of the day the only alternative was selling you into prostitution, which would never have worked.'

'That isn't funny, nor is it— Why wouldn't it have worked?'

'No one would have bought you.'

Her unnerving calm is shattered. 'PEOPLE WOULD HAVE BOUGHT ME!'

'No,' I say, 'I don't think so.'

'Would people have bought me, Simmons?'

'Indubitably, miss.'

Simmons is the bravest man I have ever met, but in this one respect he is a coward. He never can bear to hurt Lizzie, even at the expense of telling her the truth. But Lizzie is rather a magical creature who exerts a strange pull over mere mortals, and I resolve not to think less of Simmons.

I find I must continually stop myself from contemplating her dalliance. I am not a prudish man, let it be understood. This age of morality is not one I have an affinity for, nor is it one I deem good.* But be that as it may, when one hears that one's sister is— As I say, I must stop myself from thinking on it. It is best unthought, unspoken, and unheard.

Lizzie meanwhile seems pleased to have found an ally, and appeals to his good sense on the matter at hand. 'How could you have let him do this, Simmons?'

'I cautioned him against it, Miss Elizabeth,' he says. 'In-

---

*For my part, I find little to admire in this frankly anarchic sentiment. This age of morality, as Mr Savage refers to it, has I believe done more to better the world than any age before. This may be a controversial opinion, but I have spent many hours in study and contemplation and I am convinced of the truth of it.—HL.

deed, I did my uttermost to dissuade him, but he was resolute.'

Lizzie looks at me with a mixture of pity and annoyance. 'Nellie,' she says, 'I've never thought of you as stupid, but you're forcing me to reconsider.'

'Her parents were desperate for a poet. If I didn't marry her, Pendergast would have.' It is my last-ditch vindication, and I expect it to carry weight.

It doesn't.

'Where is she?' demands Lizzie without acknowledging that I have spoken.

'Who?'

'Your wife.'

I wince at the word. I do not like the word. I do not like the woman, and so I do not like the word. 'Out,' I say.

'Out *where*?'

'She's throwing a party tonight. She's picking up her costume.'

Lizzie's eyes light up. 'A fancy dress party?' It occurs to me that she has probably never been to one.

'I recognise that may *sound* fun,' I say, 'but let me assure you it isn't.' My wife has a passion for fancy dress parties. It is a passion I do not understand. Everyone wears masks, so no one has any notion to whom one is speaking. She says she finds it exciting and that the masks return some mystery to life in an age when nearly all the mysteries have been or are being solved, but I say that does not make sense. Masks muddle things. I have not infrequently found a top hat or a cane or even a pair of men's gloves left about after such parties. This is to me proof of the muddlement—society men only leave their things lying about when they are muddled or when they are embarked upon affairs of passion, and as no one lives at Pocklington Place save for myself and my wife and Simmons and some footmen and a few exceedingly plain maids and Mrs Davis the cook who frightens me to death, I doubt that gentlemen are having affairs of passion here.

Lizzie ignores my remark. I am not sure she even heard me. She is already far away, somewhere in the Orient no doubt, dreaming of silks and turbans. She is distractible. 'What's she like?' she asks.

'Who?'

'Your wife.'

I am surprised by her single-mindedness. She is usually more lively of thought; I wonder if school has begun to soften her wits. I answer her honestly, all the same: 'Rich.'

She glares at me. 'When I think that you make your living through your verbal prowess, it shocks me. What's she *like*, Simmons?'

I can see that Simmons is about to say something other than what he should—but as I believe I have stated before, Simmons is the best butler in Britain and perhaps the world: so he says instead, 'Given the circumstances, miss, I think it best if I don't answer that question.'

Lizzie narrows her eyes, and it is quite plain that she has no intention of letting the matter lie. 'What is going *on*?' she demands. 'What's her name?'

I tell her.

'Vivien what?' she asks.

'What?'

'What's her last name?

'Savage!'

'What *was* her last name?' she snaps back, and I realise what she meant but do not apologise. I am not in an apologetic mood. Lizzie is wearing on my nerves today in a manner she usually does not. I wonder if it is because she is older than when I last saw her (which thought makes me laugh to myself, for it occurs to me that every time one sees *any*one, he is older than when one last saw him), but I am not sure if this is the reason. I try to remember myself at sixteen, but I cannot. I was doubtless very much the same.

'Lancaster, Miss Elizabeth,' says Simmons. 'Her name was Lancaster.'

'Lancaster,' repeats Lizzie, tasting the former name of her sister-in-law. 'Vivien Lancaster.' Then her eyes light up again. 'Wait,' she says, as though I were going somewhere. '*The* Lancasters? You married into the Lancasters?'

I had hoped that by some miracle she would be unfamiliar with the family. 'I don't want to talk about it,' I say, but she carries on.

'You married Ashley Lancaster's little sister?'

'Yes.' I feared it would come to this. It always does when the Lancasters are brought up.

'Ashley Lancaster is my— Is my *brother-in-law*. Oh my God. Oh my *God*.'

'Don't curse,' I tell her.

'I'll curse if I damn well please! Have you met him?'

'Who?'

'Ashley!'

'No,' I say. 'He's in Africa somewhere. Or South America. I forget. Where is he, Simmons?'

'Tibet, I believe.' says Simmons. 'Or is it Pago Pago?'

'Yes, that's it,' I say. I do not know if it really is it or not, and I do not care to know.* It is likely somewhere very cold or very warm, and likely all in all very unpleasant. I do not understand why a person would subject himself to such travails, and I understand still less why a country would follow with bated breath reports of said unpleasantries. I recall when he sent back dispatches from his time among the horsemen of central Mongolia—they were the talk of the town, and I found myself quite baffled why anyone should care.†

Lizzie has stopped listening to Simmons and me, and is babbling again on a predictable path. 'My brother-in-law is the greatest explorer who ever lived. Nellie, have I told you that I love you?'

Her obsession with the man wearies me. This country's obsession with him wearies me. I refuse to believe that he is truly the paragon the newspapers make him out to be. No one is so tall, so broad, so handsome, so generous of spirit, so full of life, so ready to do whatever must be done despite the danger and hardship and weather. I simply refuse to believe it. Lizzie is now discussing my wife.

---

*It is not.—HL.

†What is amusing is that even as I prepare this manuscript for publication, Mr Savage is preparing to accompany Mr Lancaster on one of his expeditions. Thus the whirligig of time brings in his revenges, which is something that Mr Shakespeare once said.—HL.

'Is she very much like him? She must be. Is she very tall? I'll bet she is. And beautiful. I'm sure she's beautiful. Is she very beautiful? I don't have anything to wear. What am I going to wear? The Lancasters! That means we must be very rich, doesn't it? Are we very rich?'

'Yes, little sister,' I tell her. 'Whatever else we may be, we are now very, very rich.'

'I don't care about the money, of course,' she goes on. 'But it is nice to have, isn't it? I'm so glad. She must be very intelligent. I hope she likes me. Will she like me, Nellie?'

I answer truthfully that I have never yet encountered anyone who doesn't like her.

'Well, I *hope* she likes me. Why didn't you tell me you married Vivien Lancaster? Why didn't you tell me you got married?'

The fact of the matter is, I don't know why I didn't tell her. Even when I believed myself happy I considered telling Lizzie but always put it off for some reason. Someday I'll have to contemplate it. I haven't the time now. I avoid her gaze and mumble, 'I'm sure I must have mentioned it in one of my letters.'

'You didn't,' she says. 'I would have remembered if you had said you were married. You didn't. I think it very bad manners of you not to have told me. Why are your wife's things in my room?'

I am suddenly on very treacherous ground. Unfortunately, I am not quick-witted in such situations.

'It doesn't make sense,' says Lizzie. 'Why don't you share a room? If I ever get married I'll want to sleep next to my beloved every night of my life.'

'. . . Yes,' I say. I am aware that there can be no stay in execution, and that in very short order Lizzie will know my entire secret and think less of me. But I am doing my best to put off the inevitable if even for another too brief few moments. Though I am six years older than she, Lizzie is the dearest friend that I have—and to lose her friendship would be more than I could bear.

'Does she just store her things in my room?'

'No. No, she lives in your room.'

'Why?'

'It's difficult to explain.'

'Does it have to do with the physical act of love?' Lizzie asks. If I were not so low already this would certainly sink me. Were there a cliff nearby I should throw myself off it. 'Because if it does,' carries on my baby sister, 'you don't have to tiptoe around it, Lionel. I know all about sex, as I believe is evidenced by my very presence in this room. In fact, I am quite well versed—do you know, the dean's son said that behind closed doors I could almost be French.'*

I had forgot about the dean's damned son. It is too much. 'LIZZIE!'

'What?'

---

*This exchange and others like it—the ones, I mean, regarding certain matters of the body—make me uncomfortable. However, I have generally left them as they were written because I believe they serve the valuable purpose of elucidating the free-thinking nature of the household at Pocklington Place.—HL.

'Discovering that my little sister is a skilled harlot at sixteen does not improve my outlook on life!'

'I'm not a harlot! If I were a man you would be congratulating me on my virility and very likely teasing me for having gone so many years without knowing the pleasures of— Oh my God. You don't love her.'

There it is, alas. She has found me out, and if I am ever to be of my former stature in her eyes I shall be very much surprised. I wish to upbraid her for her sluttish ways, but I cannot even do that, for I am fully occupied in defence of my own callous ones.

'You don't love her, do you? You don't! That's why you have separate bedrooms. Oh no. Oh, Nellie, what have you done? This is awful! You've married yourself to the richest and most interesting family in Britain and you don't love her. How could you be so hateful?'

I knew it would come, but I am all the same unprepared for it. To lose the respect of one's sibling is a most dreadful thing, and for me it is doubly dreadful for the reason I have already mentioned. All the same, though, there is a part of me that is defiant to the last. 'You have no idea what you're talking about!'

'Of course I do! You seduced a young girl who fell in love with you because you're a famous poet and you married her just for her money and you don't actually love her and I can't believe we're related and I hate you and I wish I'd never been born.'

Even in my despair I marvel at her grasp of the world—she is indeed changed. She has quite found me out. I tell her so, and add gloomily, 'And now my vapid wife hates me almost as much as I hate her.'

'I don't believe you,' she says. 'Is she really vapid?'

'Painfully so.'

'Is that true, Simmons?'

Simmons is once again the soul of discretion. 'In matters of love, miss, you know I hold my tongue.'

'I don't think she can truly be vapid.'

'She is,' I say, weary of the conversation but also somehow glad to be speaking of what I do not speak to anyone. 'We never talk about anything. And timid. And sickly and pale and prone to inexplicable weeping. And when she isn't snivelling she's throwing parties. It's awful. I want to die. And I can't write.' I hadn't meant for all of that to come spilling out, but it has done so and I feel better for it. It is like the letting of bad blood. (I recall that leeching has long since been proven not only ineffective, but actually detrimental to good health. Alas.)

'What do you mean you can't write?' demands my indefatigable sister. 'When was the last time you wrote a poem?'

'I don't want to talk about it.'

Lizzie is peering at me again in an unsettlingly maternal way. 'Lionel, I'm worried about you. You really don't seem well at all. I'm going to call a doctor.'

'I don't *want* a doctor.' I find myself rallying. Speaking my sorrow aloud has mitigated it somewhat, or at least held it briefly at bay. 'Lizzie,' I say, 'we need to talk about school. You can't just run around uneducated—'

'I am *not* uneducated,' she cries hotly.

'All the same, you must go back.'

'I can't, silly—I've been kicked out.'

'I know that, Lizzie,' I say with vast and I think impressive patience. 'We need to find you another school.'

'That sounds dreadful,' she complains. 'They haven't anything new to teach me, any of them.'

'Now Lizzie,' say I.

'Don't "now Lizzie" me!' She is becoming rather angry. 'YOU try going to one of those dreadful places!'

'I have done,' say I, 'and I'm better for it.' She rolls her eyes and is very near to stamping her foot. I press my advantage. 'I don't care if you don't like learning—'

For the first time in my life, Lizzie strikes me. I put a hand to my stinging face, too shocked to do anything else. We blink at each other. Then Lizzie begins speaking in a torrent, furious and indignant and near to tears. 'The minute I walked into this house I suspected something was dreadfully wrong, and now my suspicion is quite confirmed. As if it is not bad enough to tell your little sister you have gone off and gotten married without her permission, you seem to believe it is also necessary to insult her in the worst possible way. You don't care if I don't like *learning*? God! Do you remember that you used to read Shakespeare aloud to me before I knew how? And that you taught me Latin? And that you used to love ideas almost as much as you loved me? That was the brother I came home to see, but you seem to have murdered the poor dear— and if you really are as senseless as you are pretending to be right now and if you really have forgotten in the midst of your marital self-pity that I was put on this earth to follow knowledge like a sinking star beyond the utmost bound of human thought,* then we have nothing more to discuss and don't bother helping me to unpack because I'll be on the next train to the Hesperides.'

Before I can think of a response, we hear the front door open. 'My wife is home,' I say.

---

*This sentiment and phrasing Miss Savage borrowed from Lord Tennyson.—HL.

Three

In Which My Wife Throws a Party & I Entertain a Mysterious Gentleman with Whom I Discuss Poetry, Friendship, & Marriage.

'If you'll excuse me, sir,' Simmons says, 'I'll help her prepare for the guests.'

He leaves.

'Oh God, the guests,' I say, remembering all at once that there is to be a party tonight. I cannot face them. It is enough to face my sister and inevitably my wife. Guests are simply too much. (I have said already that I do not like callers.) I decide that I shan't attend the party. 'Lizzie, you must stay here and help me hide.'

'Absolutely not,' she says, still flushed from her little speech.

The doorbell rings again. I am quite certain that there is something not right and probably supernatural about the doorbell at Pocklington Place. It rattles the nerves as ordinary doorbells do not. I have inspected it personally many times, and can see nothing amiss—it is a simple contraption which when pulled from without causes a small bell to jingle within. But somehow, I know beyond doubt, there is malice in the little thing. It jars me such that I cannot recall what I was thinking on before it rang.

I listen. There are footsteps, the front door opens, there are voices, it shuts. More footsteps, by which I mean both that there are again footsteps and that there are more of them: I can hear that the number of the steppers is multiplied. Where only one set went toward the door—that of Simmons or a footman—several have returned.

Guests.

'Good heavens, they're coming.' I hear the desperation in my own voice. 'This is awful.'

'What's so terrible about a party?' Lizzie asks. I stare at her, aghast. She blinks at me bovinely. How can this person, so much more worldly than myself in certain deplorable ways, not know why society parties are terrible?

The doorbell rings again, and my train of thought is derailed and several passengers are killed. I hope none of them were poetical. The door opens and shuts again. More guests. Many of them. At least a hundred. Perhaps a thousand.

'Lizzie,' I say, 'have you ever been to a society party?'

'Obviously not, because I was raised by you, the most boring man on the planet.' I resent the allegation, but before I can reply, the infernal doorbell rings for a third time. This time the door is open for longer and is hardly shut before the bell rings yet again. I am becoming very agitated. I wish to crawl under my desk and put a pillow over my head. Lizzie, though, isn't finished with me.

'I have yet to meet your wife and I have nothing to wear and have been travelling all day and look a fright. This is a calamity.' She fixes me with a glare that plainly implicates me in her troubles. When she has satisfied herself that I am feeling suitably remorseful (I'm not), she says, 'I'm going to my room to put myself together.'

With some trepidation, I say, 'Your room—'

She cuts me off. 'Oh yes, my room is no longer my room. How could I have forgotten? Very well, I am going to *your* room. Have I mentioned that I hate you?'

Then she sweeps out of the study without a backward glance. I know that she wants me to feel chastened, and it irks me that somehow I do. Lizzie has an unattractive habit of making you feel precisely the way she intends.* I wonder if it is possible (I have wondered it often before) that she was not switched at birth with a fairy child.† It would make sense of many things I have never understood if she were a changeling.‡

My study, if I have not already mentioned it, has two doors on its lower level, one leading upstairs to the bedchambers by a back stairway and another opening into a corridor which leads to the foyer, from which one can choose either to go upstairs by the main staircase or into the rest of the house. If one were cruel and perverse, one could also go up the spiral staircase and pick one's way through the armchairs on the bal-

---

*This is the truth.—HL.
†I, too, have wondered this.—HL.
‡It would.—HL.

cony and out one of three doors upon the upper level; but I do not like the noise on the iron of feet that are not mine, and so I discourage that path. Members of my family, by which I mean Lizzie, for she is the only member of my family—I do not count my wife for obvious reasons, though I suppose the law would—often use this when they mean to annoy me. My wife often uses it as well, but I do not believe she knows it annoys me; she is neither intelligent nor observant enough.*

Lizzie, though angry with me, has spared me the clamour of the iron spiral and gone up the back stairs. Through the other door drift the voices of a handful of party guests. The clock above the mantel tells me they are early. I do loathe people who are early to parties.†

I have not yet decided what to do. Killing myself seems ill-considered with Lizzie newly arrived, and quite out of the question during a party. It wouldn't do to gas an entire household of society folks. There is a certain wicked part of me which thinks it could be just the thing—'Society Murdered by Poet,' Pendergast could write, damn him—but I do not in earnest wish them dead.

So I cannot kill myself yet, but neither can I face the guests. I am not mentally equipped at this time. Until further notice, I am resolved to hide in my study. I have a moment to consider what Lizzie said to me. It *is* true that I am not as carefree

---

*While I do not mean to sway the reader, I would like very much to call his attention to my earlier note about whether or not 'gentleman' is the correct descriptive for my cousin by marriage.—HL.

†I myself love promptness. I often arrive early, occasionally on time, and never, if it can be avoided, late. It has earned me the nickname 'Timely Hubert,' which I like, though there are not many who call me this.—HL.

as I once was, but I do not believe I am quite as hopeless as she thinks.

I resolve to write a poem. I have found it impossible for six months, but I am not yet so broken that I shall go down without a fight. I search for a subject and recall my exchange with the priest. If ever there were matter suited to a poem, it is that. I have a queer fondness for tales of morality, and the public always embraces narratives with theological undertones. I begin.

'Without the Devil, we'd both be out of a job,' I say to myself. (I frequently compose aloud.) I attempt to render it into blank verse, alternating unstressed and stressed syllables into a pleasing configuration.

I could here bore you with a lengthy digression on iambic pentameter, but I will not. I trust you are familiar with it, and if not you need only consider the name. It is a poetic metre which consists of five iambs. An iamb is a pair of syllables, the first of which is unstressed and the second of which is stressed. It is the poetic metre which most closely replicates the rhythms of English speech, and has been the mode of poetic expression favoured by English poets for half a millennium. It is a beautiful thing, and one upon which I could discourse at great length, but I will not. I will only mention that it stirs within me great feeling. It provides structure and form for the greatest thoughts ever expressed in our language, and without it ours should be a meagre sort of poetry. There are of course some persons who choose not to utilise it—even I have at times succumbed to the enticements of other metres—but by and large if you say to yourself, 'I am going to write a poem which will endure for a thousand years,' you do not then sit down and attempt to write it in anything other than iambic pentameter.* Even Pendergast is not such a fool as to forsake it. It is a very beautiful thing.

And so I begin to compose. I speak in a singsong manner, hitting the stresses of the lines with exaggerated emphasis. 'With-OUT the DEV-il WE'D both— Damn it.' You observe that I am off the metre. Blank verse (which is of course un-rhymed iambic pentameter) at its finest fits its words like a glove. Take, for instance, 'To FOL-low KNOWL-edge LIKE a SINK-ing STAR / Be-YOND the UT-most BOUND of HU-man THOUGHT.' It seems effortless. It becomes effortless—when I am consistently poetical for a stretch, I find that I begin to think in iambic pentameter. (i FIND that I be-GIN to THINK . . .) Alas, I have not been poetical / For such a long long while that I begin / To wonder if I ever shall again. I take a breath and reconfigure some words. 'We'd BOTH be OUT of A . . . job.' It's awful. Drivel. Worse than drivel. I call for Simmons, who enters with impossible promptitude—was he listening at the door? I sometimes think he must be for the speed of his en-trances, but I know that eavesdropping is not in his nature.

He is wearing a turban and a mask. He is doubtless re-quired by my wife to wear them at her absurd party. I am grat-ified to note that his butler's weeds are otherwise unaltered.

'Simmons,' I ask, 'how many syllables in "Devil"?'

---

*Though I am no poet, I cannot refrain from pointing out that this is not necessarily the case.—HL.

'I believe there are two, sir,' says he, confirming my worst fears.

'Can there be just one?' For some unnameable reason I am feeling desperate about it. It is as though if 'Devil' could be considered a single syllable, my poem could move forward and then so too could my life.

Simmons thinks for a moment, and tries pronouncing it several different ways. 'Dev-ill. Devl. Dev-il-ish. Dev-lish. Dev-il-ry. Dev-lry. Devl.' He sighs, and at length says, 'I'm not sure, sir.'

An idea occurs to me. It is an excellent one. I am all at once prodigiously excited. 'If I write D-E-V apostrophe L, will people understand what I mean?'

He moves his head from side to side in equivocation. 'What's the context, sir?'

I answer him in iambs: 'With-OUT the DEV'L we'd BOTH be OUT of-a JOB.' I elide 'of' and 'a' to fit the verse, but I believe it sounds quite well.

'I don't know that it scans, sir.'

'No, no, it does! That's why I made it one syllable.'

Simmons frowns, and says, 'But you just said "Devil."'

'No,' say I, a little annoyed, 'I said "Dev'l."'

'Forgive me, sir, I heard "Devil."'

'Well damn it, it doesn't matter what you heard: it'll be written "Dev'l."'

'I thought you were going to make it one syllable.'

'THAT WAS ONE SYLLABLE.'

'Oh,' he says dubiously, 'I see.'

It isn't much of a concession, but I don't need much of one right now. Even a little one will do. I take it as tacit encouragement and feel a surge of elation. I haven't been excited about a project in months, and I plunge forward in explanation.

'I've decided to write a defence of the Devil,' I tell him. 'It's a dialogue. A man is walking down a road and sees a priest—'

'Who has tripped over a cobblestone and is cursing the Devil and the man defends the Devil?'

I hate when Simmons finishes my sentences. It makes me feel unoriginal. But I acknowledge that, yes, such is in fact what I was going to say. I ask him what he thinks.

He surprises me by replying, 'I think it's very good, sir,' and then surprises me not at all by going on: 'I've heard that when one runs out of inspiration, it can be very helpful to whore out one's own experiences.'

When my parents died, which happened in a manner at once absurd and poetic, Simmons took over the rearing of Lizzie and me. It was not strictly speaking usual, but then nothing in our family has ever been so. We are eccentrics. Simmons is, you will have already apprehended, not a butler in the usual sense. He frequently does unbutlerly tasks, but when I point it out to him he simply sniffs and says that he prefers to know the work is sound. I admire him greatly for it.

(I am at heart a revolutionary.) I mention all this only to make clear that though I am furious with Simmons, the thought of dismissing him is quite inconceivable. I do however consider striking him—but refrain, as I have never in my life hit a man, and it seems a foolish thing to begin upon my septuagenarian butler.

Instead, I mumble, 'I wish you hadn't said that, Simmons.'

'Yes, sir.' There is no contrition in his voice. I believe he is cross with me, but I am not certain why. I am behaving in quite the manner I always do. His attitude, however, seems quite changed. In fact, as I reflect upon it, he has seemed rather off since my wedding. I wonder if perhaps he finds Vivien as upsetting as I do. It is not a thought which has occurred to me before. I realise for the first time that in a sense when I married her he did also—not of course in the physical sense, but in the sense that she is now a constant presence in his life and has complete authority to make his existence miserable—and he was not even consulted upon it.*

'By the bye, sir,' he says, 'your wife is asking for you.'

That is how I know Simmons is displeased with me: he is acting as her messenger. I refuse to submit. 'Tell her I'm working.'

'Very good, sir.'

Simmons turns on his heel and begins to leave. I know that he is sulking and I feel slightly ashamed of myself. I do not

---

*What Mr Savage speaks of is true of any servant. For instance, Mrs Savage brought with her to Pocklington Place a cook, one Mrs Davis, whose services were a wedding gift from Lord and Lady Lancaster. The poor woman is devoted to Vivien, but because of the marriage must also endure Mr Savage.—HL.

like it when Simmons and I are at odds. It seems elitist and wrong. I search for something to say which will allow us to part on better terms.

'Are there many people out there?' It is not all that could be desired, but as an overture of peace it will serve.

'There are, sir,' he replies, and I can tell that he is not so angry at me as he may have been a moment ago. There is forgiveness in his voice and manner, even if no one but myself could discern it. I have that gift—faces and demeanours are to me an open book. I know of no man more adept at reading other people. 'We're nearly out of champagne,' he adds.

I sigh. He is waiting for me to say something, and I know what it is. It is what he would call my duty. At length, I say as cheerfully as I am able, 'I suppose I should go out and make sure no one's stealing anything.' It is the last thing in the world that I would like to do, but there comes a time in a man's life when he must stare a bullet in the eye, and if this is mine then I shall not shrink from it.

I expect Simmons to be mollified by my courage, but he is not. He says, 'Do you have a mask, sir?'

I am taken aback. 'Excuse me?'

'No one is allowed at the party without a mask. It's strictly enforced.'

'It's my own home,' I cry with indignation. Does he want me to do my duty or not?

'All the same, sir.'

He is being contrary on purpose, and it annoys me greatly. I have striven to make myself agreeable even in the depths of my foulest of moods, and all he can tell me is that I cannot leave my own study without a mask! 'Lend me yours,' I say coolly.

'I'm afraid I can't, sir. It would baffle the guests.'

'Well damn it, then go and find me one, Simmons!'

'Very good, sir,' he says, and begins to leave.

I am determined to show him that I am not cowed by his belligerence, and so I continue composing immediately. I say, 'With-OUT the DEV'L we'd BOTH—' and then break off. I cannot maintain the act in the face of such wretched poetry. 'It's not any good, is it?' I ask his back. There is a part of me which wonders if perhaps it *is* rather good, and I am simply unaccustomed to good poetry and can no longer recognise it. It is a small part of me, but it is there all the same.

'Not very, sir,' he says, sounding pleased. Then he opens the door and plunges out into the swirl of silk and satin and noise.

I sink my head down upon my desk. I reflect that if I had killed myself three hours ago, I should not have had to speak with Lizzie or fight with Simmons or confront my own inferior poetic efforts. If I could go back in time I would surely hurl myself into the Thames without consulting anyone, Froggy children be damned.*

There was a time, and it was not so long ago, when my poetry was respected very widely.† I commanded a large read-

---

*I trust that my views upon such language and sentiments are by now quite clear.—HL.

†Respected is not, I think, the correct word. Of the most recent collection, *Daydreams and Digressions,* Mr Pendergast wrote, 'The best one can say of this packet of poems, for such Mr Savage assures us they are, is that it is but seventy pages long.' For a time it did sell tolerably well, however.—HL.

ership, and from book to book I did not let down the expectations of press or public. Admittedly, my work was not Keats. Nor, I suppose, was it Byron, Shelley, Wordsworth, Coleridge, Milton, Blake, or Shakespeare. And it was certainly not Tennyson. But it was not bad. I was young, agreeable, unpretentious, and wrote prettily and wittily, even if I had not I suppose altogether overmuch to say. I amused myself and I amused my readers, and what else can a man wish for? I do not care for poets who spin solemn stanzas of lost love and theology. Ours is not a solemn age, on the whole, and so it puzzles me that our poetry should by and large be characterised by its solemnity and lack of humour.

Why, given the choice of subjects and voices, would a man choose to write about, say, the moral virtues of chastity? Chastity is not *interesting*. Moral virtue is interesting sometimes, but only sometimes! It is only interesting when an author or poet *notes that it is in general uninteresting,* and then works actively to counteract that. For instance, when someone (and it has not yet been done, even by my lord Alfred)* decides to set out and write an epic about King Arthur—not about the exploits of the knights and damsels of his court, but about the man himself—they will have to grapple with what the literary world has been grappling with since Chrétien, which is that Arthur Pendragon himself is by nature boring because he is an exemplar of virtue; whereas Lancelot (or Gawain or Yvain or Tristan or Perceval or Gareth or really anyone else for that matter except perhaps Galahad) is by nature

---

*That is, Tennyson.—HL.

interesting because his is a tale of virtue gone awry. When a great writer tackles Arthur himself directly, something quite interesting may result, if he proves equal to the task—how is virtue made compelling?

Well, I do not know. I am not myself virtuous, so it does not trouble me. I once wanted to be, but that was long ago. I am now a cowardly poet hiding in his study, hoping vainly to escape the slings and arrows of a society party. (Pendergast is here. I can sense it.)

I imagine what will happen when Simmons returns with a mask for me. I believe it will go something like this. He will come into the study and hand it to me without saying a word, because he is a good butler and does not use words unless they are necessary. I will say, 'Thank you, Simmons,' though I will not in fact mean it because I do not want to leave this room.

But I will leave it, for though I rail against society I cannot entirely break free of it for the sake of those I hold dear. I will open my door, the only barrier between myself and the horrors of the modern world. I will be caught up in the current of sweaty bodies pretending to be having a better time than they are.

In the hallway I will run into Sir Francis Babington, who has never entirely forgiven me for not marrying his Agnes. He will be wearing a costume of harlequin motley, holding a flute of champagne, and cackling like the Dev'l. He will say, 'Decided to honour us with your presence, eh Savage?' and I will know it is him because no one else I know is quite so fat nor half as abrasive.

'Sir Francis!' I will exclaim with insincere delight. 'How did you recognize me beneath my mask?'

'A mask cannot mask your air of smugness, Savage,' he will say, and he will dart off after a sylph who is likely Mrs Frazer, though because of her costume (an Egyptian getup which hides her face and not much else) I will not be able to tell for certain.

(I was mistaken before—a self-satisfied chuckle outside my door reminds me that Pendergast is more abrasive than Sir Francis, but only just.)

I will have to avoid Pendergast—who I suppose is here only to spite me, for he does not frequent parties. He spends most evenings following the press. He has an unfortunate predilection toward Contemporary Matters, which makes his poetry even worse than it would be otherwise. I knew a man who once joked that a fellow could dispense with ever reading Pendergast if he could afford the morning paper. I am not similarly enticed by reality.

I may encounter Vivien. She will be very beautiful, and very cold. 'Hello,' I might say.

'Hello, Mr Savage,' she might reply.

'Quite the party,' I might say.

'I looked for you earlier,' she might say.

'I was in my study,' I would reply. 'Writing.'

'Ah,' she'd say to that in a disapproving way. She would almost say something more—perhaps even take a breath to do so. But then she would let it out. She does this often, and I do not know why or about what she is thinking. That done, she would tug at a sequin on her gown (she will be dressed as something fantastical and romantic, I imagine—a princess or something similar) and look vacant. She will have nothing more to say, for she neither appreciates nor understands poetry. We never do have much to say to one another. I will fumble for words and try to think of some complimentary remark about the party, though I have forgotten why she threw it in the first place. I will almost come up with something, but just then she will exclaim, 'Mr Murray!' or 'Lord Eisley!' or 'Is that you, Algie dear?' and she'll dash off and I will feel wretched.

I will wander about like Dante, but without a guide. I will bump everywhere into lost souls who will clutch at me and try to make me join their ranks. I will deflect conversational attempts as though they are fiery snares which tug at my ankles. I will avoid Pendergast's nose. Eventually, if I am lucky, I will find Lizzie.

'Lizzie!' I will cry, and we will shoulder through the press of bodies and grasp each other by the hands and find a secure corner and retreat to it. She will raise her mask, and wear beneath it a look of horror. I will say, 'Do you still imagine society parties to be fun?' And she will apologise with her eyes and say, 'Nellie, they are hideous! How could I ever have thought otherwise? And how have you managed to stay sane with these travails? You say something of this magnitude happens once every week or so? How dreadful! How frightful! I was quite wrong to doubt you when you said that you were cast down by fate.'

And despite the previous harsh words between us I will accept her contrition readily, because she has now stared the beast in the eye and knows what it is I am burdened with.

We will begin plotting our escape. Possibly we might make it to a window, which we could hurl ourselves through, landing bloodied and battered but free upon the cobblestones outside. Or we could maybe achieve the roof, and watch the pale disk of the moon, gently obscured by the fog, rising behind the grey dome of St Paul's. But as we begin to sneak from the room, a man in a mask will grab Lizzie by the waist and whisk her off to dance, and I will be alone again.

I will blunder about some more, adrift amidst the sea of false words and insincerity. It will be awful, and there will be no escape, and I will feel again the crushing sense of doom I have felt since my marriage.

I do not know how it is that I wooed Vivien with so few words passing between us, but I must have done—for it was not until after our wedding that I tried talking to her and realised the mistake I had made. We had, it turned out, nothing to talk *about*.

I ought to have been tipped off on the day that I proposed to her. It was raining. We were taking a turn about the Park. (I had ulterior motives.) I pretended to trip, and meant to land upon one knee and propose to her in a flash of planned spontaneity. But I was forestalled—Vivien, displaying unexpected reflexes, caught my arm. We stood for a moment, pressed together, not speaking. There was something in her eyes which I could not interpret. I deliberated. I resolved to take the bull by the horns: I knelt down. I tried to speak, but my mouth had suddenly gone dry. I swallowed, but choked upon my own saliva and coughed. I tried again to speak.

'Vivien,' I began, but dissolved into a fit of coughing. She looked down at me, saying nothing. 'Vivien,' I said again, 'Vivien, I am—'

On second thought, I am not going to tell you what I was. I had intended to record what I said, but I will not. It is private. Suffice it to say that I went on at some length, chronicling my love for her in the most poetical terms you can imagine. I have never been more poetical than I was in that moment. I wish I could remember my exact words, for they would be canonised as classic words of love. But—and looking back, I cannot believe such a thing happened and did not serve to warn me of the horrors to come—Vivien interrupted me. She looked down at me and laughed—actually laughed at me!—and pulled me to my feet, and said only, 'Peace! I will stop your mouth.' Then she kissed me.

At the time it seemed the most romantic thing that had ever happened. But looking back, I see it to have been the beginning of the end. I was composing poetry, and Vivien interrupted me in a way which brooked no further converse. So there you have it.

I courted a goddess, but married only a woman. I hear that this is how it often goes, and I must pause here to note that marriage seems to me a most awful institution. If only we could carry out eternal courtships! I believe then I should be content, for the weeks courting Vivien were the happiest of my life. When every glance makes one's heart beat quicker and one's breath come short, and when a shy smile or spirited toss of the head makes one's eyes lose focus, the world becomes more vivid. Even London becomes a welcoming place, a lovely place, a town of beauty instead of filth and parties.*

I am not looking forward to Simmons's return.

The door creaks open. I do not lift my head. 'Did you find me a mask so I can attend my own party, Simmons?' I ask with some bitterness.

'Oh,' comes a querulous, stammering voice I have never heard before, 'I'm not Simmons.'

I look up. The stranger has entered my study and closed the door behind him. He is absurdly thin, well dressed, and wears no costume but a bird-beaked Venetian carnival mask which he holds on a stick in front of his face. His shoulders are sloped as though with inexpressible weariness, but he does not appear to be elderly. As I study him, I find that I cannot in fact age him within a decade.

'Indeed,' I say. 'You're lost.'

'Not lost, either,' he says. The stammer wears upon my nerves.

'No, see, in fact you are. This is my private study. The party is out there.'

'I'm not here for the party, Mr Savage, though it does seem to be an excellent one.'

'Then what *are* you here for?' I demand. I do not like strangers, interlopers, stammerers, uninvited guests, or gentlemen travelling incognito.

'Only to thank you,' he says with great politeness, lowering

---

*I believe this must be true, as I have read as much elsewhere. I do not, however, have any personal experience with it. There was once when I believed I had—but I was mistaken.—HL.

the mask absently. There is nothing in his face of note. It is a perfectly ordinary face, one with a nose, two grey eyes with lids to them, a mouth, a chin, and everything else one would expect to find upon a face. I still cannot determine his age.

'To thank me?'

'For the kind word. I had been in a dark place, you understand, but hearing a friendly word can work miracles, and I'm feeling jolly much better.'

I stare at him, quite at a loss. At last, I say, 'I have no idea what you're talking about.'

'Earlier tonight you defended me from a particularly short-sighted priest, for which I came to thank you.'

I am utterly confused. He keeps looking at me with significance, but I do not understand the look. 'You must be mistaken,' I say. 'All that happened is that a priest tripped over a cobblestone and was cursing the—' Then I understand all at once. It is an unpleasant sensation, the sort of thing I imagine a man must feel who has had legs his whole life and then finds them abruptly amputated. 'Oh,' I say dumbly. 'Then you are—Really?'

He says only, 'Indeed.'*

I have never spoken to a supernatural entity before, and do not know precisely how to proceed. The Prince of Darkness—for I am reasonably certain it is he—simply looks at me. I study his face again. It remains ordinary. I wonder if this is his

---

*Though it is scarcely credible, I have examined and cross-examined many people who assure me that the conversation which dominates this chapter did indeed take place. Make of that what you will. For my part, I am still grappling with it.—HL.

body, or if he has appropriated it. I try not to shudder at the thought. My mind conjures up images of a perfectly ordinary fellow walking home when suddenly the Devil floats up out of the dusty roadway and through his leather soles and along his shins and past his knees and around his hips and into his heart, rather like smoke into a smoker's lungs. I glance at him again. I am waiting for something, but I am not sure what. Flames to spurt up, I suppose, or horns to sprout from his forehead, or a dead angel to plummet through the roof. None of these things happen, and the longer I look at him the more uncomfortable he seems to become and (strangely) the less uncomfortable *I* become.

'Well I say,' I venture at last. 'This is unexpected.'

'But not unwelcome, I hope?' he asks eagerly.

'No,' I say, thrown off by his diminutive demeanour. He seems really quite tame, and what's more, even a trifle melancholy. 'No, of course not.'

'Oh good!' he exclaims with feeling. 'I do so hate to be unwelcome!'

I scratch my head. I have reason to believe I am standing in my study hiding from the guests of a fancy dress party conducting an interview with the Devil, but for some reason there does not seem to be anything particularly odd about it. He is very polite, and I am very polite, and what more I expect I cannot say.

After a very long and awkward moment in which I find speech impossible, the Gentleman says, 'Well, I'd best be going. But again, I thank you, and I wish you a happy life free from care.'

'Alas, sir, I am already married!' I say without thinking.

'Oh sir,' he cries in horror, quite taken aback. 'What, and a fine poet like you?'

I grin ruefully at his boyish chagrin. 'I'm afraid so.'

'Oh dear,' he says, with what sounds like genuine concern. 'Why?'

I find myself beginning to like the old chap, and so I tell him the truth: 'It was a financial thing.'

'You married for money?'

'I blush to admit that I did. Otherwise I never would have done it. I never planned to marry—in fact, I planned never to marry. I am not made of marriageable stuff. My mind is not a marriageable mind and I do not come from marriageable stock. My parents died upon their anniversary, you see.'

'Indeed, indeed,' he says, nodding sagely.

'You see, sir,' I carry on, the floodgates now open, 'as you say, I'm a poet, and poets aren't meant to marry! Poets are meant to dream and dance in the moonlight and love hopelessly! And in short, sir, I found that as soon as I had married I quite lost my ability to write and have been losing my already tenuous grasp on my reason ever since—for I find that no matter what I try—and believe me, I have tried everything: I stopped speaking to conserve my apparently limited supply of verbiage, I stopped sleeping so as to not waste creativity in dreaming, I even considered burning my library, thinking that without reading material I should be forced to generate my own. But no matter what I try I cannot, come—excuse me—Hell or high water, write, and it seems that the well of my genius has run dry and I am left bereft at twenty-two with neither words nor ideals to sustain me. And in short, sir, since my marriage I cannot write, and but for my little sister—no, in fact, regardless of my little sister—I wish I were dead.'

There is a pause after my speech, and I wonder if it had been ill-advised. I meant every word, but it occurs to me that revealing one's inmost heart to Satan may not always be the wisest course of action. At length he says with quiet feeling, 'I'm so sorry! That sounds dreadful.'

'It is,' I say, deciding that Satan or no, this gentleman is especially reasonable and quick to apprehend.

'All the same,' he adds after pensing a moment, 'one can't help but point out that it's your own fault.'

'I don't follow.'

'Hang it, man, you're a *poet*! And you married for money instead of love!'

He is perfectly correct, of course, and I know it—indeed, I have said as much myself. But something in his manner irks me. I do not like it when I am preached at, and I am feeling contrary—too contrary even to appreciate the irony of being preached at by the Devil. I say, 'That has nothing to do with it. It's my wife's fault.'

'I don't mean to offend you, Mr Savage, but that's not the case.'

I am becoming upset. 'It is!'

'Please don't be angry,' says the Gentleman. 'I don't want to quarrel with you.'

'Then don't give advice regarding matters of which you are plainly ignorant! I take it you are not married?'

'I am not, but I—'

'Of course you're not, or you wouldn't be so damned impatient to pass judgment!' I wonder fleetingly at my choice of words. Can one say 'damned' to the Devil? Is it proper?* I do not know. Nor do I know why I am arguing with notions I have myself set forth already. I feel as though I am a sleeve unravelling.

'I am not married, sir,' says the Gentleman with more resolve than I had expected of him, 'but I have some small understanding, I think, of human nature.'

I do not know why I am yelling at the Devil. Perhaps it is a residual effect of my recent self-endangering impulses. 'I don't care about human nature!' I cry, my voice breaking. 'I am married to a harpy and you tell me it's my fault I'm losing my mind!'

'I didn't say that,' he says soothingly. 'I said—'

But the madness is upon me, and I have lost my head. 'What are you *doing* here, anyway?' I demand.

He looks hurt to be so interrogated. 'I have told you already. I am here to thank you.'

'And steal my soul while you're at it, no doubt,' I mutter. As the words pass my lips, I think perhaps that wouldn't be such a bad thing. No matter what method of suicide I resolve upon, it will leave something of a mess for those I leave behind me—but if I were to descend bodily to Hell it seems that all compli-

---

*I have often wondered about this, and things similar, such as whether or not one ought to say, 'You see,' to a blind man, or 'If you follow,' to a man with no legs. It is a complicated question, and one which has not yet been satisfactorily answered.—HL.

cations would be allayed. (Could I go bodily? Or would he rip out my soul and just take that?)

'What on earth would I want with your soul?' he asks with genuine surprise.

'Isn't that what you do? Collect souls?'

'I have quite a surfeit of souls, sir,' he replies. 'I'd be happy never to see another soul as long as I live.' So much for that.

'Indeed?'

'Assuredly.'

'I find that fascinating.'

'You do?'

'Certainly.'

'Why?'

'Well,' I say, wondering how best to put it. 'It goes rather against common wisdom, you know.'

'Does it?'

'It does.'

The Gentleman looks so downcast that for a moment I fear he will weep. He says with a sigh, 'There are times when I feel as though humanity misunderstands me.'

'Sir,' I tell him wryly, 'you suffer the plight of a poet.'

'You're too kind,' he says.

'No, but truly.'

'Do you know,' he muses, 'Alighieri once told me the same thing.'

I must have misheard. It is too extraordinary. 'Excuse me?'

'Oh,' he says offhandedly, 'the fellow who takes care of my flowers. Something Alighieri. Don, Donald, something. He once told me I understand poets better than most poets understand themselves.'

'Dante?' I say in shock. I was only just thinking of the man. 'Dante Alighieri?'

'Yes, that's it,' says he.

'Dante the poet?'

'Yes. Wonderful with the roses. Less so with the rhododendron.'

I can only repeat the name like an idiot. 'Dante Alighieri— is your gardener?'

'I believe I just said that.'

'Well good Lord.'

'What?'

'Well—' He seems not to understand how extraordinary this is. I search for words. 'He's quite famous, you know.'

'Is he?' asks the Gentleman, with evident surprise.

'Indisputably.'

'Fascinating. Indeed?' He seems doubtful. 'Don't misunderstand me, he does a perfectly adequate job; but I keep him on more because I enjoy talking to him than for his gardening skills—which are, between you and me, spectacularly mediocre.'

I cannot tell whether I should laugh or cry. 'He isn't famous for his gardening,' I manage to say with offended poetic dignity. I do not in fact much care for his work (allegory does not agree with me). But the *Commedia* is after all something of a standard around which all poets rally—and if I do not care for it, I can at least appreciate it.

'Well I should think not,' laughs the Gentleman, relieved. 'That would have been quite inexplicable. His poetry, then?'

'Quite.'

'Fascinating,' he says again. 'That drivel about Hell and such?'

'Yes.'

'He got it all wrong, you know.'

If I pause to consider that I am discussing the poetic merits of Dante Alighieri with the Devil, I believe I shall lose what is left of my mind—so I simply carry on with the conversation as if it is one I have every evening in my study. 'Did he?' I say.

'Well of course!' says the Gentleman. He seems eager to talk about it. 'Don't think it's really that awful, do you? Couldn't live there if it was, could you?'

'What's it like, then?' I ask.

'Well, first off, I rather prefer to call it Essex Grove.'

'Call what Essex Grove?' I ask, just to be certain.

'Where I'm from.'

'You mean—Hell?'

The Gentleman shudders and says, 'Oh, I do hate that word! It sounds so vulgar. And uninviting.'

'So you call it Essex Grove.'

'I do.'

'To make it more inviting.'

'Indeed.'

He is so blithe about the whole thing that all I can say is, 'How extraordinary.'

'Thank you,' he says.

'If you'll pardon my asking, why Essex Grove?'

'As opposed to . . . ?'

'I don't know,' say I. 'Milford Haven or Pocklington Place or Pemberley. What I mean to say is, does the name Essex Grove have any especial significance to you?'

'Oh,' says the Gentleman, 'certainly! I like it.'

Which, really, is as good an explanation as I could wish.

I am aware that I am not alone in my curiosity regarding certain matters metaphysical in nature—so for the sake of posterity I ask him, 'And you live in a palace? A mansion? A Grecian temple?'

'But you *do* have a flair for theatrics, don't you!' he says with a little laugh. 'Of course I don't live in a palace. Just a simple cottage on the edge of the Elysian Fields, a stone's throw from the River Styx.'

'And Dante is your gardener,' I repeat.

'Yes.'

I have run out of things to say. The enormity of the situation threatens to overwhelm me, and I simply gape at him. He stares back, quiet and awkward. This goes on for several minutes.

At length, desperate to break what has become an uncomfortable silence, I blurt, 'Look, please forgive me for being blunt, but I have no idea what you're doing here.'

'Well I say,' says the Gentleman, mildly offended. 'I've told you—I wished to thank you.'

'Which you have done.'

'Which I have done.'

We stare at one another again. I feel compelled to add, 'It's not that I object to your company. But you must admit this is a damned peculiar sort of encounter. If you'll pardon me.'

'I suppose it is, yes.'

'So what is it that you want?'

'Actually,' he says, enormously uncomfortable, 'I was rather wondering—' He breaks off, and shifts from foot to foot. I try to look encouraging. Finally he takes a breath and says all at once, 'Could we be friends?'

I stare at him.

'I've always wanted a friend,' he blunders on. 'I've heard all about them, and I think they sound splendid. But I've never had one. And I don't know how to go about obtaining one. One reads stories and they are made out to be very easy to come by—in fact people seem to take them for granted—but I've never had one. And I'd like one. And so at the risk of sounding provincial, I would like to ask you to be my friend.' He reddens and quickly adds, 'I mean, if you'd be agreeable to the notion. I don't mean to impose terms on our relationship. I'm afraid I must seem the soul of tactlessness. I'm sorry.'

'No, no,' I say hurriedly, for he looks more mortified by the moment. 'No, I'd—' I hesitate, then say, 'I'd like that.'

The Gentleman looks up sharply, searching my face for traces of mockery. He finds none. 'You would?' he asks.

'I would. I am at the moment suffering from a dearth of friends.' It is no lie. I have never been what one might call a social chap; but I was not always as isolated from my fellow man as I have been of late. It was not so long ago that I had numerous acquaintances—admirers, colleagues (though the bond of fellowship between writers has always been a fraught thing),* even here and there a few of what you might call friends. Never perhaps of the intimate sort; but all the same men and women whose company gave me pleasure. Over the last six months, however, these have one by one fallen by the wayside—and this conversation, irrespective of the hellish nature of my interlocutor, is the first pleasurable exchange of words I have had with a like-minded person in a very long while. And so I tell him genuinely and without a thought to personal danger, 'I would.'

'That's— That's marvellous! And very kind of you, sir.'

'Not at all,' I say. There is more emotion in the air than I care for.

'No, no, it is! You have treated me handsomely this evening, Mr Savage. I have been as I think I mentioned in a dark place these last— Well, for a rather long time. And your kindness moves me, sir. It moves me very much indeed.'

I see that he is very near to being overcome, which I fear will lead to me being overcome. 'Steady on, old boy,' I say with alarm, 'I've had a run of it lately, too, and I don't know if I can handle any more emotion tonight.'

'Forgive me,' he says, turning from me. 'A moment, please. There. Apologies.'

'Not at all. Handkerchief?' I offer him mine.

'Thank you.' He takes it and dabs at his face. I avert my eyes. This is definitely not the evening I had expected it to be.

---

*A wise man of my acquaintance once said, 'Between writers there is no friendship possible. There is passion, enmity, worship, love, but no friendship.' —HL.

'What is that book on your desk?' the Gentleman asks. I am grateful for the change in subject, and look to where he points.

I smile to see the title indicated. *'The Idylls of the King,'** I say.

'What is it about?'

'You've never read it?' I ask with surprise.

'No. Is it very good?'

'It is,' I say, struggling to imagine how dreary life must be without my lord Alfred.

'Who wrote it?'

'A great bear of a poet named Tennyson. But unlike any poet you've met. He's taller than any man I've ever seen. At school they say he used to sneak into the stables and steal a pony which he'd put on his back and parade around the grounds. When queried about this remarkable habit, he replied that we should never recover the nobility lost us since the age of Arthur until we learn to bear our mounts as willingly as they bear us.'†

'I would like to meet that man someday,' he says with enthusiasm, and I try not to think mordant thoughts. 'I do so love books,' he goes on. 'I have a great many. I flatter myself

---

*I like this work very much.—HL.

†I have met one very old man who went to school with Tennyson and who swears this is not true; and one who swears it is. So I do not know. I do know, though, that my cousin Ashley once carried a mare across a stream because it was pregnant and Lady Lancaster was worried it would take a chill and miscarry. (I may add that, gratifyingly, the mare delivered without mishap—and that the foal went on to become Falling Star, whose exploits on the racetrack can scarcely be overstated. The reader will recall his famous victory against Persian Emperor at Alexandra Park.)—HL.

that my library is one of the finest anywhere. But I haven't that one.' He looks mournfully at the small volume.

'Would you like to borrow it?' I ask.

'May I?' he says with trepidation. 'I would be in your debt.'

'Please. The only thing more pleasurable than reading perfect poetry is sharing it.' He still looks nervous, so I pick up the book and hand it to him.

'I begin to understand the premium placed on friendship,' he says with feeling. Then he shakes himself and says, 'I regret that I must go.'

'Are you sure?' I ask. I find myself disappointed that the interview is at an end—somehow I have become quite attached to this slender Gentleman, and will be sorry to see him go. His company has been like a bit of wreckage from a sunken ship which a drowning man might cling to. His departure will plunge me back into the trackless ocean of despair which I have swum for so many months already.

'Yes,' he says. 'I've tarried too long already. Your kindness tonight will not be forgotten, Mr Savage. I wish you a very pleasant night.'

'You forget that I am married,' I reply, gloomy once more.

The Gentleman looks at me queerly, with a sort of half-smile playing across his face. 'Chin up, old boy,' he says. 'These things have a way of working themselves out.' He raises the book to me in salute, opens the study door, and vanishes back into the party.

I scarcely have time to blink and none at all to think before Lizzie flounces in, a swirl of black velvet and pearls. I haven't the slightest idea where she found the dress, but it suits her better than I am comfortable with. No sister should look so well.

'Who was that?' she demands, removing a silver domino mask. She must have passed the Gentleman in the hall.

'It's really rather difficult to explain,' I say. I have no desire to speak to her about my encounter until I have had time to properly think about it, and I do not know when that might be. Then I recall our earlier harsh words and I tell her, 'You look beautiful, little sister.'

'Thank you,' she says with womanly graciousness, twirling to show off her gown. It is alarming to me how lovely she is grown, and how very old. It isn't a thing little sisters should do, grow up.

'I wanted to apologise,' I say. 'About earlier.'

'Oh no, no!' she exclaims. 'I was going to do the same!'

'I love you, you know,' I say.

'And I love you, of course. I brought you a mask. Simmons said you needed one.'

She holds out to me a small, plain black mask, just such as I would have chosen for myself. 'Thank you,' I say. 'Where is he?'

'Simmons?'

I nod.

'I'm not sure. There was some sort of upset among the guests which he was seeing to.'

I imagine the possible causes of said upset and shudder. Several scenarios chase one another through my mind. General Hallam might have had a heart attack and fallen dead on the table and caused a mess which would take a week to properly clean. A servant might have made eyes at a lady and been shot by a jealous husband. Or perhaps Babington became truly drunk and pinched a maid who squealed and jumped and upset a soup tureen which emptied its contents onto the lap of the Duke of Cumbria who fell backward and into the way of Mr Moncrieff who tripped over him and whose mask upon falling was pitched across the room and stabbed Lady Lazenby in the bosom causing her to drop her champagne flute which shattered on the carpet and a shard of which bounced and impaled Lord Earlsmere who dropped to his knees in pain and over whom Mrs Frazer, who was all this while preoccupied with jealousy for the pinched maid and was looking behind her at Babington instead of in front of her at the body of Earlsmere, pitched headlong, landing in a fireplace which immediately set her costume ablaze which in turn set the curtains alight and which will by and by burn down the whole house.* I loathe parties.

'Did you meet my wife?' I say.

'Not yet. There are lots and lots of people, and everyone's wearing a mask.'

'Isn't it horrid?'

'Oh no!' she cries. 'I've never had such a lovely evening. I feel as though I could dance until my feet bled. Everyone's so beautiful and mysterious and romantic in their costumes. I'm upset with you, Nellie. I feel as though you've been holding out on me. Society parties are wonderful.'

---

*I was present at this party, and so I can say with authority that this is not what happened. However, I have heard that something very similar did occur once at a party given by the Count and Countess de Guiche in Paris.—HL.

It is a dreadful speech, one which I never feared one of my own blood would ever make to me. I must look pained, because Lizzie says to me sternly, 'Lionel, you are an old humbug, and I cannot believe—'

I do not learn what she cannot believe, for she is interrupted by the entrance of Simmons, who looks (though it is hard to tell beneath the turban) grave.

'Excuse me, sir,' he says.

'Hello, Simmons. What was the matter out there?'

'No one can find your wife, sir.'

'What do you mean?'

'Just what I said.'

'She's probably gone up to her room,' I say.

'*My* room,' puts in Lizzie.

'No, sir, I've checked all the rooms. The guests say one minute she was dancing and laughing and generally hostessing, and the next moment she was gone.'

I stare at him. 'What do you mean, "gone"?'

'I mean *gone*, sir. They say it's as though she just— disappeared.'

Four

In Which I Write Dreadful Poetry & Discover Two Other Dreadful Things.

I have just had an interview with the Devil. Is not that strange?

What is stranger still is that I leave the interview not fearful, not awestruck, not cast down—but, rather, feeling a little sad for the fellow, and wondering how I might contrive to sometime have him round for tea. He seems to me on the whole a decent chap, and I am struck that perhaps we (by which I mean humanity) have misunderstood him. Of course I could be wrong—perhaps this is all a ruse and will end in my eternal damnation. But if so, at least I have had a pleasant conversation with a stimulating partner.

I am not a religious man by inclination—I have time to worship only one deity, and Thou, Poetry, art my goddess—but I am born in England, and I have been brought up in a God-fearing English society. To suppose that things Up Above—or more to the point, Down Below—might be different than we have in the past supposed is, I admit, a bit of a reorientation; but not an unpleasant one.

Nearly as soon as the thought enters my head it is replaced by another, which is that perhaps my visitor wasn't the Devil at all. He could have been mad, or he could have been playing a practical joke on me. That seems on the whole unlikely, however. If he was mad, he was unlike any madman I have ever met—and I have, to be candid, spent some little time with madmen. (I find them especially poetical, and have made it my business on occasion to visit Bedlam in an observatory capacity.)* No, I do not think him mad. An imposter, then? Sent, perhaps, by Pendergast? It is doubtful. I would not put such a thing past my rival; but if the fellow I just spoke to was counterfeiting, he did so better than any actor I have ever seen upon the stage.

If he was neither lunatic nor confidence man, logic if not reason tells me that he was then the Devil. Besides, he knew of the incident with the priest and the cobblestone. As no one besides he and I (he the priest, I mean) were present for the exchange, and as I have told no one of it but Simmons and Lizzie, how could he have discovered it other than by supernatural means? I have an acquaintance—friendship being not my forte or his—who says that when one eliminates the impossible, then what is left, no matter how improbable, must be the truth. Well then, the Gentleman was the Devil.

And *if* the Devil (which fact I have just resolved upon) then

---

*These visits were not always in an observatory capacity. See the first note on page 83.—HL.

he was either counterfeiting docility or not. But what reason had he to feign friendship? The man left without my soul—without anything, in fact, save the finest volume of poetry published since the First Folio.* His diminutive demeanour gained him nothing—except my sympathy, which I do not know why he would have needed if he were secretly the terror we think him.

So, then, I again am led to the conclusion that the encounter I have just had was genuine. The Devil is not, in fact, a wicked stealer of souls and ravisher of virgins—he is, rather, a melancholy man of between five and six feet tall (I have no eye for those things), who stammers slightly and enjoys books and wishes himself better liked.

This of course alters the last two thousand years of literature. Most notably, it casts the exploits of one Johann Faustus in an especially dubious light. If the Devil is the Gentleman I have just met, then what precisely happened to the Wittenbergovian necromancer? It seems poor Mr Marlowe and Herr Goethe were misinformed. And what then? Ought I to publish something saying so? It could be the making of me. On the other hand, it might not be viewed in a strictly serious light. It could, in fact, lead to a deal of ridicule. I do not like to be seen as ridiculous. I suppose I will not publish an article. A poem, though, could be acceptable. The public rarely views poems as wholly factual affairs. A poem, then! It will be an epic in the

---

*Oddly, my poetic tastes in this instance align with Mr Savage's. It should be acknowledged, however, that we are not in the majority in this judgment. I say this because Mr Savage presents his view as hard fact, when it is truly nothing but opinion.—HL.

Miltonian vein, though with perhaps a touch more Byron or Ariosto. A comical epic, but with serious and indeed existential undertones.

Here, though, I encounter an unfortunate stumbling block. I believe I have mentioned that my literary fame is of the passing, rather than lasting, sort. I am (I am perfectly aware) a strictly momentary sensation. Already, in fact, I have noted my waning reputation. I have published nothing in eight months, and the world is forgetting the tame wit of Lionel Savage. For me to compose an epic, even a comic one, would not do—it would confuse my readers. I might perhaps work my way to a place where I could publish it; but I am not there now. I have not written in a long while. If I attempted something on the scale I am considering, I would doubtless fall short of the mark. It would not be quite good enough to be good and not quite bad enough to be bad and would rather be simply mediocre, which is to me the single worst fate that can befall a work of art. I have no intention of being mediocre.

If, though, I were to regain my talent— to begin with trifles, at length advance to little amusements, from there to small gems, onward to ambitious flights of fancy, thereafter to— Yes, I believe that is the way it must be done.

I will write my way from impending obscurity to national hero.

And so I write all night. I do not spare a thought for my wife. She will return soon, no doubt, which is a pity; but until she does I will consider myself a condemned man handed a reprieve. I turn off the gas-jet (O metaphor!) and light candles and arrange my writing things with a care I have not taken since my marriage. To call it bliss would be to call Heaven pleasant. (I pause at that—the Gentleman had said Hell was more pleasant than one might suppose; and if there is a Hell I suppose there truly must be a Heaven: and what, then, is it like?)

I begin with trepidation. What if after all my jealously nourished hopes, I find myself still unable to write? But my hand seems to move pen across paper of its own accord. My brain has no conscious control over its speed. I am like a man who has wandered through the desert for an eternity and is suddenly confronted with a limitless expanse of cool, fresh, clean, blessed water. It is strange to me how easily the words flow. My wife will surely return home soon, wherever she may have gone; so why this sense of freedom? I do not know. But I take full advantage of it.

The sun rises and the candles are puddles on my desk, and I have finished a sheaf of poems. They are not masterpieces, but they amuse me and are sure to amuse a public long deprived of my words. I am composing aloud, as I do. 'i WALKED a-LONG the STRAND as EVE-ning FELL / And

SAW to MY sur-PRISE a GIRL who DID-n't . . . look . . . well?'
I crumple the page and begin again. It is not quite right, but
that is no matter. This is the sort of thing that happens when
one writes: one expects it. Iambic pentameter is an unforgiv-
ing mistress. Ten syllables and five stresses a line—there is not
room for fools or amateurs.

I am about to begin again when I hear the front door open
and shut. My wife, I suppose. I sigh. It couldn't last forever. I
resolve not to let her reappearance dampen my mood or in-
hibit my verse. I plough ahead.

'Life WAS re-STORED—' No, no, no. The advent of the sun
has thrown me off my rhythm. I am a creature of the night.
The day is not made for poets. I begin again. 'The MASQU-er-
ADE re-STORED to ME my LIFE: / Re-STORED my MUSE
and TOOK a-WAY my WIFE.'

I am chuckling to myself as Simmons enters. This night
has improved my disposition as no night has in I do not know
how long. I am feeling vastly better. That I contemplated suicide barely twelve hours ago seems to me most strange and
wondrous. I feel so well this morning that I could sing. I am
exhausted but exhilarated.

'Good morning, sir,' says Simmons, setting down a tray of
tea. He is accustomed to my erratic hours of old. 'Did you
sleep well?'

'No, Simmons, I didn't sleep. I thought it best to take advantage of any wifely reprieve to write. Where was she?'

'Excuse me, sir?'

'My wife. I heard her come in just now. The door slammed.
Did you find out where she'd been?'

'That wasn't your wife, sir,' says Simmons. 'That was Miss Elizabeth going out for a morning walk round the park.'*

I am surprised by this news, but cautiously optimistic. 'Then where *is* my wife?' I ask with bated breath.

'She's still missing, sir.'

My heart leaps. 'That's marvellous! Thank you, Simmons, you've taken a load off my mind.'

'You aren't worried, sir?' says he.

'Worried? No, why on earth should I be? Maybe she has a lover. That would be brilliant! Get her out of the house once in a while, give me some peace. Do you know I wrote all night?'

Simmons looks queer, as if he wants to say something, but he does not. Instead he asks only, 'Is it good?'

'What an awful question, Simmons!' I exclaim, laughing— my heart feels buoyed aloft on butterfly wings. 'Of course it's good!'

'May I read it?'

'Certainly not,' I snap. I regret my brusqueness, but Simmons has an unpleasant habit of making my writing seem much worse than it really is. I do not like it when I am composing and feeling grand and then someone comes along and reads my work and finds it wanting. It takes one down so quickly. It is like when one has a dream of flying, and then just as the world below looks its most marvellous and one feels the freest, it suddenly occurs to one that one hasn't any wings

---

*Pocklington Place is located just across from a small park. I will not say which one out of respect for my cousins' privacy.—HL.

and that humans aren't built for flight and that the laws of physics decree that one must fall—and then with a sickening sensation one begins to plummet to the earth so far below. That is what I always think of when I feel pleased with my poetry and then Simmons reads it. He is an astute critic, of that there is no doubt—but he is not always a gentle one, and my constitution requires gentleness.

Simmons has that queer look again, and says at length, 'Do you really think Mrs Savage has a paramour, sir?' It is an indelicate question, and asking it is unlike him.

'Well, how else do you explain it?' I counter. 'Lovely though it would be, wives don't just disappear. It is strange, though—devilish strange. Or "dev'lish," if you will. I've decided it *is* only one syllable, by the way. Dev'l.'

'Very good, sir,' he says, and leaves the room to continue his duties. He asks no questions and pushes the subject no further. Damned good man, Simmons.

I am struck by a poetic feeling, and extemporise: ''Tis DEV'lish STRANGE when WIVES just DIS-a-PPEAR.' I like it. It has some panache. I wonder if there is something in it—a story in blank verse about disappearing wives, some devilry, a dash of the supernatural. It would not be the epic of which I have spoken—but in later years it could perhaps be viewed as a sketch of it, an early consideration of wives, the Devil, heartbreak, the follies of youth, perhaps abductions—

Very abruptly, something quite awful occurs to me.

'SIMMONS!' I cry.

He enters with his usual promptness. 'Sir?'

I cannot say it. It is too terrible. Simmons will never forgive me. 'Nothing. Nothing, Simmons. Never mind. Please let me know if my wife comes back. That will be all.'

'Very good, sir,' he says, looking perplexed. He leaves again.

My stomach is doing all sorts of peculiar things—whether from fear, excitement, guilt, or hunger, it is impossible to tell. I try to consider the situation, but I am too disturbed to think straight. Before I can order my thoughts the door slams again. I wonder if it is Vivien, and my stomach does even more strange things.

It is not Vivien; it is Lizzie. She skips into my study, holding a rather crushed baked good which she deposits on my desk and a sheaf of papers which she does not. Vivien is still missing. The unspeakable consideration still stands.

Lizzie says, 'Good morning, you look like death, I brought you a pastry, and we need to talk.'

I can see that she's in a lecturing mood, so I tell her that I'm a bit preoccupied this morning, which I am. I cannot focus my thoughts. They are swirling and purling through the whirling world without pause or consideration for my delicate sensibility just like my sister.

'You lied to me,' she says.

'What are you talking about?' I demand. I do not lie. I do, however, sometimes omit the truth. I wonder to which particular truth she may be referring.

'You said you couldn't write.'

'I can't!' I cry. I do not want to think about what I wrote last night; it already seems lacking. The light of day is a most awful thing.

She waves the papers she's holding at me. 'Then what are these? I found them in my room, locked in my desk!' Her voice is abruptly tender. 'You could have told me, Nellie. I'm so proud of you. I read them while I walked this morning—I believe they're the best you've ever done.'

I do not recognise the papers. What is she talking about? I need her to leave. I need to think. Strange things are happening. Have happened. I need a moment alone. 'They're not mine,' I tell her.

'Don't be silly, whose else would they be?'

Whose *what*? I have no idea what she is talking about. I have not been attending. I am not myself. I am distracted. I ask to look at them. She hands me the papers. More unpleasant things happens in my abdomen. They are poems. They're in Vivien's handwriting. I tell her so.

'Surely she transcribed for you?' enquires my ever-loyal sister. I feel an overwhelming sense of goodwill toward her, which is in turn immediately overwhelmed by my sense of wretchedness. I have not time to peruse them at length, but the words I see are quite good. Perhaps better than good. Oddly arranged, but good.*

'I haven't written anything since we got married.'

'Then whose are they?' asks Lizzie. 'Is she copying out Tennyson?' I am appalled that Lizzie could even ask the question. What *have* they been teaching her at that school? If it is the sort of place which takes perfectly sensible girls and renders

---

*Rather better than good, I would venture. But you needn't take my word for it—their quality is now generally acknowledged.—HL.

them unable to tell whether or not a scrap of verse is written by Tennyson, then perhaps it is better she was expelled.

'This isn't Tennyson,' I tell her icily.

'Browning?'

For God's sake. 'No.'

'Either of the Rossettis?'

It is self-evidently neither of the Rossettis. Lizzie is growing stupider. 'SIMMONS!' I yell.

'Sir?' he says, entering promptly. I believe he does listen at my door. It does not bother me, but I note it. He is still the best butler in Britain, and a damned good judge of poetry besides.* He will provide answers.

Without a word I hand him the poems. He peruses them briefly, then makes his pronouncement.

'They're charming, sir, if not what you might call structurally sound.' I *knew that already*. He is not giving me the answers I need.

'Yes, yes, but do you recognise them?' I demand.

'Ought I to?'

'I had rather hoped so. Could they be Morris?' I am grasping at straws. They are clearly not Morris.

'You know they couldn't be.' There is disappointment in his voice—he sounds as I did a moment ago answering Lizzie's absurd questions.

'Arnold?' I ask him. It is even more ridiculous. What am I saying?

---

*Both these assertions, contrary to others my cousin sets forth in these pages, are hard fact.—HL.

'I rather think not,' he says, offended by the very thought.

'Swinburne?' I wish I could stop myself, but I cannot. If I accept the reality of the situation it may break me.

'Really, sir!' he says, now terribly disappointed and a little hurt by the depths of my stupidity. I am desperate.

'Then WHO, damn it?' I cry.

'Someone new, sir,' he replies.

Lizzie, who has been observing the exchange with the breathless excitement of a gambling man watching a tennis match, begins to ask a question I would rather not consider. 'Could it—'

'No,' I say in a tone that brooks no argument.

'But—' protests my tone-deaf sister.

'NO.'

'This is Mrs Savage's handwriting,' says Simmons. Damn him. I should sack him on the spot for even suggesting such a thing.

'I know that,' I reply acidly.

'Though I hesitate to suggest the obvious explanation, sir,' carries on my soon-to-be-former butler, 'I cannot in the name of reason and logic let it lie. When one eliminates the impossible, what is left, no matter how improbable—'

I cut him off. I *know*. I do not want to hear it. 'Give them back,' I say petulantly. He hands me a few pages, but keeps a few for himself. We both read Vivien's poetry for a moment. I will not comment on its quality any further than I have already done. I cannot. It is painful.

'These are quite good, sir,' he says. I glower. They are.

Though something is the matter with their structure. They are written in no metre I have ever encountered; in fact, they look rather like *vers libre,* and it is an affront to me that anyone living beneath my roof would dare compose in *vers libre.*

'If you think about it, Nellie,' says Lizzie, 'the situation is really very funny.'

'NO IT'S NOT,' I say hotly. I am feeling the level ground upon which I once thought I stood sliding out from under me. Too many things are happening at once. I do not like it. I am not an adventurous soul, I am an Englishman. I desire things to remain quite the way they have always been; but suddenly everything is changing. It is awful.

I have dabbled in madness,* but what is wonderful about madness is that there *is* no ground to shake beneath your feet. When there is nothing that is level, then there can be nothing that is *not* level. (If that is complicated to you, I suggest you walk into a very dark room and shut the door. Look around. There is nothing. Close your eyes. There is no difference. Stand on your head—the world is not upside down; it remains only black. Spin in circles until you fall over. Still the world is black. Do everything you can manage to disorient yourself— try as you might, you will not be able to for the world *is still black.*)† I am not at present in Bedlam, however.‡ I am in my

---

*By this Mr Savage means that he once contrived to have himself admitted to Bedlam, where he stayed for some time because none of the doctors noticed that he was perfectly sane. If not for the Herculean efforts of Mr Simmons it is likely that he would be there still.—HL.
†I have tried this. I became disoriented.—HL.
‡See the first note above.—HL.

study, and am standing on what I had presumed to be level ground, but it is abruptly shifting beneath my feet. It is intolerable. I cannot live like this.

Lizzie notices my night's work on the desk. 'What's this?' she asks.

'Nothing,' I say. I am not eager for her to read it, in light of the things just revealed.

'Let me see it,' she says.

'No.'

'Please?'

'No!'

While I have been guarding it from Lizzie, Simmons has come behind me and plucked it off the desk. By the time I notice, he is reading it and looking unwell.

'Damn it, Simmons,' I cry, 'give it back!' After a long moment he does. He doesn't say anything. If there's anything worse than Simmons passing judgment on my work, it's Simmons remaining silent. He simply stands there, looking aggrieved and a little affronted. Finally I say, 'Well?'

'It's not your best, sir,' he says.

'I know that, damn it!' I wish he had not read it. I wish I had not asked his opinion. I wish this day had not happened. I suddenly feel that yesterday afternoon I was not so miserable as I am now. If I could go back in time and simply be unhappily married I would leap at the chance. It is funny how every time one thinks things can get no worse, they do. I think it is a metaphor for life. Or perhaps it's not a metaphor at all and simply *is* life. I marvel that I used to be considered a happy person. You would not think it reading this, but it is true. I was once untroubled and light of heart.*

Lizzie asks what is, at the moment, the single least useful question she could ask: 'Where's your wife?'

'I DON'T KNOW!'

Lizzie and Simmons are silent, taken aback by my volume. They look at me in what seems a most accusatory manner, though that is perhaps only a projection of my own guilty and unstable mind. I did not mean to yell at them. I never used to yell.

'I might know,' I amend.

Expectant silence.

'This is going to sound much worse than it really is.' I consider the best way to put it. 'Yesterday evening before you arrived,' I try, 'I was walking home and I met a priest—'

'Who had tripped over a cobblestone and was cursing the Devil and you said without the Devil we'd both be out of a job, yes, you told us.' Lizzie may be growing stupider, but even if she cannot tell what is and is not written by a Rossetti her mind is still quicker than most.

---

*As I have said, I am not convinced of this. I have made enquiries of his intimates, but Mr Simmons equivocates decorously and Miss Savage changes the subject. But as this is characteristic of both of them in most conversations, I cannot take it to mean one thing or another. I wish I had known Mr Savage in our youth—I would have been curious to see him as a boy. I believe he would have been very much like he is now, only his virtues (wit, sensitivity, imagination) would I think have been fresher and his vices (narcissism, vanity, cowardice) less developed. But this may not be so. He may have been precisely the way he is now, only shorter.—HL.

'Yes. Well. You remember the gentleman last night you met coming out of my study?'

'What's he have to do with anything?'

I hesitate. 'Well. He said that he came to thank me for the kind word.'

'I don't understand,' says Lizzie. She is thick. I can hear the gears turning in Simmons's head. Perhaps he is made of clock-work. This would explain his inhuman correctness in things.

I take a breath and it all comes tumbling out. 'And then I complained about my wife and told him I couldn't write and gave him a book and he said everything would be alright.'

Lizzie's face is still blank, but Simmons has apprehended. 'Oh sir,' he says.

'What?' demands Lizzie.

Simmons almost looks like he is going to laugh, but I suppose that must be nervous tension. 'Sir, *really?*'

'Shut up, Simmons,' I snap.

'What's going on?' says soft-witted Lizzie.

'He believes he gave Mistress Vivien to the Devil,' says Simmons. Lizzie's eyes widen, and I can see that she is about to say awful things to me. I rush to cut her off.

'I *may* have given— Actually, no, no, wait, there was no *giving* involved. The Devil *may* have *taken* her. Possibly.' I am running backward desperately. I do feel I have given Vivien away, though as I think of it that seems unfair to myself. I certainly never *asked* the Gentleman to take her. At least not directly.

'Oh, Nellie,' says Lizzie in a tone of voice that makes me want to find a hole and crawl into it and die. 'You really are an awful person.'

'I would have thought, given the situation, that the two of you might show a trifle more understanding,' I say bitterly.

They just stare at me. I cannot bear it. I try to find the silver lining, try to make them see it, try to regain some of my former stature in their eyes. (*Had* I any stature? Perhaps not, not in recent days or weeks or months. I had once, I am certain. For Simmons maybe not in a long while.)

'Don't you see?' I exclaim. 'This is a good thing! I'm free! I can write again! I wrote all night.'

Simmons, damn him, has taken another poem from my desk and dashed my hopes. He reads it aloud: '"I said to her now please disrobe yourself / And she complied and said here's to your—"' He pauses painfully, then finishes, '"—health."'

'IT'S WORDS ON THE PAGE!' I yell like a cornered animal. 'That's the first step! When there are words on the page then one can revise them until they are *good* words! But until they're there, there is nothing!'

They stare at me some more. Lizzie eventually says, 'I cannot believe you sold your wife to the Devil.'

I consider pointing out that I didn't actually *sell* her, but the difference is so slight I do not even bother. I am in a very peculiar, rather misty area in which I could become quite lost if I am not careful. And so I try to rationalise. 'Lizzie,' I say, 'I had no choice. I have been unable to write since I married her—this was the only alternative to a life of misery and perhaps madness.'

'But you still can't write!' says she. Which is true.

'I'm working on it!' say I. Which is also true, but rather pathetic.

She takes a matronly tone I do not like. 'You've been wifeless almost a full day, Lionel. If you haven't written anything in that time, you're not going to.'

I protest automatically, but I grasp her point. Is it possible that my wife is not in fact the reason for my declining talents? I must think on it someday.

'You have to tell them,' says Lizzie.

'Tell who what?' How her mind hops about. Perhaps *she* is mad.

'Tell her parents you sold their daughter to the Devil!'

'Absolutely not,' I say. It is clearly out of the question. I hate her parents as I hate her. Her father perhaps a trifle less; he is a kindly soul, just trapped. Lady Lancaster, though, is the awfullest human who ever lived. I am actually a little scared of her.*

'You must,' she says.

'I wish you wouldn't talk about my wife's family.' I do not know why Lizzie insists on bringing them up. There is nothing to be gained from talking about them. The Lancasters are society folks, emblematic of everything that I do not like about this age. That they are now my relations is an awkward truth I do not like to consider.

'You have to tell them sooner or later.'

'I don't see why,' I say. 'The whole thing was a mistake. I

---

*I considered excising these disparaging sentences (and others like them) from this manuscript. However, upon reflection I decided to leave them. I did this not from lack of respect for Lady Lancaster, but for the very opposite reason. When this reaches publication, I look forward to seeing what she might do to Mr Savage.—HL.

certainly probably wouldn't have done it if I'd been aware of what I was doing.'

'You have to tell them,' Lizzie says again. She is stubborn that way. It is an unattractive quality.

'No.'

'You have to.'

'No.'

'Yes.'

'Absolutely not! Simmons understands—don't you, Simmons?'

'I am afraid, sir, that I have in this instance only a limited understanding.'

'I cannot tell any woman's parents, not even my wife's, that I did what I did!' I do not like saying what I did, even to my sister and Simmons, even in the privacy of my own study. It seems more terrible when spoken aloud. I wish we could just forget all about it and have tea.

'Then tell her brother,' Lizzie presses.

'I can't, he's off conquering Borneo.* Besides,' I say, 'I've never met the man and now there's no one to introduce us.'† I omit that I hate the very thought of him. I have heard far too much of his virtues to ever think him anything more than an utter fool.

'Write him a letter.'

---

*This is not where he was.—HL.

†I am surprised that no one thought of telling me. If Mr Savage had contacted me, events would have unfolded differently. I cannot say if they would have ended up better or worse, for who ever can?—HL.

'"Dear Mr Lancaster,"' I say, '"I seem to have misplaced your sister. Satan may have been involved. Warmly, Lionel Savage."' (Actually, it would be an amusing letter to send. I said it only to annoy Lizzie, but I wonder if I oughtn't to send it after all.)

Lizzie glares at me. 'Did you do it because she's a better poet than you?'

This is too much. 'SHE IS NOT!'*

'You know very well that's a lie.'

I am apoplectic. 'She writes without form! Her line breaks are arbitrary! She may as well be a—novelist!'

'Now you're just lying to yourself,' Lizzie says. She appraises me unnervingly. 'You look like you're about to cry. I think you miss her.'

'I do not miss her!'

She raises her eyebrows. 'I don't know that I've ever seen anyone so unhappy in my entire life. I love you, and I wish you'd let me help you. I'm bored and melancholy and sick at heart. I'm going to go lie down.' And she leaves. I have never heard Lizzie to voice boredom or melancholia. I did not think her afflicted by them as other people are.

I hit my head against my desk several times, hoping it will clear my mind. It doesn't.

'SIMMONS!' I call.

'I'm right here, sir,' he says at my elbow.

I start—I had forgotten he was in the room. Simmons is like that.

---

*She is, as is now common knowledge.—HL.

'Simmons,' I say, 'do I seem unhappy to you?'

'Of course, sir,' he says.

It was a poorly phrased question. I am very obviously unhappy. I rephrase it. 'But do I seem *more* unhappy since my wife left?'

'Indeed, sir,' he answers promptly.

'Ah.' That is queer—I had thought that as she was the primary source of my sorrows, her disappearance would immediately lift my spirits. That it has had the opposite effect is very odd. I had suspected it, and hearing Simmons's confirmation I can but accept it as so.

After a moment, he says, 'Will that be all, sir?'

'Yes. Thank you, Simmons.'

'Very good, sir.'

He starts to leave. My mind is spinning and my head hurts. I wish I hadn't banged it against the desk. I call after him, 'Simmons!'

'Sir?'

'Do you consider me morally reprehensible for inadvertently selling my wife to the Devil?'

'I do, sir,' he says. I had feared as much. I was feeling morally deficient, but wondered if that was only because of my weariness.

'And do you consider me yet more reprehensible for refusing to notify her family?'

'I do, sir.'

I sigh and slump forward. I press my cheek against the desktop. 'Simmons,' I say at length, 'I believe I am miserable.'

'That is just the word I would have used, sir.'

For the first time in a long time I do not think about anything. I simply lie there being miserable.

We remain in silence. Then I think of another question I am not sure I have the courage to have answered, but I ask it anyway. 'Simmons?'

'Sir?'

'Is my wife a better poet than I am?'

'I am compelled to tell you that she is, sir,' says the man who raised me.

I am silent. What is there to say? Outside my window, I watch the little park. Rain is falling, which ordinarily pleases me, mist is rising, which ordinarily cheers me, and the trees all look like mysterious sculptures stolen from other worlds. But instead of finding the sight lovely and poetical, today it seems to signify imminent doom of some sort.

Then Simmons adds, 'Considerably.'

'Excuse me?'

'I said, "Considerably." She is considerably better than you. The poems Miss Elizabeth found display an imagination and verbal dexterity that you have never shown even in your most inspired spells. And if you'll forgive me, sir, you have not been in a truly inspired place since you were about sixteen.'*

'Then you are implying,' I say, reeling, 'that my fame—'

---

*The informed reader will note that Mr Savage's first collection of poetry, *Pasquinades and Peregrinations,* was published shortly after his seventeenth birthday. It is my favourite of his books. The following two collections—published at two-year intervals—grew progressively repetitive, though I still found some small enjoyment in them. The most recent was subject to an especially scathing review from Mr Pendergast.—HL.

'Is based largely upon the ignorance and poor taste of the reading public at large.'*

'Why have you never said these things before?' I say, too defeated to move or think.

'Because you never asked, sir.'

I sigh. I am worn out, overwhelmed, done. 'You think I should tell the Lancasters.'

'I do.'

'Her parents won't understand.' It is a feeble protest. Not even a protest—I am too weary to protest, and I begin to suspect that he may be right.

'I believe that is so, sir.'

'Well, then what am I to do?'

'You could try telling her brother, sir.' Him again.

'No one has seen her brother in two years!'

'You could write him a letter, sir, as Miss Elizabeth suggested. Your wife used to do so frequently. She sent letters to the last town in which he was seen, in hopes that he would receive them upon his emergence from the wilderness.' I didn't know that. I was not aware Vivien had any correspondents.

'I can't put it in a letter,' I say. I recall my brief cheer at sending him one line about diabolical abduction; it now seems childish.

'You would feel better, I think, if you did.'

---

*I believe Mr Simmons to be an excellent literary critic. However, he is in this instance an uncharitable one.—HL.

'I can't!' I cry. 'Look, Simmons, if he were here, I'd tell him—I don't know how, but I would find a way. But Simmons, HE ISN'T HERE!'

Before Simmons can reply, the doorbell rings.

'Excuse me, sir,' he says, and goes to answer it.

I am left alone with my thoughts and my wife's poems. I pick them up and begin to read. They are very good. They are mystical in subject, but only just. They are not the maudlin, self-pitying things you would expect. They are vigorous and feather-light and impossibly quick-minded, and unlike my own verse their quickness does not disguise want of depth. She writes of joy and wonder and sunrises and adventure, and through it all are somehow answers to life's mysteries, though even suggesting such a thing sounds silly from my pen. It is the sort of poetry I admired when I was younger and somehow forgot about along the way. I find that I cannot see the words through my tears. I must get hold of myself. I try hitting my head against the desk again. The pain gives me at least something to grab onto.

I hear Simmons open the door, and I hear a booming voice I do not recognise call, 'VIV! VIVIEN! VIIIIVIEN!' The whole house shakes as someone very large jogs down the hall. Then the door to my study bursts open and Ashley Lancaster bounds into the room.*

---

*My cousin Ashley had returned to London that very morning. He has since told me that his first stop was his club, where he changed clothes because he could not tolerate his own smell but refused all tonsorial advances in the name of haste, and his second was Pocklington Place.—HL.

Five

In Which I Meet an Adventurer Who Informs Me That Things Are Not at All How I Had Thought.

He is scruffy, sunburnt, dressed immaculately in evening clothes, and the most enormous man I have ever seen. He must be six and a half feet tall, and so broad he has to turn sideways to fit through the door frame.*

He is, if anything, handsomer than the papers would lead you to believe. His face is wide and ingenuous, his nose is small, his blond hair comes to a rakish widow's peak. He has premature crow's-feet from squinting in glacial sunlight, and small wrinkles at the corners of his mouth from smiling too much. His eyes are the same piercing blue as his sister's and radiate goodwill. He is in his early thirties.

'Hello!' he bellows upon seeing me. I rise, alarmed. 'My God, you must be Savage!' he goes on, his voice rattling the

---

*This is less of an exaggeration than you might think.—HL.

paintings on the wall. 'It's a pleasure, sir, truly a pleasure! Viv's told me all about you in her letters!'

He sweeps me up into a bone-crushing embrace, releases me, and kisses me soundly on the mouth. I had not expected that.

All I can manage is a shaky 'Hello,' as I wipe his saliva from my lips.

'I'm sorry, old boy,' he says, 'I'm accustomed to the customs of Krakatoa!' He claps me on the back so hard I nearly fall. His hands are like shovels. 'Afraid my manners have seen better days! Always like this when I get back from a trip. I'll be up to snuff and fit for polite company in a week or two. In the meantime I thought I'd stay with you, if you don't mind. My parents aren't fond of the re-entry process, truth be told. But this is all for later, by Christ! Where's my sister! Viv! VIVIEN!'

I am too shocked to do anything but gape at him. I do not know why he is wearing nice clothes.* It seems incongruous. He looks like he ought to be in desert khaki, or stripped to his waist on a raft somewhere in the Pacific, or dressed in sealskins wrestling polar bears.

'You feeling alright, old boy?' he asks, gazing at me solicitously. 'You're looking poorly. 'Course I don't know you—though I feel I do, from Viv's letters, damn if that woman doesn't have a way with words—but I'd venture to say you look as though you've been trampled by a yak! Isn't she taking proper care of you? VIVIEN! YOUR HUSBAND LOOKS LIKE DEATH! WHERE THE DEVIL ARE YOU?'

---

*See the note on page 94.—HL.

He is nothing like what I had expected. 'Mr Lancaster—' I croak, but he cuts me off.

'Come, man, don't insult me! No one calls me *Mister* Lancaster but the press and rich mothers looking to buy me for their daughters.' (I wince.) 'It won't do—my sister's in love with you, by Christ! Call me Ashley, or just Lancaster if you really must—that's what they called me at school, before I quit.'

He has such a bluff, good-natured manner than I do not know what to do. I am struck by an overwhelming and entirely absurd desire for him to like me. 'We have to talk,' I say.

'We *are* talking!' cries this garrulous giant. 'And it's about time, too! Read all her letters on the boat back, and Christ, it's Lionel this and Lionel that—I feel as though we spent the entire voyage together! Where IS she? VIVIEN! But listen,' he says, leaning in conspiratorially so that our foreheads are almost touching. 'As long as we've a moment alone, I wanted to thank you. God knows it isn't easy being an older brother—but I forget, you know all about that! I'm sure it's the same for you. I'm a pacifist—too much time in Tibet, ha ha ha!—but by God if the wrong man *looked* at Viv I'd rip his heart out and eat it raw.' I blanch. He doesn't notice, and continues. 'But the way she talks about you, I know you treat her right. And it's a load off my mind, by Christ, to know she's found a good man who loves her the way she deserves to be loved!'

I am reeling. I do not know what he is talking about. Does he not know that Vivien and I hate each other? To what letters is he referring? What has Tibet to do with anything? Where did he come from? Why is he here? These thoughts chase each other through my brain, followed closely by wonderment that the papers were right about him after all. 'Mr Lancaster—' I begin, but am again cut off.

'She's not a frivolous woman, mind—she thinks things through. Never was impulsive, not even as a girl. Never even *looked* at a man that way—though not for lack of men looking at her, God knows! I never imagined she'd find anyone worth her. But the way she talks about you, Savage! I'm not a sentimental man, but damn me, I was moved. She *respects* you, you know. It's more than just love—love's fine, but it fades—but she *respects* you! And I wanted to— Well, Savage, I wanted to thank you. It's a relief to know she's in good hands. Now where the Devil is she?' (Oh God.) 'VIVIEN!'

I must read these letters. 'Listen,' I say, but he does not.

Instead, he says, 'VIIIIIIVIENNNNNN!' and several books fall from their shelves.

'LISTEN TO ME, DAMN YOU!' I shout.

He is brought up short, and for the first time since he entered the room he stops moving. 'I say, I'm sorry, old boy. What is it?'

'She isn't here.'

'Well why didn't you say so!' he cries with a grin. 'Popped out, eh? Well it's been two years; another hour won't hurt anything. Give us a chance to talk, what?'

'Yes,' I say, 'quite. Well, you see—'

'I envy you, Savage,' says Lancaster, lying down on the sofa and stretching his long legs out before him with evident pleasure. 'I wasn't cut out for marriage; but damn me do I envy you. Do you know I haven't even spoken to a woman in eighteen months? Not that I'm complaining, mind—in my profession a woman's the kiss of death. Truth is, I don't even look at women anymore. Think marriage would kill me. And you get used to bachelorhood. But all the same, in another life, God what I wouldn't give for a soft pair of arms attached to a quick mind and an adventurous heart. Eh, but as I say, not for me! No, old boy, I don't believe there's a woman on this earth who could make me truly regret my freedom.'*

At that moment Lizzie comes into the room with a sparkle in her eyes. She says, 'Nellie, I'm sorry, I've tried my utmost to be melancholy, but it's no good: melancholia bores me.' She notices my guest. 'Hello, who are— Oh my God, you're Ashley Lancaster.' Roses bloom upon her cheeks and her breath comes a little quicker.

Lancaster, who has not taken his eyes off her since she entered the room, turns very pale, then very red, then very pale again. He tries to rise, becomes tangled in his own feet, sits down heavily, and rises again like a breaching whale. He is staring at Lizzie in a way I do not like. He opens and shuts his mouth several times, but doesn't say anything. Finally he nods.

'Nellie,' says Lizzie to me with a disapproving look, still a little breathless but trying to pretend that she isn't, 'why didn't you tell me we had company? Please forgive my brother, Mr

---

*This statement has been seriously questioned. In the time I have known him, I have met no fewer than three women who have made Cousin Ashley regret his freedom very much indeed—and I beg you to note that I say these are only the three I have met.—HL.

Lancaster, he is at times shockingly impolite. I'm Elizabeth, and you don't need to—'

'Mr Lancaster and I were just—*talking*,' I say with a significance which I hope Lizzie will notice and Lancaster will not.

'Oh!' says Lizzie, noticing. 'Oh. Good. I'll leave you to it, then. Mr Lancaster, it was a pleasure. I trust I'll be seeing more of you.'

Lancaster still has not said a word. He nods again.

Lizzie sweeps out of the room. She casts one last glance upon him before she shuts the door behind her, and I feel uncomfortable having witnessed it.

As soon as the door is closed, Lancaster locates his tongue. 'That's your *sister*?' he says with wonderment.

'Yes,' I reply tersely. I would like to move on to another subject—*any* subject—very quickly. But he is not finished.

'She's *beautiful*.'

'We need to talk,' I say.

'You don't mind my saying that, do you?' I mind very much. The goodwill I feel toward the man has gone up in smoke. I wonder that I could ever have supposed him charming. The papers were hopelessly mistaken. He is a lascivious cad. 'I have travelled, Savage—I mean, I have *travelled*. But I have never, *never* seen anyone— Good Lord.'

'LANCASTER!'

He comes back to the present. 'What?'

'Vivien's been abducted by the Dev'l.' It is a gamble, but I have been trying to get the words out for ten minutes and I am through with subtlety. If he may ogle my sister I may sell his.

He looks confused and says, 'By the what?'

'The Dev'l.'

'Once more?'

'The Dev'l.'

'I'm sorry, old boy, I don't have any idea what you're saying.'

I decide that this once it can perhaps be two syllables.

'For God's sake don't ask how,' I say, annunciating very clearly, 'but your sister has been abducted by the Dev-ill.'

I expect him to explode, but he does not. Instead, he becomes very businesslike. His eyes, which have been wandering around my study vaguely, as if on reconnaissance, snap into sharp focus. 'Oh,' he says, 'the Devil. Wonderful. Yes, I see. How long ago?'

'Fifteen hours, give or take.'

'Are you sure?'

'Quite sure.'

'The Devil?'

'Yes.' I am still waiting for the explosion. I wonder if perhaps he hasn't quite understood. It is a bit of a shock, I suppose—the sort of thing which any man could be excused for not processing entirely.

He is musing almost to himself. 'My sister has been—*Really?*'

'Indeed.'

Suddenly, he smiles. 'Poor chap,' he says. 'She's a handful, as you know! Do you mind if I bring in my things? I'm going to be staying here for a few days.' What is the matter with this man? Does he not understand plain English? Is he somehow demented? Perhaps he has ingested some tropical worm which has caused him to take leave of his senses.

'You seem unperturbed,' I say.

'Why on earth should I be perturbed?' he asks with what seems to be genuine curiosity.

'Because your sister's gone!' I say. His lack of concern is increasing mine.

'Gone?' he says dismissively. 'She isn't gone, she's just . . . missing. The Devil! Really?'

'Yes, for God's sake, the Devil!'

There is a glint in Lancaster's eye I am not sure I like. It is the sort of glint I used to see in my mirror when I had found a poetical subject. I wonder what is going through his head, and if it is dangerous. He says almost mischievously, 'Savage, this is a little bit exciting.'

'What are you *talking* about?' I cry.

'Listen, old boy,' says he. 'There's no problem without a solution. And luckily for us, this solution is particularly simple.'

'It is?' I say.

'Of course! We just have to go get her!'

'We *what*?' I don't know what I was expecting, but it wasn't this. Humans are continually surprising me today.

'Come on Savage, show some spirit!' he says. He seems almost bursting with happiness. 'This is a great day! We've found ourselves an adventure!' He pauses and looks at me, making sure I have understood fully the greatness of the day. I attempt to smile. I do not know what he means when he says that we have to go get her. How does one get someone back from the Devil? It does not sound like something I would be interested in, even if I had the slightest desire to get her back, which I have not. I am perfectly content with her absence. Or mostly content. Somewhat content, at the very least.

'And you're certain it was the Devil?' he asks.

'Quite certain.' I say.

'Extraordinary,' he says.

'Yes, I suppose so,' I say absently. I am not really attending. I am wondering why it is that I do not feel more content—why I am, frankly, feeling rather wretched.

'My God, man, you seem not to understand just how wonderful this all is. Is anything wrong?'

'Oh, I'm fine,' I say. 'I suppose I'm waiting for the storm to hit.'

'I don't understand,' says Lancaster.

'Your little sister was just abducted by the Devil,' I point out. I feel as though I am prodding an unexploded bomb—aware that it is an awful idea, but somehow fascinated by what the precise moment of explosion will look like.

Still it does not come. 'Oh yes, yes, by all means. Don't get me wrong, old boy, it's perfectly dreadful what happened,' he says, though he doesn't sound full of dread. 'Not very sporting of him, I daresay. But all the same, I can't imagine any lasting harm will come of it, and it's the most fantastic thing, by Christ!'

I am unclear how it is fantastic, but I say only, 'Quite.'

'And besides,' ploughs on Lancaster merrily, 'it's hardly your fault!' My gut wrenches. It *is* my fault. I do not say so, however. The man is clearly capable of crushing my head in one of his massive hands. 'But come, you must tell me exactly what you said to one another. I'm terribly curious. The supernatural's rather my area, you know.'

'Oh?' I did not know. It at least explains his morbid glee.

'Surely Viv's told you what I do.'

She has not. She could not have, for the simple reason that we never spoke. I do not know how to explain this to him, however, so I say instead, 'Oh yes, she must have done. But then— You'll have to excuse me if I . . . Be so good as to refresh me?'

He settles back onto the couch and becomes a storyteller. I suppose it must be a habit of his to pass time on long Arctic nights—in any event, it is clearly much practised. He stretches and clears his throat and says, 'Well, I started with the Royal Geographical Society, of course. That was the beginning of it all—the first Tibet trip, the Peruvian debacle, the Greenland rambles. Surely you read about them?'

I have no idea what he is talking about. 'Naturally,' I say.

'You didn't read about them, did you?'

'No.'

'Well never mind, old boy. Don't have to lie about it. No shame in a little ignorance now and again.' I consider objecting, but he is already describing his trips and I cannot get a word in edgewise. 'They were your standard expeditions: sunburn, frostbite, sleeping on rocks, maggots in your flesh, near starvation. You know.'

I do not know. How would I know? Why on earth would I have any notion? 'Delightful,' I say.

'Oh, but it is!' he exclaims. 'You have no idea. Most wonderful thing in the world, travelling. What was I saying?'

I am not interested in his stories, but I am making mental notes on his person. He strikes me as a perfect specimen upon which to someday base a character. He is poetical in the extreme, and the creative part

of my mind, which is most of it, considers ways I could utilise him. The trouble is, no reader would ever believe the almost godlike beauty of the man. It is as though light radiates from his skin. 'The Geographical Society,' I say.

'Oh yes! Well, things were going along nicely until I found El Dorado.'

'El Dorado doesn't exist,' I say. Though I suppose maybe it does after all. My wife *was* just abducted by the Devil. Surely El Dorado isn't as fantastical as that.

'That's what they said, the faithless beggars!' cries Lancaster. 'I told them I'd found it and they laughed in my face and told me to prove it.'

'That sounds reasonable,' I point out.

'Well maybe so, old boy,' he says, frowning, 'but it's not strictly speaking polite. Anyway, I went back with a bevy of 'em, but couldn't find the damn place again, and that was the beginning of the end. The trouble with the Geographical Society is, they've no imagination. Well, I'd had quite enough of the whole thing, and it wasn't as though I needed their money, so I left the Society and ever since I have independently been finding remarkable things which the scientific community blithely assures me don't exist.'*

I do not voice my scepticism, and he goes on.

'Now, I tell you all this not to toot my own horn, as the saying goes, but because I want you to understand that I'm with you, by Christ, and we'll see this thing through to the bitter end. I've been to El Dorado and I've stumbled across Shangri-La and I'm damn near to finding Atlantis, so if you're looking for a chap with whom to storm the gates of Hell then don't worry, old boy, you've found your man!'

He is breathing rather heavily—if his words have not roused me, I believe they have at least stirred his own blood a little. I am glad, for it was a pretty speech—and if not for the fact that I do not like going out of doors if it can be avoided, I would doubtless have been inspired to seek the sunset. 'Well that's very kind of you,' I say, 'but I'm afraid it's more compli-

---

*The debate which has raged around the topic of Cousin Ashley's discovery of El Dorado deserves a volume of its own. Suffice it to say that the controversy still rages—but that he and Mr Savage are currently outfitting an expedition in hopes of settling the thing one way or the other.—HL.

cated than that.' I still do not know how to tell him exactly what I mean.

'I don't see why it should be,' he replies. 'She loves you, and you love her, and she's my little sister, and she's been stolen. God knows we'd go after them if it were the Frenchies who'd taken her,* so why not the Devil?'

I do not know why he keeps talking of love. There is no love in this household. I do not love my wife, and she does not love me. It is a loveless marriage, which is why I cannot write and why she confines herself to her room except when she's throwing parties. The man is delusional. Where has he gotten these notions? 'Well of course,' I say, 'but—'

'But what? She dotes on you. You know damn well she'd never leave you to rot if it were the other way round.'

I know no such thing. I believe were it the other way round she would dance a jig. It's finally too much for me. 'Yes, so you keep saying. You'll excuse me for pointing it out, but you haven't even *seen* her for two years. For all you know we hate each other.'

'Now there's a thought!' laughs Lancaster, dismissing it out of hand. 'I told you, Savage, I read her letters, and it's not every couple that's got what you've got.' There's something about him which tells me that, I am almost certain of it, he is not lying. He truly believes that she loves me. How can this be? What is in those letters? I must read them. Immediately. My life may depend upon it.

---

*I should say we would!—HL.

There are very strange happenings inside me.

'I'd show them to you, if I could—the letters, I mean, they'd warm you right from the inside—but they were all lost when the ship went down off Spitsbergen.* Damn shame, that. Never met anyone who can use words like my little sister. What was it she said? "The fact is, I'm his, all of me, and he is mine—and whatever the difference in our temperaments, we are souls entwined." Makes a man glad to read those words, glad to know such a thing's possible, eh?'

Something is wrong with my chest. I cannot breathe. I do not know what is happening. My blood is not pumping properly, my eyes are not focusing, my ears are ringing, I can feel a feverish flush rising to my cheeks.

'You alright, Savage?' asks Lancaster, eyeing me with concern. 'You're looking poorly.'

'Indeed,' I say. 'I'm feeling . . . peculiar. Peculiar feelings. I'm going to lie down. Make yourself at home. Lizzie will come find you.' I raise my voice and call, 'LIZZIE!' Then, without a backward glance, I flee.

---

*Record of this shipwreck has been made elsewhere. I will remind the reader only that Mr Lancaster single-handedly saved no fewer than seven Danish, four Norwegian, and two Algerian sailors from drowning.—HL.

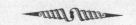

Six

In Which I Visit the Grandest Shop in the World, Where I Meet a Very Poetical Person, After Which I Have an Earth-Shattering Epiphany.

I hurry up the stairs and into my room. I lie down on my bed. It is a great four-postered monstrosity that used to belong to my parents. I hate it. I have never spent a night in it with Vivien. I have never spent a night anywhere with Vivien. The week of our wedding I was in a fit of composition, and I dared not waste any time consummating our marriage. I wonder if things would have been different if I had.

It is a silly thought. Vivien is now in Hell, and I am lying on this wretched bed thinking of her. I do not understand Lancaster's words. His talk of letters. Could there truly have been letters?* I do not know. I was not aware that my wife writes—wrote—letters, but I was also not aware that she wrote poetry. One learns the most alarming things.

I hate my room. I hate my house. I hate being indoors. I need to get out of doors. I still cannot breathe. I need to be outside. I tiptoe to the door, open it a crack, peer through. No one is on the landing. I can hear faint voices from the study and a shout of laughter. Lizzie must be entertaining Lancaster. I wish them well, and if he touches her I will kill him. I do not know where Simmons may be.

I creep down the stairs. I do not like creeping within my own home, but I cannot bear to see anyone. I do not want to speak. I do not believe I would know what to say. I do not know what to think. Something inside me is broken. I slip into my overcoat, for it is a chilly November day and my smoking jacket will not be warm enough and I hate being cold, and I slip out the front door.

The yellow fog is wrapped round the house waiting for me, and I plunge into it. I love the fog. The sounds of the city are muffled by it, made mysterious and poetical. It is a poetical city. Why have I never noticed that before? Perhaps I have. I do not remember. I do not know. I do not know a great many things, I find. Everything seems somehow different. Perhaps I am dreaming. I wonder if that is the case. It would make explicable many things currently inexplicable. I pinch myself. I do not wake. I am not asleep. I am not dreaming. Unless I am

---

*There truly were letters. I was privileged to read one or two of them before they were posted. They were moving.—HL.

in a waking dream. I may be mad. I may have stumbled into a fairy tale, but I see no dashing princes about, unless Lancaster be one. I imagine him holding a sword leading an army. It is easy to do. If I were a great painter I should paint him as St George. I have never had a care about my body, but watching the way Lancaster moves I was struck for the first time in my life that I am small and weak. If I were otherwise, would Vivien have loved me? I do not know.

Seeing her brother makes me think of Vivien differently. They look so similar that I could not help thinking of her as I watched him. They have the same unconscious grace. Why did I never notice it in Vivien before? It occurs to me that I *did* notice it, but that I preferred not to think of it after our courtship.

Briefly, I wonder what it would have been like to see Vivien without her clothes on our wedding night. Would she have moved with the same ease and grace then?

I banish the thought with something like panic. I will not think of it. I cannot. It will drive me mad. I focus on my feet. They move of their own accord, without conscious thought or effort or command from me. That is a marvellous thing. Why have I never before noticed what a marvellous thing that is?

I have not known where I am walking, but I know now. I need to see Tompkins. (Tompkins is my second sage. If Simmons is my Ector, Tompkins is my Merlin.* He owns a bookshop.) I cannot see my course through the fog, but my feet know the way. They skitter across the damp cobblestones, my

---

*It is typical of Mr Savage that in his own mind he is Arthur Pendragon.—HL.

heels clicking like hooves. I wonder if the Gentleman had hooves. I did not think to look.

I pass illuminated house-fronts which grin at me mania-cally through the fog, gaslight blazing from their windows. It is a dark afternoon (the sun for sorrow will not show its face), and the lamp-posts are being lit. I tip my hat to the lamplight-ers. I hurry past the smell of clustered humanity. I still find perverse poetry in it all, even in the sewage in the gutters and garbage in the street. I do not know what is wrong with me.

Mine is a city in transition. Signs of Progress are all around me—the steel girders spanning the Thames, the omnibuses clattering by, the modern policemen standing on every corner of this modern metropolis—but still there is history beneath my feet, sneaking out from cracks between cobblestones and darkened alleys forgotten by the tide of time. I know of no other era when life was so exciting, unless it be the glory days of the Roman Republic.* We have the world before us, but have not yet outrun our past. It is a good time to be alive.

I walk through respectable neighbourhoods which turn abruptly into disrespectable ones. The respectable are quiet, on this foggy and inhospitable day. The disrespectable are noisy, for despite the weather it is a day like any other and there is work to be done. There is much a poet might learn from this. I pass into commercial neighbourhoods, which are even noisier than were the disrespectable ones. People are ev-

---

*I would submit, at random: the height of Athenian democracy; the Crusades; the great Age of Discovery; Constantinople in 1453 (though not exciting in a pleasant way, perhaps); Renaissance Italy; and the year 0. I could go on, but I shall not. (I am something of an amateur historian.)—HL.

erywhere, and horses, and carts, and cabs, and policemen, and advertisements. I have no desire to purchase a new top hat, nor a miraculous spring-loaded shoehorn (my boring one serves just fine), nor a corset made with the bones of an elephant. I am bumped and jostled and sworn at. I bump and jostle and swear back, which is the only way to survive in a city such as this.

I am sweating by the time I reach the small shop. It is sandwiched between a haberdasher and an apothecary. Above the door a peeling sign says, 'Phoenix Used Books And What Have You, Prop. Wm. Tmkns.' The windows are crusted with a thick layer of soot, but I can just make out a flickering light inside. Tompkins reading by his hearth.

Abruptly I find myself face-to-face with Whitley Pendergast, who is leaving the establishment. 'Hullo, old boy,' I say, 'the Hell are you doing here?'

'Purchasing a racehorse,' he replies automatically. 'What else would I do in a bookstore?'

'Thought you might've come to pick up *Platitudes*.* There's a stack of unsold first editions that have been gathering dust in the corner for a month.'

'Savage,' says he, 'words cannot express the acute pleasure I will feel when at last I drive my rapier into your belly.'

'When that day comes, Pendergast, I've instructed my lawyer to hang a black banner from St Paul's to mark the death of poetry.'

---

*Mr Savage refers to Mr Pendergast's most recent book, which is in fact titled *Maxims*.—HL.

'Speaking of poems, Savage,' he says, 'I've written you one just now. "The savage fool does vainly rage and cry / But foolish Savage imagines how he'll die."'

'Better a witty fool,' I tell him, 'than a foolish wit. Cheerio, old boy.'

He storms off into the night and I push open the door with my shoulder. Rusty hinges groan loudly in protest. Why the treasures of this magical cave are not more widely known I have never been able to conceive. It is the most marvellous place in the world. It should be the most popular spot in town; but I am glad that it is not.*

'It's Savage,' I say, entering the shop. It is at first glance a tiny place, a narrow storefront barely wide enough for a door and a window looking out upon the street. But once your eyes grow accustomed to the gloom, you are able to see the teetering towers of books which vanish into the dusty darkness of the rafters, and that the room, though not wide, is very deep. Looking down the stacks it seems as though the shop has no end. It simply goes back, back, back, into some sort of musty, misty, magical hinterland of crumbling pages and lost knowledge. There's a cat, too. Its name is Boadicea, and I do not like it. I do not like cats. They return affection with indifference. But even its presence cannot diminish my love of the shop.

Before the fire, engulfed by one of his colossal wing-backed

---

*This is another of those instances where I must put away whatever personal antipathy there is between Mr Savage and myself and confess that he and I are in complete agreement. Mr Tompkins's shop has excellent selections both of History and Law, which are subjects about which I am particular.—HL.

armchairs, the ancient bibliophile himself sits squinting at dusty pages. He doesn't look up. (The shop seems otherwise deserted, which is not uncommon. I do not know how it turns a profit, if it turns a profit. Perhaps Tompkins is fabulously wealthy and has never told anyone and runs the shop purely for the pleasure of it.)

'Tompkins,' I say, 'I have a problem.' I always call Tompkins 'Tompkins.' Once I tried to call him 'Mr Tompkins' and he threw a book at my head.

He continues to read. He is maybe two hundred years old, though to see the agility with which he climbs a ladder to reach a distant book would astonish you. His eyes are sunk deep within wrinkles, and are very dark and tend to glitter. His hair is perfectly white.

'Tompkins!'

'Eh?' He turns a page. His voice is not as feeble as you would suppose, looking at its owner—he is a trifle deaf, and talks loudly.

'Damn it, Tompkins, I need your help!'

'I'm in the middle of a chapter,' he complains.

'I don't care if you're in the middle of a sentence!'

'I am.'

'Tompkins, something awful has happened.'

Grumbling, Tompkins lowers the book. 'What do you want?' he says, fixing me with a keen-eyed glare.

'I need advice.'

'I hope it's worth the interruption.'

'I am having peculiar feelings about my wife.'

'Let me guess,' he says without enthusiasm. 'You hate her.' (I often confide in Tompkins.)

'Tompkins, I'm serious! I don't know whether I hate her or not, that's the trouble!'

'Well, boy, we live in troublous times.'

'Tompkins, I sold her to the Dev'l!'

'The what?'

'The Dev'l.'

'Speak up, Savage, I didn't quite catch that.'

'THE DEV-ILL!'

'Ah,' he says, closing the book entirely. 'And why did you do that?'

He doesn't display any surprise at my pronouncement; only interest. That is something I especially like about Tompkins—he is never astounded by anything. I believe that is a by-product of living one's entire life within books. He has read about every conceivable happening upon this earth, and so the notion that one might sell one's wife to the Devil is not inconceivable. Indeed, it is even rather commonplace.

'I didn't mean to!' I say. 'It just *happened*. He dropped by to thank me—'

'He did what?' Tompkins says, intrigued. I believe he thinks more of me than he has hitherto.

'I don't have time to explain! Lizzie is holding Ashley Lancaster at bay in my study, and they think I'm in my room, but I'm not, I'm here, and—'

'Ashley Lancaster is back in England? I didn't know that.' There is self-reproach in his tone. Tompkins doesn't like not knowing things. (It is from him that Lizzie got the trait. We spent a considerable portion of our childhood in Tompkins's bookshop. He and Simmons are very old friends.)*

'Yes! He's hiding from his parents in my study! He wants to know where his sister is, but I couldn't tell him, but I finally said she was abducted, but he wasn't angry he was excited because the supernatural's rather his area, and he—'

'Breathe, boy,' advises Tompkins.

'I don't have time to breathe! I don't know what to do! There are letters, and he says she loves me!'

'Who says who loves you?'

'Lancaster says Vivien loves me! She told him so in a letter! And now I don't know what to do!'

'What are your options?'

'I don't have any options.'

'Lionel Savage, one always has options. Let us begin at the beginning. First, sit down and please stop yelling. You are upsetting the books.'

I apologise and sit down. Boadicea promptly jumps into my lap and begins to purr. Tompkins hands me tea. I shove the animal onto the floor, then master myself and take a sip. 'That's better,' he says. 'Now. What precisely is your quandary?'

---

*I have often endeavoured to ascertain the precise circumstances (and date) when Messrs Simmons and Tompkins first met, but I have been unable to do so. Both men are peculiarly absent from public record, and unaccountably reticent about certain details. My own private notion is that they met many decades ago in the army—they have an unconscious ease with one another which is to be gained I think only by military comradeship or physical intimacy—but I hasten to add that this is based upon nothing but a feeling.—HL.

I stare at him, trying to put it into words. I realise I cannot. I mumble something about hating my wife.

'Who you never have to think about again, for you have sold her to the Devil.'

'Well, yes,' I say, 'I suppose so. But— But those letters to Lancaster!'

'What about the letters?'

'Is it possible she actually loved me?' I loathe the wheedling, pathetic tone of my voice.

'I know of nothing impossible when speaking of love.'

'Don't joke, Tompkins, it isn't funny.'

'I wasn't being humorous.'

If I wondered in childhood whether Lizzie wasn't somewhat magical, I knew it for certain of Tompkins. He has a way about him which is not of this world. To be in his company is to be put preternaturally at ease. I begin to feel my stomach unclench. My chest, though, is still doing odd things.

'What would it mean if Vivien loved me?' I ask.

'It would mean you have been very selfish and very blind.'

'But if she loved me, why didn't she ever *say* anything?'

'Perhaps she hadn't the words.'

'She did! She wrote poetry! Did you know that? Poetry that is lovely.'

'Well,' says Tompkins, 'let's ask Mr Kensington. He sometimes has an excellent grasp of these things. What do you think, lad?'

'Maybe she hadn't the heart,' says a voice from the stacks. I look around in surprise—I hadn't realised there was anyone else in the shop.

A person I do not know emerges from the gloom. He is very young, perhaps eighteen, but tall (not Lancaster tall, but a little taller than me) and pretty well built. He has bright green eyes which look older than the rest of him, and dark hair, and ears that stick out just a little bit too far. He looks too well bred for me to accuse him of eavesdropping, but he seems to have misplaced his eyebrows.

'Hello,' he says, extending a hand which I take and shake. 'I'm Will.'

'Savage,' I say. 'Lionel Savage.'

'It's a pleasure, sir,' he says. He has a trace of a northern accent. 'I have a brother who is a great admirer of your poetry.' He looks awkward, and hastens to add, 'Which isn't to say that I am not—I am sure it is quite good as poetry goes, only, I do not know much about poetry and so cannot judge. Algernon, though, is a great scholar and says it is excellent, which is why I only say that *he* admires it.'

I cannot but smile at his open-faced sincerity. 'No offence was taken,' I assure him. Then I ask, on a notion, 'You are not related to Kensington the inventor, are you? I believe he is from the North.'

He blushes and says, 'I have been called inventor.'

'You are he?' I cry. 'I have read of your experiments with the greatest delight!'

'Have you indeed?' he says, blushing deeper. 'I am glad of it.'

'But your name—?' I say.

'Fitzwilliam-Lewis is not a fit name for a young man,' he replies. 'It was a curse from a misguided grand-aunt. I much prefer Will.'

I smile again. 'Well then, let it be Will Kensington,' I say. 'I am very happy to meet you.'

'And I you,' he says, returning my smile a little shyly.

'You must tell me all about your experiments!' I say, looking to distract myself from any consideration of my wife and the odd sensations in my chest.

'Oh,' says he, 'I would not know what to say. I believe the press have misrepresented things.'

'They have that habit,' I say with a touch of ruefulness. I recall the many notices of praise my own work has received.

'Indeed they have!' he exclaims. 'I feel as though I no sooner build something than there are a dozen articles hailing it as the future of British excellence and ingenuity, and all the while I am searching high and low for my poor eyebrows, which have vanished in a puff of smoke, and then there are articles of rival inventors and the ascendency of coal and the importance of our South African interests and so on and so forth and I have still not managed to regrow my eyebrows and certainly have not had time to devote toward making the invention that started the whole clamour in the first place actually *work*!'

'I know exactly what you mean,' I tell him, laughing. I like this Will Kensington very much—he reminds me of Lizzie. I must introduce them. 'It's just the same with poetry.'

'Oh, I have no doubt!' he says. 'Algernon says that is the case. He is very wise about such things.'

'But what are you doing in London?' I ask.

He looks embarrassed. 'Truthfully,' he says, 'I crashed.'

'You crashed?' I repeat, not sure I heard correctly. 'What do you mean?'

'I have been working on a flying machine for some time,' he says reluctantly. I do not think he wants to talk about it, but he does so from politeness. It would be good form to change the subject, but I am interested and I am selfish and I am momentarily distracted from my own plight, which is a feeling I like immensely. Besides, this is almost inconceivably wonderful news.

I say, 'A flying machine?'

'Yes,' says he. 'Of sorts. Thomasina helped.'

'Who is Thomasina?'

'Oh! Thomasina is my sister.'*

'I have a sister,' I say.

'Do you?' says my young friend. 'That's splendid! I think sisters are excellent. Is she older or younger?'

'Younger,' I say. 'By six years. Yours?'

'Oh, older,' he says. 'I'm the baby of the family. I have another brother, too—Bernard. Have you any brothers?'

'No,' I say. 'Only Lizzie. But you were speaking of your flying machine . . . ?'

---

*I consider Miss Thomasina Kensington to be a person of enormous capacity and great depths of friendship. We are acquainted.—HL.

'Oh yes,' says he. He seems more willing to talk about it,
now that we are on intimate terms. 'Well, Thomasina and I
have been building it for ages. She taught me everything I
know, you know.'

'I didn't know,' I say.

'Oh yes—the press never mentions her because she's a girl,
but that's a crime—everything I've ever done I've done with
her. It was she who first posited the usefulness of steam. She
makes the most amazing clockwork gadgets you've ever seen!'

'I have never seen a gadget,' I say, unfamiliar with the word.
I do not like to seem ignorant, but I am compelled to ask after
an awkward pause, 'What *is* a gadget, exactly?'

'Oh, I'm so sorry—it's a word of Thomasina's; I believe she
stole it from the French or something. She uses it to mean a
little mechanical device.'

'"Gadget,"' I say again. 'It is a good word. I believe I shall
use it in a poem someday.'

'That will make Thomasina monstrously happy!' says Will
Kensington. 'Algernon, too.'

'So you and your sister built a flying machine,' I say. 'Is it a
balloon, or what?'

'Not at all! You can't steer a balloon! It is much similar to—
Well, you are familiar with da Vinci's devices, no doubt?'

'No,' I say. I am not well acquainted with art in general—
words have been my domain, not pictures. They seem to me
to have much greater value on the whole. Whoever said that a
picture is worth a thousand words has clearly never read *good*
words.

'Well, da Vinci drew all sorts of ingenious gadgets, many

of them for flight,' says the boy. 'Not balloons at all, but things more like mechanical birds. The trouble was, none of his flying machines quite worked. They were all human-powered, but you see, humans don't actually have the strength to make them fly.'

'So you substituted steam for humans?' I ask, beginning to catch on. It seems incredible, but after the events of the last twenty-four hours I am prepared to accept anything.

'Exactly!'

'And it worked?'

He looks a little embarrassed again, and chooses his words carefully: 'I hope that one day it will work better.'

'So you came to London to test this machine?'

'Oh no, I flew from York.'*

'You *flew* from York to London?'

'Yes,' he says without a trace of pride. 'I had hoped to make it to Paris, but something went wrong and I crashed in a field not far outside of town.'

'You *flew* from York!' I exclaim. 'That's astonishing, Kensington!'

'No, no,' he says modestly, 'it's really not. It was rather— It was rather an ignominious end. I'm afraid my poor *Cirrus*— that's her name—is in pretty awful shape.'

'Where is it?' I ask.

'In a barn outside of town.'

'Why haven't I heard about this? Tompkins, did you know anything about it?'

---

*This claim has been substantiated and confirmed.—HL.

'Hmm?' says Tompkins. He has reopened his book and is lost again.

'I prefer not to get the press involved,' says Will Kensington. 'They have that beastly habit we spoke of earlier.'

'Of course, of course,' I say. 'Beastly.' I am in my head already halfway through the composition of a paean to this young aeronaut.* He has quite captured my imagination.

'But you were speaking of your wife?' he says. From his tone I can tell he has been wishing to mention it for some time, but held himself back from good breeding.

'Indeed,' I say. 'My wife.'

'I didn't mean to overhear. But I did, and it can't be helped now, and I believe I should die of curiosity if I kept silent. Did you really sell her to the Devil?'

'I did,' I sigh. 'I am not proud of it. But what was it you were saying earlier—that she hadn't the heart to tell me she loved me?

'Yes, yes, exactly!' he says. 'If I may offer an observation . . . ?' I nod. 'Well,' he goes on, 'would you give voice to a love you knew to be unreturned?'

'But I *did* love her!' I cry. It is a strange thing that I am sitting in Tompkins's shop discussing my most intimate problems with a complete stranger; but somehow that makes it easier. I believe what I have needed all along is someone quite unacquainted with the whole issue.

---

*Like so many of my cousin's poetical notions, this work has yet to see the light of day.—HL.

'If you loved her,' says the young inventor, 'why didn't you tell her so?'

'Because— Because— I don't know! Because she seemed so cold! How could I tell her I loved her when she so obviously didn't care a jot for me!'

'But you mentioned some letters—proof that she indeed *did* love you.'*

'Yes,' I say, at a loss. I am furious. Not with Will Kensington, who is doing his best to help me navigate a frightfully complicated situation, but with the situation itself. It just doesn't seem *fair*. I tell him so.

'No,' he says, 'it's absolutely not fair. But isn't that what's so wonderful about love? I mean, I don't really know because I've never *been* in love—but that's what I'd imagine, from hearing about it. My brother Bernard is often in love, and he says that's what makes it such a grand thing—that you never really know what anyone else is thinking and so all you can do is trust that when they say they love you, they really do.'

'But she *didn't* say she loved me!'

'She married you,' he points out.

'Damn it, Kensington, don't turn sophist on me.'†

'I'm sorry, sir.'

---

*Proof seems a strong word; it is at most circumstantial evidence. If a case were built upon the letters alone, I do not believe it would hold up in court. It did not in the case of Musser vs Van Dyke.—HL.

†The discerning reader will have noticed that here Mr Kensington displays not sophistry but astute apprehension and keen insight into the human heart.—HL.

'No, no,' I say, at once sorry myself, 'I didn't mean to aim that at you. I'm just— I'm rather down lately. I apologise.'

'I understand,' he says.

We stare at the fire in moody silence for a while. From time to time Tompkins turns a page of his book. The feline stalks me.

'Kensington,' I say eventually, 'I'm glad I've met you.'

'And I you, sir,' he replies. 'Algernon will be quite jealous.'

The clock on the mantel strikes, and my stomach plummets. I rise abruptly. 'I need to go,' I say. 'I intend to see you again, Kensington.'

'I'd like that, sir,' he says.

'Goodbye, Tompkins,' I say, setting down my teacup.

'Hmm,' he says, and turns the page. From his engrossed demeanour and the subtle way he hides the title of the book, I gather that he is reading about Elizabeth Bennet. She is a great favourite of his.

I shoulder open the door and vanish into the fog.

I walk blindly. My mind is stormy, but my steady feet take me home. I cannot tell whether or not I am satisfied with my sortie. I am certainly glad to have encountered Will Kensington—he may be the most poetical person I have ever met. I would very much like to continue our acquaintance. I do not remember the last time I felt the stirrings of friendship, and now I have felt them twice within twenty-four hours. Perhaps the day is not as dreadful as I had imagined.

I reach Pocklington Place, let myself back in, tiptoe up the stairs, creep into my room, and flop down on my bed which I

THE GENTLEMAN

still do not like. I still do not know what to do. I still do not know if I hate my wife or not.

How is it that she could have loved me? Or (this occurs to me abruptly and unpleasantly) is this all some elaborate hoax—is Ashley Lancaster tormenting me deliberately? I do not think it possible; I have known him only an afternoon, but I do not believe he is capable of subtlety.* No, I am forced to believe that Lancaster believes his intelligence is sound. If this is the case, then—

Then I am a cad. Worse than a cad. But how can it be true? I do not believe it. During the last six months we have said barely six words to each other. She *cannot* love me. *I* could barely tolerate me! I do not believe it is possible that another human could have loved me.

But if she did. If, defying reason, sense, and all wisdom, *if* Vivien truly loved me, then I am a lost soul.

I have deciphered the feeling in my chest. It is passion. Passion such as I have never felt before. Passion of the sort one reads about in poems, but such as I have never myself been able to write. Passion of the old-fashioned sort, passion true to its roots—from the Latin *patior,* to suffer. It is not what might be called a pleasant feeling. It is rather as though my skin has been flayed from my bones and my entrails have been

---

*In our youth, Ashley, Vivien, and I spent a great deal of time together. Their father, Lord Lancaster, is the elder brother of my father. I mention this only to state that never, in all our time together, did Ashley Lancaster display toward me, or any person or thing in my sight, deliberate cruelty. He is not a man who torments for pleasure.—HL.

used as boot laces by a troop of soldiers walking through the mud in the rain at midnight. It is a horrible experience.

I gasp for breath, inhaling the musty air of my bedroom in great, gulping mouthfuls.

Good God, I think to myself, as the awful realisation strikes me with its full weight. There can be no other explanation but that*

---

*Mr Savage believes himself fiendishly clever for ending a chapter mid-sentence, *sans* punctuation. I vainly endeavoured to have it changed, but he smiled at me in that odd way he has (which I truthfully find a little unnerving) and said, 'Hubert, the same was done by Cervantes—so why not by I?' I had not time to compose the dissertation necessary to reply.—HL.

Seven

In Which I Very Nearly Fight a Duel.

I LOVE HER!' I have flown down the stairs, crashed through my study door, and hurled myself into the room. 'LIZZIE! SIMMONS! ASHLEY! I LOVE MY WIFE!'

'Oh God,' says Lizzie. Lancaster is not there. I do not know where he is. I do not care where he is, but if he were present I should embrace him as a brother and beg him to share in my joy.

'Lizzie, this is extraordinary!' I cry. 'I was lying on my bed, trying to figure out the peculiar thing happening in my chest. I thought I was dying. I thought, "Oh dear, twenty-two and it's all over." But the longer I lay there *not* dying, I began considering alternate possibilities, and finally I realised. I love her! It's the only possible explanation! And do you know what's awful? I think I've got quite a bad case of it! I think I love her more than anything in the world. I don't know how this could have happened. How could I never have noticed? My God. This is—'

I am cut off by Lancaster's voice. It breaks like thunder and rolls from the foyer down the hall and through the study door. 'SAVAGE!' he bellows. His person follows upon the heels of his voice. He is carrying an intricately carved wooden box. I do not know what it contains. I do not care. I am transported.

'Ashley!' I exclaim, ready to fling my arms around him.

'Mr Savage,' he says stiffly, 'as a brother and an Englishman—'

'Ashley!' I say again. I care not for brothers or Englishmen. 'I've just made the most spectacular discovery! It turns out I'm in love with your sister!'

'Would you hold these?' he asks Lizzie, handing the box to her. He is not smiling, which I find peculiar. How is it possible that anyone should not smile on this great day?

'Isn't that marvellous?' I continue. 'I've only just realised, but I think—'

Lancaster punches me in the face. It hurts. I fall down.

'Oh God!' cries Lizzie.

'Sorry,' Lancaster says to her.

'Carry on,' replies the traitoress.

'Bully!' he says.

I've never been in a fight before. I have often had cause, but never inclination. It has occurred to me more than once that I am not physically suited to it. My legs are the size of most men's arms, and my arms flail like ropes in a breeze.

'Get up,' says Lancaster, standing over me. He really is a tremendously large person. It's like looking up at the chap from Rhodes.

'Not really able to, old boy,' I tell him. I have no idea why he has hit me, but my face hurts prodigiously. I believe it will bruise. My jaw seems to work, though, which is something. Not even unprovoked physical abuse can dampen my spirits. I am in love! I feel startling goodwill toward all men—even this angry one.

'You sold my sister,' he says with menace, peering down at me spitefully. I now understand why I am lying on the floor. I suppose Lizzie must have told him the truth of my exchange with the Gentleman while I was with Tompkins. That was bold of her, and not altogether sisterly. Someday I will discuss the matter with her.

'You sold my sister,' Lancaster says again.

'Well, yes,' I admit, 'in a manner of speaking. But—'

'You sold my sister—to the *Devil!*'

'Now wait just a minute!' I wish I could make him understand what a ghastly mistake the whole thing was. I feel like Romeo talking to Tybalt. I say, 'Things have changed significantly in the last quarter hour or so. Help me up and I'll explain everything.'

'By all means,' he says, and offers me his hand. I am gratified that he will listen to reason after all. He helps me to my feet. I have scarcely begun to mention the virtues of civilised converse when he hits me again. This time it's one of those instances where his right fist hooks around from behind his head and whistles with the speed of its approach.

I renew my acquaintance with the floor. Lizzie is watching with one eyebrow raised, but does not intervene. She seems amused. Her eyes twinkle. She *is* amused, damn her.

'You lied to me,' says Lancaster. 'You said you were happy.'

'*She* lied to you!' I protest. I grow weary of looking up at him from below. (Of course, even when I'm on my feet I must still look upward; never mind.) '*She* said we were happy! All I did was fail to deny it.'

'You said she was *stolen*. Abducted. Taken. Not bloody *sold*. Get up.'

'Why?' I demand. 'So you can hit me again?' I do not respond to the obvious truth of his accusation. That was an atrocity committed in a time of war; but it was long ago, and things are much different now!

'I can't hit a man when he's down, it's not sporting,' Lancaster complains. 'Get up.'

'No! I'm sorry, but dash it all, I'm a POET. If I wanted to be punched I'd have been a boxer.* Stop hitting me and let me explain.'

'Absolutely not,' said Lancaster. 'Damn it, man, I'm not a violent sort of chap by inclination, but see here. You've impugned my sister's honour, lied to me, and generally been a blackguard of the highest order. Now GET UP.' It is true. I cannot deny it. But that's not the *point*. The point is that I've had an epiphany!

He helps me up again, then punches me again. Surprisingly, I do not fall. Even more surprising to us both, I hit *him*, and knock him down. I would not have thought it possible. When he lands, the entire house trembles.

'There we go, by Christ!' he exclaims from his back. 'Now

---

*Lancaster family legend holds that we have a shadowy, possibly illegitimate great-uncle who was a famous boxer. I do not know if that is true or not. But it is an undeniable fact that we Lancasters have a rather devastating uppercut.—HL.

you're showing some spirit! I could like you yet. I demand satisfaction.'

My hand hurts tremendously,* and I am not sure I heard him correctly. 'Excuse me?'

'For the offences you have done me and my family, I demand satisfaction.' He says it with a feral grin which two hours ago I would have thought him quite incapable of. The laughing-eyed sun god is gone, replaced by something altogether more fearsome. I had thought his divinity Grecian—I see now that it is Norse.

'Are you—' I break off. My hand hurts like the Dev'l, but I am strangely elated. 'Are you challenging me to a *duel*?' To fall in love and within ten minutes have an opportunity to fight a duel for it is more than any poet could ask for.

'No, I'm inviting you out for oysters. What the deuce do you *think* I'm doing?'

'I've always wanted to fight a duel!' I say. 'Never thought I'd get the chance!' As a boy I engaged in magical duels with rival magicians I concocted out of dreams and dust motes, but I have never actually duelled a real person. I always half-supposed that sooner or later Pendergast or I would say something truly dreadful to one another and a duel would be required, but I never seriously considered it. It was more the sort of happy sleepythought that brings a smile to one's face as one drifts off at night. The closest we ever came to an alter-

---

*Mr Savage does not record it, but he in fact broke three bones in his left hand—I do not know why he used his left, but he did—and was compelled to wear a plaster cast for the next several weeks. As he makes no mention of this, I can only assume it was an embarrassment to him.—HL.

cation was at Lady Whicher's dinner party when I threw his review into the fire and he responded by throwing my most recent book in after it. I tried to challenge him on the spot, but a piece of ham was lodged in my throat.

Lancaster has taken the wooden box from Lizzie and laid it on my desk. He now opens the lid. Within lies a matched set of duelling pistols. My heart begins to beat with excitement. They are exquisite objets d'art, entwined with gold filigreed vines and each bearing upon its hilt, if that is the word for the handle of a gun, which it probably isn't, a lion proudly rampant.

'There,' he says. 'The pistols are identical, but the choice is yours.'

I take one of the weapons eagerly. I have never held a gun before. It is cool to the touch, and fits in my hand with a feeling that is alarmingly sensual. The thing hypnotises me, and I stare at it as though in a trance. Lancaster takes its mate and walks to the far side of the room.

'Now hold on a minute,' I say, considering. 'A duel sounds marvellous in theory, but the thing is, I don't actually want to kill you.' I realise I'd never really thought it through.

'Don't worry,' he says, with that feral look in his eye. 'You won't.'

'Don't be naïve—if we're fighting a duel, one of us isn't going to leave this room alive. Isn't that how a duel works?'

'It is.'

I suddenly grasp his meaning. 'And you think that the chances of you being the man on the floor are . . . marginal.'

'I do.'

'In which case, *I* would be the man on the floor.'

'That's more or less how it works, yes.'

'Well,' I say, intrigued, 'this is a conundrum. Because the fact of the matter is, I don't want to kill you; but I also don't want you to kill me. And of course you don't want to die, and I don't believe that you truly *want* to kill me, either. Whatever I may have done, you don't strike me as a bloodthirsty fellow. Yet you feel it your fraternal duty to challenge me, and as an Englishman and a poet I am honour-bound to accept your challenge. If either one of us could avoid the whole thing we would, but our social standing, nationality, and chosen professions forbid it. This really is a philosophical paradox.' I study the gun. 'Is this where the bullet goes?' I observe him load his weapon, and follow suit. I make a mess of it of course, and he is forced to cross the room and do it for me. I watch his feet on the carpet and imagine poor Simmons trying to scrub out my blood.

Lizzie, who has been supervising the proceedings in silence, stands up. 'Give me the guns,' she says. Well, she is too late. If she had planned to intervene, the time to do it was back when Lancaster was batting me about like a toy. Now, however, we are in the realm of gentlemen.

'Lizzie,' I say, 'you're out of your depth. This is a matter of honour, and far beyond—'

'Shut up,' she says. 'Ashley, give me your gun.'

'I'm afraid I can't do that,' he says. 'Your brother is right—where honour is concerned—'

Lizzie stamps her foot. 'Honour be damned! I've sat here

and watched you two hit each other for the sake of your silly honour for the last ten minutes, and it was perfectly amusing, but now you've had your fun and quite frankly my patience is exhausted. It's time for both of you to grow up. Give me the guns.'

Lancaster and I glance at each other. Then at Lizzie. She eyes us flatly. Her jaw is set and her nostrils are flared.

We give her our weapons.

'Careful,' says Lancaster as he hands his to her. 'They're still loaded—'

Lizzie brandishes the pistols with some negligence, and both Lancaster and I drop to the ground. Lancaster mutters unprintable things, and I cry out.

'I don't trust you not to try to hit each other,' she says, ignoring our terror. She gestures to me with one of the guns. I

cower. 'Lionel, hands to yourself!' She points to Lancaster with the other. 'Ashley, go over there.'

'WOULD YOU STOP POINTING THOSE AT US!' he cries. 'For God's sake, unload them!'

'Ashley,' says Lizzie, 'you know I haven't the slightest idea how to do that. You'll please to stay on your side of the sofa. Nellie—'

Lancaster interrupts her. 'If you promise not to point them at me, I'll explain how to unload them. First, you're going to very carefully—'

'Sorry, Ashley, I haven't the patience.'

Lizzie spreads her arms and fires both pistols at once. Plaster flies from the walls and the simultaneous reports make my ears ring.*

'Well now, that wasn't so complicated after all. Oh do get up,' she says, 'you look so silly down there.' We rise. 'Now. It seems there are some things you two need to discuss, only I'd rather the discussion didn't include one of you getting shot. So because someone has to be an adult, I hereby decree that we are going to sit down right now and have a family meeting.'

Simmons used to make us have family meetings when one or both of us had misbehaved. They were never my favourite activity, and usually ended with deeper feelings of resentment than they began.

Lancaster and I give voice to our displeasure. Lizzie

---

*The holes in the walls at Pocklington Place have yet to be filled. Attempts have been made, but the study is Mr Savage's domain and he has forbidden it. He says that the holes serve to remind him of the 'marvellous eccentricity' of his family.—HL.

stamps her foot again. There is as much threat in the stamp of that little foot as in the negligent handling of two loaded weapons.*

'Don't speak,' she says. 'Sit over there.' She directs me to a chair on the near side of my desk. 'Ashley, you go there.' He sits on the sofa where she points. 'And now we'll talk like civilised human beings.'

We object again.

'Oh shut up!' she cries. 'You are *children*! Here. Only the person holding the magic gun may speak. Ashley's the guest, so he goes first.'

She hands one of the pistols to him. 'Thank you, Lizzie,' he says smugly.

'Don't call her Lizzie!' I say for no particular reason.

'I'm sorry,' he says, 'I'm holding the magic gun.'

'Oh, for the love of—'

'NELLIE!' says Lizzie. I stop speaking. She says, 'You were saying, Ashley?'

'I was saying that Lionel married my little sister for her money and sold her to the Devil. And then lied to me about it.' All of which is true, but had I the power of speech I should add that that was all a very long time ago, and that things are significantly different now.

'Anything else?' asks Lizzie.

---

*This is unquestionably the case. I have become very dear friends with Miss Savage, and I do not think she would be offended to hear me say that her anger, on the rare occasions it is displayed, is more frightening than anything I have yet witnessed.—HL.

Lancaster takes his time considering. I believe it is only because he enjoys holding the magic gun. At last he says, 'Not at the moment.'

'Very well,' says Lizzie, 'then give the magic gun to Lionel and let's hear what he has to say for himself.'

Lancaster hands me the gun.

'Am I allowed to speak in my own study now?' I demand sulkily.

'Don't pout,' says Lizzie.

I am resolved to be the bigger man. I turn to Lancaster. I say, 'Ashley, listen to me. You're right—'

Lancaster cuts me off. 'You'd bloody well—'

'LIZZIE!' I cry. 'I have the gun!' He is breaking the rules, and if he thinks he is going to get away with it then he does not know Elizabeth Savage.

'Ashley,' she reprimands, and there is a dangerous set to her dainty shoulders.

Lancaster holds up his hands in mute apology.

'You're right,' I continue, 'I have behaved . . . badly. But something incredible has happened. I have discovered that I am in fact overwhelmingly in love with your sister. And I will do anything in my power to get her back.'

I think it is very handsomely said, but Lancaster grabs the gun from me and says, 'Listen, Savage, it's all well and good to be contrite, but for heaven's sake—'

I snatch the gun back, if only to shut him up. 'I know that what I've done is unforgiveable. I'm not asking for your forgiveness. All I'm asking is that you let me help to look for her. Anything after that . . . Well, we can only engage one problem at a time. Like Horatius.* But in the meantime let me remind you that your sister has been taken by the Dev'l, and that for all we know he's doing horrible things to her.' I do not mention that he seems on the whole quite a decent, rather bookish chap. It seems at the moment to be extraneous information.

Lancaster takes the gun and says, 'I trust you're aware that if a single hair on her head is harmed, I'm going to end your life with a roll of baling wire and a dull spoon.'

'I'd assumed as much, yes,' I say when the gun is again in my hands.

He takes it back. 'And when we find her, if she hates you I'm not going to say a word in your favour. And if she wants me to kill you I will. And if she wants to kill you herself I'll load the gun for her. And if she wants you to take her place in Hell, I will personally escort—'

I grab the gun. 'Yes, yes, you've made yourself quite clear!' I say, and hand it back.

He thinks, then he says, 'Very well, then.'

We both look at Lizzie. She nods. Lancaster puts the gun down.† We enjoy the silence, knowing we once more have the ability to say anything we choose at any time we choose. At length Lancaster holds his hand out to me and says, 'Help me

---

*Mr Savage of course refers to Lord Macaulay's hero who single-handedly held a bridge against an army by forcing it to engage him one soldier at a time. Mr Savage claims to deplore Macaulay's verse as simplistic and pandering, but I do not think that he can truly mean it, as his is very much the same.—HL.

†This gun is still in Mr Savage's study. It has a place of honour on the wall, beside a pair of crossed sabres. Mr Savage refers to it as 'the only gun which ever *began* a friendship.'—HL.

move in my things from the foyer—I'm going to be staying here indefinitely.'

My heart, which was for a moment brought down to earth by the punching and the duel and the accusations, is once more borne aloft by thoughts of my wife. She really is the most wonderful woman in the world, I reflect—and that I should devote the rest of my life to winning her back from Hell, if it should take that long, sounds perfectly marvellous. My equanimity restored, I am inclined to once again look favourably upon Ashley Lancaster. Far from ruining my good opinion of him, the past quarter hour has made me view him as a much more interesting human than I had hitherto supposed. I wonder if perhaps I could not make *three* friends today.

'Very well,' I say, and shake his hand warmly. (I believe my knocking him down raised me up in his eyes also.) 'Lizzie, we need to know all there is to know about how to retrieve one's wife from the Devil. I leave it in your keeping, and put my library at your disposal.'

She looks at the shelves for a moment, then says, 'I'm not entirely sure how we're going to go about this, Nellie.'

I hesitate. 'To be honest, neither do I. It sounded so simple in theory. Gather the troops and march right into Hell and grab my wife. Didn't think about that fact that you need to find the bloody place first.'

'It *is* an interesting dilemma,' says Lancaster. 'Makes you wish you could talk to Dulle Griet, doesn't it?'

'Who?' says Lizzie.

'Dulle Griet,' he repeats. 'Mad Meg? The woman who rounded up the peasant mothers and stormed the gates of Hell to reclaim the souls of their sons that were killed in battle.'

I am drawing a blank, and I can see from Lizzie's face that she is, too. She says, 'Who wrote it?'

'Oh, no, it's a painting,' says Lancaster. 'Bruegel, I think— or is it Bosch?'*

There is a brief silence. At length, Lizzie says, 'I don't know,' in a small voice.

I don't either. It is unlike us not to know something. I move forward quickly. 'Here's what we'll do,' I say. 'Together we'll pull out all the books which might have information on Hell, the Devil, supernatural abductions, and missing wives. We'll split them up into three stacks, and we'll look until we find something. I'm in love and I've the best private library in Britain. I have never known books or love ever to fail, so I don't see why they'd do so now. Come on, Lancaster, let's get your things.'

As we head toward the foyer, he says almost to himself, 'Never thought I'd have to break *in* to Hell.'

---

*Bruegel.—HL.

Eight

In Which Lancaster Discovers a Breach in Lizzie's Defences for Which I Am Unjustly Held Responsible, & We Search for a Way to Hell.

Lancaster's things are in the spare bedroom, and we are once more in my study. Books are strewn everywhere. It is very late at night. I sit at my desk, paging through *Paradise Lost*. Lizzie and Lancaster lounge on the sofa. I am trying to concentrate, but I cannot because they are chattering wantonly. (I like Lancaster, but I do not approve. Lizzie I believe needs a hiatus from men.) They reach the subject of his expeditions, about which he is very eager to talk, and Lizzie no less so. They do their best to impress one another.

'I've read all about your expeditions!' gushes Lizzie. 'It must be so wonderful. I've never been out of England. Except in my head, of course. And in books. I think that should count, but for some silly reason it doesn't. You must tell me all about it! Simmons said you were in Tibet, but that's not right, is it? I read you were heading north, looking for Hyperborea. What did you find? Did you find it? Is it wonderful? Where exactly did you go? Tell me about the north! Does it really never get dark?' Answer me in one word, she could add. I smile to myself.

'Not in the summer,' says Lancaster. 'You see, the earth's axis is tilted so that— Well, the higher you go—the higher in degrees, that is—latitude degrees, you know—' The poor man is quite at sea. I wonder when he last carried on a tête-à-tête with an attractive woman. Lizzie seems to be wondering the same.*

'Are you trying to explain to me why in Arctic latitudes the sun never sets during the summer months?' she asks.

'Yes.'

'You really have no idea how to speak to a woman, do you?'

'No. You see, I have not been in polite company for some time. I apologise if I am— I should really just stop talking. I'm sure to be at once completely boring and horridly coarse.'

'Oh, don't be silly, Ashley! May I call you Ashley? I'm going to call you Ashley. "Mr Lancaster" just sounds so stodgy. You couldn't bore me if you tried—I've been in love with you since I was a little girl.'

I am too tired to tell her off, and not sure I have the inclina-

---

*It had been eighteen months.—HL.

tion. Lizzie seems to be enjoying his discomfort and Lancaster chokes on his tea—so I am gratified.

'Well never mind,' she continues. 'We'll teach you to speak to women yet! In the meantime, try to think of me as a man.'

'I'm afraid that's going to be quite impossible,' says Lancaster, wiping tea from his trousers. He casts me a sidelong glance. I think it makes him uncomfortable that I am present while Lizzie attempts to flirt with him. No more than I, I want to tell him—no more than I.*

'Oh, very well,' says Lizzie. 'But at least don't try to explain things to me. It's very sweet of you and almost unbearably charming, but I promise you that although I must seem a very young girl I am not ignorant.'

'No, God, no, I didn't mean to imply that—'

Lizzie wearies quickly of people who are slaves to propriety. In this she is still my sister, misplaced affinity for society parties or no. She cuts off his apology and says, 'Do you want to know a dreadful secret? I was expelled!'

'Oh,' says Lancaster, unsure how else to respond. 'I'm so sorry.'

'It's a perfect scandal!' says Lizzie with a twinkle. 'You see, I was caught having a dalliance with the dean's son.'

Oh good Lord, there it is. I can only bury my face in my book and wonder how I am ever to find her a husband.

'Good Christ!' cries Lancaster.

---

*Miss Savage was not flirting with him: I believe she was *toying* with him. She does this often with men. It can sometimes feel demeaning.—HL.

'That's what *I* said!' says Lizzie. 'They claim to be concerned with educating you, but they leave such glaring gaps—and when you attempt to rectify the situation and learn for yourself what they refuse to teach you, they behave as if you've killed someone. It's a disgrace.'

Lancaster's mouth opens and closes, but no words emerge. The trouble with Lizzie is, she does have a certain logic to her misbehaviour. What's worse, we think enough alike that when she explains something I cannot but wonder if she isn't right.

Lancaster's mouth still moves soundlessly. 'I've shocked you,' says Lizzie with pert accusation.

'A bit,' mutters Lancaster.

'I see,' she says. 'I'm sorry.' She doesn't sound sorry. Or at any rate, she sounds sorry only that he is not more liberal in his thinking.

She is being deliberately cruel, and he has not yet noticed. I am passing proud. I have said that Simmons raised us, which is true—but I like to think that, being so much older than she, in a large part it was *I* who raised Lizzie.

'I didn't mean to make you angry,' flails Lancaster.

'I'm not angry,' she replies with a dying fall. 'Just disappointed.'

Lancaster looks as though he's going to cry.

'Oh come now!' says Lizzie, breaking out in a charming little smile. 'Laugh! If I'd dreamed at thirteen you'd be this stodgy my heart would have broken.'

Lancaster is adrift. Lizzie at last wearies of her game and takes pity on him. 'Tell me about the north,' she says again.

He clutches at the question like a life preserver. 'What would you like to know?'

'Everything,' she says. 'But you could start by telling me where you went.'

'You read about Greenland?'

'Yes! Did you really ski all the way across it?'

Lancaster leans in conspiratorially and says, 'Truthfully, no. My binding broke with a hundred miles to go, so I walked the rest of the way. Then by balloon from the east coast of Greenland to the west of Iceland, where I rendezvoused with Dr Nansen. We went together on his ship, I forget her name—'

'The *Fram,*' says Lizzie promptly.

'How d'you know that?' demands Lancaster, looking at her even more intently.

Lizzie shrugs. 'I know things.'

Lancaster cocks an eyebrow. 'Well, then you know he built the *Fram* especially for Arctic waters.' She nods. I have no idea what they're talking about.* 'I'd have preferred to take my own *Daydream,* but the poor girl wouldn't have made it through the ice. When the pack got too thick I took my leave of the good doctor and skijored to Svalbard. Skijoring is—'

'When dogs pull you on skis, I know. You were saying?'

He beams at her precocity. 'From Svalbard I tried several times to punch north, but each time was turned back by weather. Damned good sport, but I'd finally had enough, and

---

*It is common knowledge that Dr Nansen's ship was designed with an egg-shaped hull, so that instead of being crushed by pack ice it should pop out of the water like a champagne cork and ride atop the ice farther north than any ship has hitherto sailed.—HL.

was completely out of supplies—I'd been living on walrus meat for the better part of a year, and between the two of us I was beginning to put on some blubber myself.'

Lancaster laughs at his own joke. It is clear that his muscled frame has never carried an ounce of blubber in his life. 'Even so,' he continues, 'I'd likely have stayed longer, but there was a blizzard and reports of a troll* and it seemed time to leave. I tramped down the spine of Norway, bought a schooner in Bergen, and set sail for home. Nothing much happened on the way—a few detours and a shipwreck, but nothing of note.'

'That sounds so marvellous,' says Lizzie dreamily. 'I'd so like to do that someday.' Which is worrisome. When Lizzie gets an idea into her head it can be a dangerous thing. I only hope that Lancaster will discourage her.

'You should,' says Lancaster. Damn him.

Listening to them makes me a little sad. They have achieved within an afternoon's acquaintance a conversational ease which Vivien and I never had. At first I think it is because of Lancaster's natural effortlessness in all things; but the more I watch, the less I think that is so—after all, he could barely say a word to her five minutes ago. Nor is it Lizzie's quickness of speech and wit; she is hardly quicker than I, and if anything her speed throws Lancaster off. No, it is something that I cannot put my finger on. Something ineffable. It is to be found in neither one of them separately, but seems to be some sort of chemical reaction set off by the meeting of their minds. Per-

---

*Such reports are common in Norway. I assume they are groundless, but cannot be certain. Cousin Ashley seems to put some stock in them.—HL.

haps had Vivien and I experienced that, things would have been different.

Lancaster is still talking, and they appear to have completely forgotten I am in the room. 'Someone, I can't recall who, wrote that exploration is nothing more than the physical manifestation of the lust for knowledge—'

'Appleblossom.'

'What?'

'Apsley Appleblossom wrote that.'

'So he did, by Christ! You amaze me. He also made a salient point, though, which is that only rarely do explorers actually enjoy themselves *during* expeditions. He notes that tramps like mine are often enjoyable only in retrospect; while you're actually on them you're generally hungry, lonely, and bloody freezing.'*

'Is that always the case, though?' asks Lizzie. 'I feel like there must be moments even as you're cold and hungry and sleeping on the ground when it's really wonderful.'

'Oh, absolutely! Don't get me wrong, you've absolutely got your Friedrich moments.'

'Your what?'

'Your Friedrich moments,' he repeats. 'Looking out at a sea of fog.'

---

*I believe this to be true. I once had the privilege of accompanying Cousin Ashley on an expedition of sorts. We were boys, and decided to have an adventure. We snuck out of Garrick Hall, which is the Lancaster estate, and spent the night somewhere in the park, under a willow tree. It was awful. But at about two in the morning Vivien found us. She had also snuck out, and had brought pillows, blankets, candles, water, and a mincemeat pie. I have the fondest recollections of that night.—HL.

'Who is Friedrich?' says Lizzie.

'Caspar David Friedrich,' says Lancaster. 'He painted *Wanderer Above a Sea of Fog*.'

'I'm not familiar with it.' There is a hitch in her voice.

'No, no, surely you've seen it. It shows from behind a man standing alone on a promontory, looking out at a vast expanse of clouds and mountains.' I brace myself. Lancaster is on dangerous ground. He is about to discover something about Elizabeth Savage which she does not want discovered. It occurs to me that I should warn him somehow, but I do not. I am intrigued. It is like watching a person walk into a patch of quicksand—you know that you really ought to call out, but you cannot; you can but watch in morbid fascination.

'That sounds lovely,' she says with gritted teeth, 'but I've never seen it.'

'Oh, I'm sure you have,' says he. 'Everyone has!' ('Oh sir!' I cry in my head. 'Oh sir, speak no more!')

'Well, clearly everyone *hasn't*,' snaps Lizzie.

Lancaster cannot let it lie. 'I mean, every educated person!' he says. 'Every art lover. I can tell just by looking at you that you spend huge amounts of time at the National Gallery. It's written all over you. I'm not wrong, am I?'

'No, actually, you are.' I have never seen her this annoyed.

'Indeed? Well my God!' he cries. 'Have I found a breach in your defences at last? This is fantastic!' I begin to wonder whether it isn't stupidity but in fact bravery in the big adventurer. He *must* know what treacherous ground he treads. My respect for him continues to grow.

'It's not a *breach*,' says Lizzie, hugely indignant. 'I just haven't gotten around to art yet. I know *books*. Art can wait. I'm sure it's lovely, and I'll get there. It's not a breach.'

Lancaster is gleeful, and does not bother to contain himself. I again imagine him with sword in hand, leading a small brotherhood in a desperate battle. It would be a sight to see. 'It is!' he cries. 'I can't believe it! You know everything in the world but you don't know a damn thing about art.'

'Of course I do!'

'Bosch and Bruegel,' says Lancaster. 'Who copied whom?'

'What?' Lizzie is becoming flustered. Lancaster charges on. 'Who's Gustave Courbet?'

'A painter.'

'What did he paint?'

'PAINTINGS.'

'Who sculpted Michelangelo's *David?*'

'I DON'T KNOW!'

'*Michelangelo's David*,' he says, and even I have an inkling.

'Oh,' says Lizzie, slumping, defeated. 'I have decided I hate you.'

But Lancaster is not done with her. 'Who painted the ceiling of the Sistine Chapel?'

'Oh, for God's sake, Ashley, I'm not stupid!' she yells, rallying. 'Even I know who da Vinci is.'

Lancaster just looks at her. I do not know who painted the ceiling of the Sistine Chapel, but from the expression on his face I gather that it was not da Vinci. (I am tempted to exclaim that I now know that he designed flying machines that wouldn't fly—but I restrain myself.)

'Damn,' says Lizzie. She turns her attention to me, acknowledging my presence for the first time in too long. 'Nellie!'

I prepare myself for the bombardment. 'What?' I say wearily.

'You have been decidedly remiss,' says Lizzie, 'and I am furious with you. I am completely ignorant about art!'

'And?' I say. I am not looking for a fight. I am tired. I want only to read my Milton and find my wife.

'And it's all your fault! As my older brother it's your duty to see I am educated in all things, but I know nothing about art!'

'Neither do I,' I say honestly.

'EXACTLY!' she yells. 'I need Simmons. SIMMONS, WHERE ARE YOU?'

Simmons enters, looking aggrieved. 'Do you know,' he says, 'there is a bell.'

'This is no time for philosophy, Simmons,' says Lizzie curtly. 'Something awful has happened. Could you be a dear and run me an errand?'

'Of course, Miss Elizabeth. Is everything alright?'

'Oh, everything's *fine*,' she says. Her voice drips with sarcasm. 'My silly brother and yourself have left a gaping hole in my education, that's all. It seems I know nothing about art!'

'Indeed, miss?'

'Don't be coy, Simmons. Who painted *Wanderer in a Sea of Fog*?'

'Friedrich, miss,' he answers promptly. 'And I believe it's *Wanderer* Above *a Sea of Fog*.' How in the name of God did he know that? I must remember never to underestimate Simmons.

Lizzie, however, is displeased with his hidden knowledge. 'DAMN IT! I am angry with you, Simmons. But I may possibly forgive you if you run out to Tompkins's bookshop and get me the two best books on art history. And while you're out, buy me an easel, some brushes, and a set of paints.'

'What are you going to do with a paint set?' I demand.

'You can't learn anything from the outside in, silly! If you really want to know about it, you have to do it for yourself.' Well, that is sound. I approve, despite myself. It is as I have mentioned—Lizzie's brain works maybe a little too like my own; I cannot for long disagree with anything she reasons out fully. 'Any questions, Simmons?' she asks.

'None, miss, but it is my duty to point out that it is approaching midnight.'

'So?' When Lizzie has possession of an idea, she sometimes does not think things through in their entirety. I do not know where she learned this trait.

'So the shops will be closed.'

'Well, then do it in the morning, Simmons!'

'Very good, miss.'

'And when you get back,' she says, her gaze softening a little, 'I'll consider forgiving your educational oversight.'

Simmons bows and leaves the room.

'Ashley,' says Lizzie after a moment, 'when Simmons returns with my things in the morning, would you like to pose nude for me?'

Lancaster turns several colours very quickly.

'A brother and an Englishman, Lancaster,' I say, laying my hand significantly on the pistol still perched on my desk. 'A brother and an Englishman.'*

---

*I am glad that Mr Savage prevented Cousin Ashley from revealing himself to Miss Savage. His motives derived perhaps more from a personal and less a moral feeling, but all the same it was well done. Sometimes I believe that Miss Savage must be protected, if I can be forgiven for saying it, from herself.—HL.

'I'm sorry, Lizzie,' says he, 'I find that I am otherwise engaged.'

Lizzie sighs prettily and frowns, as though searching for another dreadful tangent to embark upon.

'Lancaster,' I say before Lizzie can display yet more slatternly proclivities, 'how does one go about outfitting an expedition to Hell?'

'Have you discovered how to get there, by Christ?' he exclaims, leaping up.

'No, no, no,' I say. 'Hardly. With the two of you prattling like goats I haven't been able to focus. But if we're going to chatter, we may as well chatter about something useful.'

'Just so, just so,' he says, flirtation quite forgotten. 'What would you like to know?'

'Well, to begin, when we do figure out where Hell is, what's the best mode of transport?'

'Nellie,' says Lizzie reprovingly, 'that's a silly question. We can't know how we're going anywhere until we know where it is we're going.'

'She's right,' says Lancaster. He's looking at her in that way I don't like again. 'But,' he goes on, shaking his head as if to clear it, 'we can still begin outfitting an expedition. Now that you mention it, maybe that is the thing to do. Make us feel useful, eh? All this paging through books is no way to begin an adventure, by Christ!'

I cannot help but say, 'No—much better to plunge blindly into a black room.'

Lancaster looks at me steadily. 'Savage,' he says, 'I do believe you're mocking me. But you shouldn't be, old boy—you shouldn't be. Let me give you some advice. You can spend your whole life locked in a library and read every book there is to read and think you know everything there is to know—but the fact of the matter is, you won't be a whit better off than when you started, because all you will have done with your life is sit in a wooden box.'*

Lizzie cuts in before I can reply, which is probably for the best. 'So how *does* one prepare an expedition to Hell?' she asks.

'Well,' says Lancaster, 'first we need to determine what we'll need. If we're going north we'll need skis, if we're going south we'll need machetes, and—' He breaks off. 'I see,' he says, frowning. 'We haven't the slightest idea what to bring because we haven't the slightest idea where we're going. Complicated, that.'

We all look at each other. None of us know how to proceed, but it is clear that someone has to take charge. So I say, 'Well, what do we know about Hell? Let us begin with that, and perhaps we can piece together its location.'

'I don't know a thing,' says Lancaster. 'I'm a Buddhist.'

I groan. I have no patience for fads. 'Very well, then it falls to Lizzie and me. What do we know, sister?'

'About Hell? Not very much, except that both of us will probably end up there.'

'I'm being serious,' I tell her.

---

*I cannot help but feel that there must be a middle ground which is healthier than either extreme. I like to think that I live in this middle ground.—HL.

'So am I!' But she sighs, and thinks, and says, 'What if it doesn't *have* a physical location?'

''Course it has,' says the explorer bluffly. 'Everything has a physical location.'

'But that's not really the case, is it?' says Lizzie.

'Let us assume that it has,' I say before Lancaster can reply. 'Otherwise we may as well just go hang ourselves.'

'Agreed,' says Lancaster. 'It has a location, and by Christ we'll find it and go there! I'll take care of that part of things— it's rather my area, you know. But what about when we arrive? What happens then?'

'I'll handle that,' I say. 'The Dev'l and I are on excellent terms—I lent him some Tennyson—and after all, he did what he did only under the misapprehension that it would be a kindness to me. Once we arrive in Hell I'm certain things will be quite easy.'

'Excellent,' says Lancaster.

'But *how do we get there?*' asks Lizzie tiresomely.

The question still baffles us, and the conversation again dies. It is clear we require aid.

'SIMMONS!' I cry.

He enters with his usual promptness. 'Sir?'

'We need to go to Hell to rescue my wife, but we've no notion how to get there.'

'I see, sir.'

'You don't know where it is, do you, Simmons?'

'Not offhand, sir.'

'Well damn it, Simmons, then what are we to do?'

'It would seem, sir, that some research is in order. Might I suggest a trip to Tompkins's?'

'Of course!' I cry, feeling the fool for not having thought of it myself. 'Simmons, you're a miracle.'

'Thank you, sir.'

'What's Tompkins's?' says Lancaster.

'Oh,' says Lizzie wickedly, 'do you find yourself ignorant upon the subject?'

'Touché,' grins the giant.

'Tompkins's,' I say, 'is the best bookshop in London.'

'And probably the world,' says Lizzie.

'And probably the world,' I echo.

'A bookshop?' says Lancaster. 'But all the shops are closed. Simmons just said it was almost midnight!'

'All the shops *are* closed, sir,' says Simmons. 'But not Tompkins's shop. Tompkins's shop is never closed.'*

---

*I have attempted to debunk this, as it is scarcely credible. However, I have not yet been able to.—HL.

Nine

In Which We Are Helped by a Human Encyclopaedia.

The first thing Tompkins says is, 'You again?' which leads to a brief account of my afternoon ramble and my encounter with Will Kensington—about whom Lizzie and Ashley are very eager to hear. They are a trifle hurt that I did not mention him before. (I did not tell them about my ramble at first because it was a private matter, and then because I was distracted by Lancaster's fists.)

'Do you know where he's staying, Tompkins?' I ask.

'Some sort of inventors' club, I believe. The Hefestaeum, was it? It's in Pall Mall.'

'I've never heard of it,' I say, which I find perplexing. I make it my business to know things about this city which are odd or poetical, and an inventors' club sounds to me like both. 'Have you heard of it, Simmons?'

'I have not, sir,' says he. 'Perhaps Tompkins invented it.' Simmons enjoys needling his friend.*

'*Invented* it, eh?' cackles Tompkins. 'I'd've expected better of you, Simmons.' Simmons makes him an ironic little bow. 'Now,' he says, 'tell me what it is precisely that you're doing here in the middle of the night.'

We are seated before his fire. Simmons and Lancaster and I pulled four armchairs into a semi-circle, or a sort of prostrate arch of which Tompkins is the keystone, while Lizzie poured us all tea, which we are now sipping.

'To begin with,' I say, 'I realised I love my wife.'

'Naturally,' says Tompkins. I cannot tell if he is making fun of me or not.

'Quite. Anyway, we obviously have to get her back—'

'From the Devil?'

'Yes, yes, from the Dev'l—but the trouble is, we don't actually know how to get to Hell to talk to him.'

'Hmm,' says Tompkins. 'Yes, I see. Go on.'

'Well . . . That's it, really. We need to plan an expedition to get to Hell, and in order to do that it seems we need to discover the *location* of Hell—'

'If it has a location,' puts in Lizzie.

'Which,' I say sternly, 'we have agreed to assume. And so we came here to do some research.'

'Simmons,' says Tompkins, 'I am pleased to see that even if

---

*Watching these two gentle, unassuming intellectual giants spar is one of the great pleasures of any educated man's life.—HL.

they are in general quite hopeless, these children of yours do at times display some sense.'

'Yes,' says Simmons. 'At times, I suppose they do. But Tompkins, it would be well if you and I—'

Simmons is speaking out of turn, and I cut him off. He seems less than enthusiastic about our adventure, and it bothers me. 'Can you help us?' I demand of the bookseller.

Tompkins pulls at his moustache, which is a very fine one (by 'fine' I do not mean that it is thin but just the opposite) and is shaped like the business end of a push broom. 'Perhaps I can,' says he. 'I do not know. One never really does. But I am willing to try.'

'Tompkins,' says Simmons, 'you and I really must talk.'

Tompkins opens his mouth to reply to his friend, but I silence him with a look. Simmons is behaving in a most un-Simmons-like manner. He and I must have words. 'Simmons,' I say, 'are you or are you not committed to rescuing Vivien?'

He looks me in the eye. 'I am utterly committed to rescuing Mrs Savage, sir,' he says.

'Good,' I say. 'Then let's get started.' And I put the queer matter of Simmons's mutiny out of my mind. I turn to Tompkins and say, 'Lizzie and I are heathens and Lancaster's a Buddhist, so we're at quite a loss. Did you know Buddhism hasn't got a hell?'

'Now wait a bit,' says Lancaster. 'I never said that.'

'It does, then?' I demand. 'Did you not think that relevant information?'

'Not particularly,' he says. 'There are several hells called *naraka,* but they're individual and impermanent hells, really more like purgatories. They appear when you die and when you've worked off your debt, as it were, they disappear. In other words, they—'

'Have no physical location?' says Lizzie.

'Well . . . no.'

'This isn't helping!' I say. 'We need help!'

'What books shall we begin with?' asks Lancaster, looking unhappy but stoic. It occurs to me with a shock that he may not *like* books. I dismiss the thought as soon as it enters my head as too preposterous to be borne. Not like books! I cannot believe it of a fellow man.

'No, silly,' says Lizzie. 'We don't start with books—we start with Tompkins!'

Which is of course the truth.

The bookseller sits in silence for a time. I can practically hear the encyclopaedia pages of his mind turning. Then he begins. 'The notion of an underworld has been around since the beginning of recorded history. Somewhere souls go when the bodies they occupy die. Nearly every religion has some version of it. In Indo-European cults—'

'Tompkins,' I cry, 'we don't need an anthropology lesson! Give us something useful.'

He sighs and I imagine I can hear a few more encyclopaedia pages turn. 'Between the Crucifixion and Resurrection, it is believed Jesus led a successful military raid upon Hell—which at that time was not actually called Hell, but, rather—

'Essex Grove?' I say eagerly. All eyes swivel toward me and I feel myself blush.

'. . . No,' says Tompkins. 'Not Essex Grove. It was called Sheol. It was the Old Testament underworld to which the souls of all dead, both righteous and unrighteous, went. The purpose of this raid, which mediaeval theologians dubbed the Harrowing, was to free the righteous and escort them to Paradise.'

'That's interesting,' says Lizzie, leaning forward.

'Yes, interesting,' I say without enthusiasm, 'but still useless.'

'It's not useless,' says Tompkins. 'It is an example of the many stories in which a living man physically visits the realm of the dead. The Orpheus myth is another—as is the tale of Sir Orfeo, which was not his real name at all. The point being that it *is* possible. Which is an excellent place to begin.'

'Hear, hear,' says Lancaster.

'But how do we get there?' I demand.

'I'm thinking,' Tompkins barks. The thing about Tompkins, you see, is that he has so much information crammed in his head that it sometimes takes him a while to unearth the precise piece he is searching for. 'Well,' he says after a moment, 'there is of course a reason it is referred to as the "*under*world." It is generally supposed to be within the earth, probably somewhere near its centre.'

'But that's impossible,' I say, exasperated. 'It's unscientifical.'

'I'm sorry,' says Tompkins blandly, 'I thought you said you'd sold your wife to the Devil.'

A hit, a palpable hit. Lizzie and Lancaster laugh. I apologise to him.

'How would we get to the centre of the earth?' I ask.

'There was a German philologist, sir,' says Simmons, 'who some years ago claimed to have journeyed there. A Frenchman wrote a book about it.'

'Just so, by Christ!' says Lancaster. 'I recall that expedition. Bungled, the whole thing, but never mind—it reminds me of something. You are all no doubt familiar with the artistic trope of Hellmouth?'

'No,' I say, and brace myself for:

'NO I AM NOT FAMILIAR WITH IT, ASHLEY LAN-CASTER. I AM FAMILIAR WITH NO ARTISTIC TROPE.'

'Tompkins,' I say, 'you don't have any books on art history, do you? It's rather an emergency.'

'Certainly,' he says. He hauls himself from the depths of his armchair and disappears into the stacks.

I stare into the fire and think of Viv. (I do not believe I have ever before referred to my wife as 'Viv.' It must have rubbed off from Lancaster. I think I like it. It puts me in mind of two separate persons—the woman I mistreated for six months, who is Vivien and whom I loathed, and the woman I am attempting to save from damnation, who is Viv and whom I love.) I remember her hair—the way it fell in waves when she wore it down, and floated upon the air when it was up. I remember her laugh. How funny that I should recall it at all; I think of her as generally an unhappy woman. Which was, it seems, my fault. Or partially mine. I still rebel against the notion that I hold sole responsibility.

There are several crashes from the stacks, a puff of dust, and Tompkins emerges victorious, holding two large tomes. He gives them to Lizzie, who says, 'Thank you, Tompkins—at least there is one person here who is a gentleman,' and kisses his cheek.

'What were you saying about Hellmouth, boy?' Tompkins says to Lancaster, who seems to be unsuccessfully composing a witty response to Lizzie's barb.

'Oh,' says Lancaster. 'Um. Excuse me. I was— Sorry.' He regains his composure, glances at me and Lizzie, smiles to himself, and says a little patronisingly, 'Hellmouth was an image popular in the Middle Ages, though in conception probably dating from much earlier, which showed the entrance to Hell as the gaping maw of a dragon belching fire. I never thought much about it before, but it's so prevalent one can't help but wonder if there isn't something to it.'

'Alright,' I say, mystified. 'That's lovely, but how does it—'

'Oh!' exclaims Lizzie. 'Yes, I see! Of course!'

Simmons and Tompkins are both nodding as though they understand.

'What?' I demand. I still have no idea what he means.

Lizzie says, 'A volcano, silly. It could be a volcano.'

'In fact,' muses Lancaster, 'I believe that's it, by Christ! I recall now that there's an African tribe I spent some time with who worshipped a volcano—they said it was a portal to another realm, one of spirits and such. I'd forgotten about it until just now! Perhaps you're familiar with it, Mr Tompkins. Where exactly are you from, anyway?'

Tompkins becomes abruptly chilly. 'I am from England, Mr Lancaster,' says he.

'Yes, yes, 'course you are,' says Lancaster ingenuously. 'But where are you from *originally*?'

'I was born in England, sir, as was my father before me.'

'I say, old boy,' exclaims Lancaster, suddenly picking up on Tompkins's tone, 'I didn't mean to offend you! Farthest thing from my mind, by Christ! I couldn't care less if you're black, white, green, or bloody purple!'

'Oh,' says Lizzie, 'these men, these men!'

Tompkins suddenly guffaws, whether at Lizzie or at the

look of chagrin on Lancaster's face it's impossible to say. 'Never mind, boy,' says he. 'I've faced worse than that. In the old days Simmons used to fight for my honour.'

This is such a remarkable piece of news that for a moment I forget all about my wife. 'Simmons *fought* for you?'

'Good man, Simmons,' says Tompkins.

'Hyperbolic man, Tompkins,' retorts Simmons.

'Don't be prosaic, Simmons!' I cry. 'Did you or did you not fight for Tompkins?'

'There were some fellows, sir, in our youth, who said some things which a friend could not let pass.'

I command him to tell us more, but my enigmatical butler only shakes his head coyly.

'If you don't mind my asking, Mr Tompkins,' says Lancaster, whose bluff demeanour is in no way altered by his momentary embarrassment, 'where is it that your people are from? I only ask in case I've been there.'

'My grandfather, before he was stolen and sold, was born in a place called Makombologo,' says Tompkins, shooting Simmons a wink which Lancaster does not notice.

The explorer looks much more embarrassed than previously, and at length admits in a low voice, 'I have not heard of it.'

We all do our best not to laugh at his ignorance of this fictitious place, and he changes the subject awkwardly. 'What do you know about Snaefellsjökull, Mr Tompkins?'

'Good God,' I say. 'What on earth is that? Another village in Africa?'

'It's a volcano in Iceland,' says Tompkins, coming back to

the matter at hand. 'Our German friend claims to have used it as a portal to the centre of the earth, and the old pagans thought of it as an entry to the land of the dead. I'd quite forgotten that. Yes, boy, I think it just might do the trick.'

Lancaster's ego is soothed and he is grinning. It's the same grin I saw when he was standing over me earlier—feral, dangerous, and elated. 'Savage,' he says, 'we're going to Iceland.'*

'We can't go to Iceland,' I protest. 'It will take ages to get to Iceland. By the time we make it to Iceland who knows what could have happened to Vivien?'

'Hmm,' says Tompkins. 'Quite.'

'Dash it all,' says Lancaster, 'I suppose you're right. Hadn't thought of us being under the gun, as it were, but maybe we are at that. Is there a time limit on these things, Mr Tompkins?'

'There could be,' says the bookseller, 'or there could not be. It's difficult to say.'

'What are the factors?' I ask.

'Well,' says Tompkins, 'occasionally when mortals are kept in the underworld for extended periods they lose touch with mortal feelings. Sometimes they die outright; sometimes they just become sort of shades, living a half-life among the dead. But of course that doesn't happen always. I have read stories of men and women who have lived for decades in the underworld and emerged as sunny as a June morning. It all depends.'

---

*The island nation of Iceland has a history as dramatic and fascinating as our own. I recommend study of it to any reader who has an interest in such things. —HL.

'What does it depend *on*?' I press.

Tompkins shrugs.

'Is there any way to find out?' asks Lizzie.

'None reliable,' says Tompkins.

'So what you're saying,' says Lancaster, 'is that it's possible that if we don't get to Vivien in time she could die, but we don't know how long that could take, or even if we actually have to worry about it?'

'Just so. Vexing, isn't it?'

We all agree that it is, rather.

'It sounds as though we must assume the worst,' says Lizzie.

'I always assume the worst,' I say.

'What we need,' says Lancaster, 'is a way to get to Iceland very quickly.'

Which is when I have a wondrous idea.

Ten

In Which We Visit an Extraordinary Place Which Turns Out to Be Rather More Dangerous Than We Had Supposed.

The Hefestaeum Club is not a well-thought-of establishment, we discover. We ask a bobby where precisely it is located, and he frowns, spits, demands what we are doing out so late at night, and takes down our names. He doesn't know who I am, doesn't believe that Ashley Lancaster is Ashley Lancaster, and doesn't tell us where the club is. I wish I'd thought quicker and told him I was Pendergast.

'Are inventors so disreputable?' asks Lizzie a little breathlessly. I fear she is attracted to scandal.

'Inventors upset the order of things,' says Simmons.

'Like explorers,' I say.

'And poets,' adds Lancaster.

We are a strange party: Lancaster so tall, Lizzie so young,

Simmons so prim, and myself so whatever it is that I am,* all wandering Pall Mall in the dead of night. I can't entirely blame the man for having taken our names.

If you have never explored the streets of London at midnight, you should. I have already told you of my walk to Tompkins's shop this afternoon, and I do not wish to be tedious. But allow me to observe that whatever is mysterious and lovely in the day is doubly so at night. And when it is very late and there are no other people abroad, fairies dance in the shadows. (That is a secret. Do not tell.)

Pall Mall is a street which I like. Not to visit in the day, and not for its position in society—but taken on purely aesthetic grounds, it is a magnificent place. It is broad, and well paved with enormous flagstones. Upon either side, gentlemen's clubs loom.

These clubs are such a fixture of our lives and routines that I fear we are not fully attuned to their oddness. Here are organizations which exist solely for escaping the humdrum conundrums of daily life. For bachelors, they offer companionship and an escape from loneliness; for married men, the illusion of lost bachelorhood and an escape from femininity. For a reasonable annual sum, a gentleman of means can come anytime he wants to what quickly becomes his second home. At his club he can eat well and cheaply, he can sleep, he can use the library (which is generally excellent), and he can hobnob with like-minded fellows.

---

*Dissolute?—HL.

I used to belong to the Athenaeum Club, which is the club, if you are a literary man of note, to which you belong. (I could not of course technically afford it, but I am a gentleman, which means that I have a great store of imaginary money which everyone pretends is just as good as hard tender.) Since my marriage, however, I have let my membership lapse. I have craved escape, certainly, but not company. I went there once, just after my wedding—but several members clapped me on the back and congratulated me and asked me all sort of prying questions, and I left without dinner. I retreated to the solitude of my study.

Often in the last six months I have considered joining the Diogenes Club. It is a club for men such as I. In it, speaking is strictly forbidden and acknowledging your fellow members in any way whatever is strongly discouraged. It is a place to go for companionable solitude and social introspection, and is peopled by lonely misanthropes. But by the time the notion came to me, I had already entrenched myself in my study— and I have said before that I am a creature of habit.

Lizzie is thrilled to be wandering Pall Mall. It is a place which is not actually off-limits to females, but where no female would ever have reason to go—and my sister, if you have not already grasped this, enjoys flouting convention. She is flitting from one side of the street to the other and peering through windows on her tiptoes and grinning like a maniac. I see that it is time to hurry us along.

Despite my acquaintance with clubland, I have never heard of the Hefestaeum, and have no notion where it might be. We have walked nearly the length of the street and have not encountered it. We finally ask a beggar boy if he has heard of our destination.

The urchin is terrified of Lancaster's size, and refuses to speak to him—so it is Lizzie who asks our way. 'Hello,' says she. 'Do you know of a club of inventors which may be near here?'

The boy nods and points past her down an elegant side street. The buildings are a little smaller than those in Pall Mall proper, and not quite so grand—but still each is rife with colonnades and porticoes and flags. A few windows are lit, but not many. The city sleeps. There is an exception, though—one building, just at the turning of the street, is different. Eerie blue light blazes from its windows, and architecturally it is the queerest sight I have ever seen. It is taller than its neighbours, and narrower, and seems to have been cobbled together from parts of many buildings dissimilar to one another. It, too, has columns—but they stand at appalling angles and seem not to support anything but other columns. It looks as though a long time ago there stood upon the spot a small two-storey cottage; and that an ambitious but unskilled architect decided to build a tower on top of the cottage; and that some time later a less ambitious but more skilled architect converted the tower into something approximating a respectable edifice, but that before the conversion was complete he died without telling anyone the remainder of his plans; and that work was then recommenced by a demented longshoreman with a fondness for drink, after which things became rather chaotic.*

---

*I cannot better Mr Savage's description—I can but confirm that this is precisely what it looks like, and if you doubt it you may go there and see for yourself.—HL.

As we gaze at it, there is a sudden flash of orange light from the third floor. The entire building shudders, and a heart-beat later we hear an explosion. I wonder if Will Kensington has lost his eyebrows again.

'By Christ,' says Lancaster, 'it looks as though we'd better get there while there's still a there to get to. Come on!'*

Our strange group hurries along the empty street and up to the strange building. As we draw nearer, it looms above us, taller than I had realised at first. ('Childe Roland to a dark tower came,' says the poetical voice in the back of my mind that is never at quiet.) I wonder that I have not heard more of this place. It is a most distinctive landmark to be so unknown. I suppose its obscurity is an indication of the rapidity with which this city grows and changes—every day there are build-ings raised (and razed), discoveries made, new oddities at which to gasp. Small wonder that one peculiar architectural relic is forgotten.

At the door we are met by a butler. He is aptly suited to the place in appearance, by which I mean he is strange looking. He is improbably tall, gangling, with an Adam's apple which would jut out further than his nose had he not such a stagger-ingly enormous nose. All ridiculousness halts however at his eyes, which are black and sharp and brook no nonsense.

Before I can utter a word, he says, 'No women allowed in the club.' His voice is high and grating.

---

*The Hefestaeum in fact caused so much trouble for the Metropolitan Fire Brigade that the government became involved. A fine system was imposed. The club was allowed two fires per annum, which the MFB would put out gratis. Each fire after that would incur a heavy fee.—HL.

'Good Christ but you're a rude one,' exclaims Lancaster, rushing to Lizzie's defence. 'That's no way to speak to a lady!'

'I am very sorry, sir,' says the butler. 'It is not my intention to be rude, but club rules forbid women from crossing the lintel.'

'Damn your rules!' says Lancaster, clenching his fists.

'Pardon me, sir,' says the butler, 'but rules are the foundation of this very Empire of Britannia.* Without them we should be living in mud huts and eating dung. I do not care if you enter the club or no, but upon my life and honour the lady shall not pass.'

Lancaster, I can see, has reached a boil. I believe deep down he has as little regard for convention as I have.

'It's alright,' says Lizzie before her champion can do anything rash. 'I'm tired anyway.'

It's a boldfaced lie and we all know it. I see Lancaster preparing to do something gallant and stupid—but Simmons hurriedly says, 'As am I, miss. Let's go home.'

'My knight!' says Lizzie, kissing him on the cheek.

Lancaster looks a little jealous. 'We won't be long,' he says.

'Oh, take all the time you need!' says Lizzie airily. She is dreadfully disappointed to leave, and trying her hardest not to show it. 'This looks like a thrilling adventure, and I expect a full report! I'll wait up.'

'Thank you, Simmons,' I say.

'Certainly, sir,' he replies. With a venomous look at the butler (Simmons is acutely pained by lesser practitioners of his

---

*Well said, sir, and God save the Queen!—HL.

profession), he puts a protective hand on the small of Lizzie's back and the two of them start off down the cobblestones.

'Well,' says Lancaster, returning his attention to the ciconian butler, 'are you happy now?'

'I am neither happy nor unhappy, sir,' replies the gate-keeper. 'But the impasse resolved, we may now proceed.'

'Excellent,' says Lancaster, and attempts to cross the threshold. But the butler does not surrender the portal.

'I'm sorry, sir,' he says, 'but you cannot yet enter.'

'Why in God's name not?' demands Lancaster. 'We've sent away the lady, what else do you want from us?'

'You may not enter the club until you have answered three riddles.'

'Riddles?' he thunders. 'You want me to answer *riddles*?'

'I'm sorry, sir, but unless you are a member of the club you are subject to the entry rules.'

'I'm not answering riddles, by Christ!'*

'Then you are not entering the club,' replies the butler.

We all look at one another for a moment. Then Lancaster says, 'I have a riddle for you: which would you prefer—to step aside, or for me to throw you aside?'

'That isn't a riddle,' says the butler.

"Course it is,' says Lancaster. 'And I'm waiting for your answer.'

---

*What neither of my cousins grasped is that the answering of three questions to gain admittance was a typical trial undergone by questers and knights errant in days gone by. Had they borne this in mind, they would have perhaps found themselves more amenable to their situation, and much trouble could have been prevented. I have pointed this out to them, but have received in return for my pains only blank, unamused stares.—HL.

The butler does a strange shuffling sort of dance with his feet and shifts a few inches to his left. I wonder why. Lancaster tries to grab him, but the butler kicks with his left toe at a spot on the flagstones and the ground opens beneath our feet. Lancaster and I plunge into darkness.

We fall perhaps fifteen feet. Straw cushions our landing, but I nevertheless feel rather battered. I take in our surroundings—we seem to be in a sort of dungeon. The walls are lit by blue lights in sconces which do not flicker but certainly are not gas. Lancaster is on his feet in the blink of an eye, itching for a fight; but there seems to be no one *to* fight. Our cell is small and square, three walls of stone and an iron gate for the fourth. We are quite trapped.

Above our heads, the trapdoor through which we fell snaps shut.

'Damn,' says Lancaster in fury. Then, looking around for a moment, he says it again in admiration. 'This is a pretty pickle, eh?' he chuckles. He is in an abruptly excellent mood that I cannot fathom.

'It does seem rather dire,' say I, getting shakily to my feet.

'It's superb!' he cries. 'Look at us, old boy! Trapped beneath Pall Mall by a bunch of inventors and their half-cocked butler!'

I know what is coming next.

'It's an adventure, by Christ!'

I expect to be exasperated by him, or frightened by our predicament, or concerned about such-and-such. But to my surprise I discover that my heart is beating quicker than usual and my senses seem preternaturally acute and I am on the edge of entirely unhysterical laughter.

'So it is!' I say. 'So it is.'

Lancaster looks shocked, and exclaims, 'That's the spirit, Savage! I believe we're going to be friends after all!'

I cannot I think convey to you the warmth I feel upon hearing this silly statement. Something must be dreadfully wrong with me. I am not by nature a man who has friends, but then I am not a man who believed I *needed* friends. Perhaps I am ill. I have made three friends in two days, though it feels much longer. Granted, one of them belongs to an organisation which has imprisoned me in a most cowardly manner, the other is my brother-in-law who tried not long ago to kill me, and the third is the Devil; but, then, I have never been conventional.

Lancaster is pacing the room like a lion—have I mentioned before how like a lion he is? He is at times wolfish, but I believe him to be much more like a lion. There is a pride about him which is very leonine. In any event, he is pacing. He goes first to one wall, then another, looking for chinks. There are none. He examines the iron gate minutely. He tests his strength against it. It does not bend. From this, I surmise it must not in fact be iron, for I have no doubt that the man before me could bend an iron bar.* As he struggles with the gate, I begin to seriously fear for the well-being of his clothes. The muscles bulging beneath his eveningwear are waging a war with his seams which cannot end well.

---

*I have spoken with several members of the Hefestaeum, none of whom can agree on what kind of metal it was—but they do confirm that it was not iron.—HL.

'Lancaster,' say I at length, 'I do not think you are going to break the gate.'

'No,' he says in disgust. 'It seems not. Damned strange sort of metal.' He is embarrassed by his failure. 'Reminds me of a time I was in Afghanistan. Got locked up in the Shah's dungeon—you read about it?'

I don't reply.

'No, 'course you didn't. Sometimes I wonder about you, Savage. For all the books you purport to read, you can be awfully ignorant sometimes.'

'Now see here, Lancaster!'

'No, no, I'm sorry, old boy. Don't let's quarrel. It's my fault, and I retract the comment. One of the dangers of imprisonment, turning on your comrades.'

'No doubt,' I say. I am inclined to be magnanimous. 'You were speaking of the Shah?'

'Quite so. Locked up most dreadfully.'

'How did you escape?'

'Escape? I didn't. Spent eighteen months there until Mummy convinced Whitehall that I was a national treasure and they intervened and secured my release.'

That sobers me. 'But we don't *have* eighteen months! Vivien could be dead by then!'

'Vivien could be dead *now*, old boy. Don't suppose she is, but all the same let's not lose sight of the reality of things.'

I know that he says it meaning well, but it throws me horribly. It isn't a possibility that had occurred to me. That Viv could be dead even now is not something I can think about at the moment. With an effort, I thrust it from my mind.

'Well,' I say, 'this is turning out to be a different evening than I had expected.'

'I should have answered the riddles,' he says, settling himself upon the floor. 'But no use crying over the milk, by Christ! Breathe it all in, that's what I learned in Tibet, breathe in disaster and breathe out goodwill toward mankind and your utter confidence that things will turn out alright. That's how it's done, you know. Sit down, Savage, and I'll teach you to meditate. It'll do you good.'

I am saved this fate by the sound of approaching footsteps and of voices which I cannot quite make out.

'Tally-ho,' says Lancaster, springing up. 'Here come our captors.'

The voices become more distinct.

'You've done well, Benton,' says one. 'Very well indeed. These are not times to take unnecessary risks.'

'My thoughts exactly, sir,' says the other, grating and unpleasant. 'Additionally, there was a woman with them.'

'Oh dear,' says the first. 'Yes, yes, you have certainly done the right thing.'

The speakers come into view. The leader is a short man in middle age, paunchy, bandy-legged, and possessed of the largest cranium I have ever seen. He has very tiny eyes which are shadowed beneath bushy brows from which rises a forehead of Jovian breadth.* He is trailed by the butler whose acquain-

---

*The reader will be amused to note that the possessor of this Jovian forehead is the inventor of that mysterious device which has lately been the subject of so much press, the Minerva Mechanism.—HL.

tance we made previously and whose name is apparently Benton. He looks somehow at home under the earth.

'Gentlemen,' says the one who is not the butler, 'welcome to my club.' He has a jitteriness of voice and manner which give the impression that he is trapped in a zoetrope. He rubs his hands together continually and touches his face more than is necessary.

'Not what I'd call a warm welcome,' remarks Lancaster. 'And hardly sporting. Who are you and what the deuce do you think you're doing?'

'I apologize for the precautions, but these are troublous times. My name is Asquith, and I am the president of the Hefestaeum Club.'

I give a start. I have read of Asquith, who in point of fact is Lord Asquith, seventeenth Baron of Gullsworth, and whose mind and industry are responsible for many of the most ingenious of modern inventions. I had expected to like him more than I do.

'Now,' he continues, 'who sent you? Are you from the Admiralty, or are you Intelligence?'

Lancaster and I look perplexedly at one another.

'We weren't sent by anyone,' I say.

'You will forgive me,' says Asquith, scratching at his nose compulsively, 'but I find that difficult to believe. You have in the middle of the night attempted to gain entrance to my club with a *woman,* and, most damningly, you have refused to answer Benton's riddles.'

'What does that have to do with anything?' demands Lancaster.

'The riddles, as you doubtless know already, were designed by Lane, whose understanding of psychology is acute. He crafted three perfect questions, the answers to which allow Benton to tell beyond a shadow of a doubt whether a stranger's intentions are good or ill. Yet you refused to answer them. What other conclusion can we draw but that you are spies?'

'But we aren't spies!' I say.

'We're looking for a chap named Kensington,' adds Lancaster—which, it turns out, was not the correct thing to say. Asquith's face becomes bleak.

'You have sealed your fate, gentlemen,' he says, and turns to leave.

'What?' I cry. 'Where are you going? How did that seal our fate? We're acquaintances of his!'

'You are the third government delegation to try to apprehend him in the last seven hours,' Asquith says, his back still to us. 'The first two were turned away at the door, having incorrectly answered the riddles. They were warned that another attempt would be seen as a declaration of war. Benton, stay here. If they try to speak, you may beat them. I will alert Kensington that the club is no longer safe for him.'

He turns the corner and disappears from view. Benton eyes us with malevolence. 'Well, this is a pickle, by Christ,' says Lancaster.

'No speaking,' croaks Benton. He picks up a broom handle which was leaning against a wall and brandishes it threateningly. I imagine him attempting to beat Lancaster. It makes me smile to myself.

'Now see here, old chap,' begins Lancaster, but Benton

sticks the handle through the bars and delivers me a smart rap on the arm.

'Ow! You're supposed to hit *him!*' I say indignantly.

'He is large,' says Benton, and hits me again. Lancaster laughs loudly, which results in two more bruises upon my person.

'Shut up, Lancaster,' I say, as Benton lands another blow.

Thereafter we sit in silence, waiting for I know not what. I try to be indignant, but there is a mischievous voice in the back of my head which suggests I'm having rather a good time.

After several hours* we hear the sound of footsteps, and my heart leaps as Will Kensington comes into view. In the eerie blue light he looks even younger than I had remembered.

As soon as he sees me, he rushes to the gate and exclaims, 'Mr Savage! Oh sir, I am so sorry! I had no notion it was you. Benton! The keys, quickly! Come, man!'

The butler blinks. 'But sir,' he says, 'Lord Asquith and I are in agreement that these men are spies of the most insidious sort.'

'They aren't spies, Benton! This is Mr Savage who is an old friend, and I don't know his companion, but he doubtless is every bit as admirable.'

'If you don't know him,' says Benton tenaciously, 'how do you know he's not a spy?'

---

*I have consulted multiple sources, including Messrs Lancaster, Benton, Kensington, and Asquith, and am assured that in fact no more than about fifteen minutes could have elapsed.—HL.

'Damn it, man, open the cell!'

The butler stares at Kensington for several long moments, and seems on the edge of refusing—but at last he sighs, saunters to the gate, and begins trying various keys in the lock. Kensington seems paralysed. I believe he would like to thoroughly dress down Benton, but his excellent good nature forbids it.

For mine own part, I am immensely cheered to see the young Northerner. My mind, which was preparing itself for a lengthy stay in the dungeon—eighteen months! and with only Lancaster for company!—is very much eased.

'Lancaster,' I say, 'this is Will Kensington, the inventor and my—friend. The one we came here to see. Kensington, this is Ashley Lancaster.'

'But you're a baby, by Christ!' exclaims Lancaster. 'This is marvellous! It's a pleasure, Kensington'—pumping his hand through the bars—'truly a pleasure! Read all about your work, think it's damned exciting!'

'Thank you, sir!' says Kensington, no less pleased by the acquaintance. 'My brother Bernard is an explorer of sorts, too! Nowhere near your calibre, of course—but he takes great joy from climbing mountains and such. He'll be terribly jealous to hear I've met you. But did you say you came to see *me*? What on earth could— Well never mind, I'll take you to my rooms and we'll have it all out.'

Benton is entirely unimpressed by Lancaster's celebrity; but he at last finds the key and with a scowl releases us. Kensington leads us along the corridor, which seems much less sinister now that we are out of our cell. This subterranean chamber is not, as I had surmised, a dungeon—our cell is the only one in it—but more of a cellar or basement. It is cluttered with all manner of strange objects which I suppose to be the raw materials necessary for inventors to make marvellous things.

We reach a stairway, which having ascended we find ourselves just within the front door of the club. The room is high-ceilinged and rather grand. It seems much like any other club, and I am surprised by how ordinary it is.

'I'm very sorry you were received so unceremoniously,' Kensington says, leading us through a doorway. 'There has been trouble with the police, you see—we daily expect a siege. Harriston designed the trapdoor for emergencies, and Benton has been trained to admit strangers only with the utmost caution.' He turns to the butler and adds, 'Please tell the president that all has been resolved and I am taking the guests to my rooms.' Benton bows stiffly and stalks off.

'But what in God's name could the police want with a clubful of inventors?' asks Lancaster. I am listening with only half an ear. Any semblance of normalcy the place might have had vanished the moment we left the foyer, and my attention is now consumed by the peculiar sights all around me. We follow Kensington through room after room packed with work-benches and drafting tables at which sit men of every conceivable description. Their only unifying trait is the quickness of their eyes and deftness of their fingers. Everywhere are the strangest and most marvellous clockwork contraptions—*gadgets,* I should say. In the centre of one room, surrounded by dozens of hushed onlookers, is a sort of mannequin that is *moving of its own accord.* Its motions are jerky, halting, uncertain; but without a doubt autonomous. Another room is filled with smoke, and liveried footmen bustle to and fro with buckets of water and damp blankets, stamping out pockets of embers.* I suppose I must be observing the after-effects of the explosion we had heard from the street.

'The government doesn't approve of our work, I'm afraid,' Kensington says. 'They feel that we represent a threat to social order, and accuse us of anarchic leanings.'

'That's preposterous!' exclaims Lancaster.

'No doubt,' says Kensington, 'but after all, they are the government.'†

'Quite so,' nods Lancaster. 'But still, it's strange. You'd think they would want to nationalise Progress, wouldn't you?'

'Oh, they do,' agrees Kensington. 'But only at a certain speed. Exceed that and they feel things are moving too quickly and it makes them nervous. Their philosophers—'

'The government's?'

'Yes, yes, or whatever you call them. *Theorists.* They say that there is a fixed rate at which a society may evolve, particularly on a technological and industrial front. Above that rate, they say, the potential for social unrest increases exponentially.'

'And this club is full of people who invent above the rate?'

---

*See the note on page 177. What I failed to mention there is that, to avoid the fee (for the Hefestaeum has far more than two fires a year), the club has formed its own in-house fire brigade.—HL.
†I like Mr Kensington very much, and wish he did not have this unfortunate distrust of Her Majesty's government.—HL.

'I don't mean to boast, but this club is full of people who invent at such a rate that the store of human knowledge doubles on a weekly basis.'

I suppose this is hyperbole, but then I recall the automaton and cannot help but wonder. We have in this time climbed several staircases. On the lower storeys they were grand and sweeping, but as we ascend they grow narrower and narrower until they twist themselves into a spiral.

'Like Burton's painting, what?' notes Lancaster. I resist the urge to strike him.

Unaccustomed to physical exertion, I am by this time breathing heavily. Kensington notices and says with concern, 'I'm very sorry for the climb, sir. But my experiments being chiefly of an aeronautical nature, I requested the highest rooms in the club.'

His 'rooms,' when we reach them, prove to be a single garret, tiny and cluttered—but for all that, the most poetical space I have ever seen. The wallpaper is a hideous shade of yellow, but can scarce be made out for it is covered, every inch, by diagrams, notes, and calculations. There is a washbasin in a corner, a small bed buried under a pile of technical treatises, and a workbench along the western wall. The eastern is dominated by a tremendous window looking out over London, which in the glow of gaslight looks strangely peaceful. We are much higher than I had realised and the few people illuminated by streetlamps look like insects. They are policemen and beggars and prostitutes and dissolute young men out too late and staggering home, no doubt—but from this vantage they seem like so many ants, without personality, vice, or history.*

Kensington's workbench is strewn with tools and models. The tools appear ordinary, but the models are anything but. They are of every conceivable design, but every one a sort of flying machine. There are balloons, gliders, birds' wings made of cloth and the most intricately and delicately carved wood, tall ships complete with sails and masts and bowsprits but with wings sprouting from their sides, and countless notions which I do not believe have names but I wish dearly I could show to you, for they are unlike anything I have ever seen in ingenuity and wonder.

Lancaster and I are both rendered dumb by the cumulative effect of this enclave of wonders. Kensington, though, is quite businesslike, if a little awkward and darting in his manner. I believe we make him nervous. He hastily clears of impediment the two chairs in the room and offers them to us, then shoves papers off the foot of the bed and perches there.

'So,' he says when we are all properly situated, 'what was it that you wished to discuss?'

'You are aware, I think, that I sold my wife to the Devil?'

'Yes,' he says, nodding eagerly, 'you said as much earlier this evening. A most interesting conversation it was, too.'

---

*What is ironic is that I had not read this (or had not attended, if I had) when I wrote the note on page 174. Also, I beg the reader to observe that the people Mr Savage sees he imagines all to belong to the seedier parts of humanity. This is to me sad. I would have seen soldiers, scholars, doctors, lawyers, ministers, and perhaps even a poet.—HL.

'Well, something terrible has happened since then—I believe partly as a direct result of said discussion—and I have realised that I am in fact overwhelmingly in love with her.'

'Oh, but that's wonderful!' he cries. 'Felicitations!' He makes a move as though to shake my hand, then thinks better of it, evidently uncertain of the proper response to such news. He shifts awkwardly on the bed and looks politely at me to continue.

'Thank you. But it leaves us with quite an interesting situation, which is that I need to get her back.'

'Your wife?'

'Yes.'

'From the Devil—yes, I see. Interesting indeed. Potentially rather difficult, too, I suppose?'

'So it seems.'

'Where precisely does one *go* on such an errand?'

'That is the question,' I reply. He leans in, all attention. 'I believe that I have—'

Lancaster coughs discreetly.

'I believe,' I amend, 'that Lancaster and Tompkins and Lizzie—she's my sister, I think I mentioned; you'll quite like her—and I have together come to the conclusion that the entrance to Hell, or at least *one* entrance to Hell—we are not sure but that there may be more than one—is the crater of a volcano in Iceland called Snaefellsjökul. But here's the rub, Will Kensington. Iceland is a dishearteningly far way off, and we do not know how much time we may or may not have until my wife becomes permanently ensconced in the underworld.'

'Oh I see,' he says gravely. 'Yes, that *is* a conundrum, isn't it?'

'So we thought,' I say. 'But perhaps not so. You see, I heard rumours of a young inventor with a flying machine . . .'

There is a pause. Kensington looks very pensive. Lancaster and I are both leaning so far forward in our seats that we are nearly standing. Kensington rises. He extends his hand and says solemnly, 'Mr Savage, I would consider it a great honour to be permitted to help you on your errand. My person and my flying machine are at your service.'

I take his hand with equal gravity and make a small bow.*

'Well, now that's settled,' says Lancaster, 'you must tell us all about sailing the sky!'

---

*A 'great honour,' 'equal gravity,' and a 'small bow'—you will note that my cousin's politeness decreases proportionally to the amount of civility with which he is treated. I once chanced to compliment him on a poem and he replied, 'Hubert, if I cared about your opinion or thought you in any way qualified to judge such things, I would be gratified.' This shows you what I mean.—HL.

Eleven

In Which We Find Something Marvellous on Hampstead Heath.

ampstead Heath at dawn is a place of mist, birdsong, and affairs of honour. It is not uncommon for the serenity of a morning to be shattered by pistol shots, or for early passers-by to hear the clink of smallswords, the muffled calls of wounded men, and occasionally the cry of women. These glorious sounds have always evoked within me a sort of patriotic fervour. Since the commencement of my own duelling career some twelve hours ago, I note that they bring an added sensation. I feel as though I now belong to a club the existence of which I was not even aware the day before yesterday.

I am not a bloodthirsty fellow. Before my encounter with Lancaster I had never struck a man or been struck. (Except by Lizzie, but that doesn't count.) But I have all my life had a fascination with the fiercer aspects of human nature. I am quite taken with the warrior ethos—and I use 'warrior' as a term distinct from 'soldier,' which I take to mean a man whose profession is waging war. A warrior does not fight for profit, but for something deeper. Honour is a part of it, but does not I think capture the entirety. There is something more, something almost monkish, which I have always admired in an abstracted sort of way.* There is a resolve in the spirit of a warrior that I did not think that I possessed. Since the events of yesterday, however, I wonder if it mayn't in fact be lying dormant somewhere deep within me. I have found in myself a vigour of spirit with which I was hitherto unacquainted. It pleases me, and I think a little better of myself than I did before.†

As we approach the Heath, we pass duelling parties returning to town. They are typically comprised of five men: a doctor, two seconds, the victor (looking proud but restrained), and the vanquished (bandaged, assisted by the seconds if wounded in the leg, carried on a litter if struck in the torso or the head or if dead). There is sometimes a variation in the party—a lady may be present. These are my favourite groups to observe. The lady is without exception very beautiful and a little haughty, and she is often weeping or bravely attempting not to. The men of parties which include a lady are different than men of the other sort. They stand taller and their eyes

---

*What my cousin fails to articulate is that he finds beauty and wisdom in the chivalric tales of long ago. It is a knightly quality which he is attempting to describe. He does so poorly because there is no room in those tales for cynicism, and Mr Savage is made nervous by sincerity.—HL.
†I cannot speak to the truth of this. Mr Savage seems always to have thought rather well of himself.—HL.

are brighter. The wounded is not so pathetic, and the victor is humbler.

I think chivalry is a magnificent thing.*

Kensington crashed his flying machine on the Heath. With the help of a kindly farmer he dragged the wreckage into an old barn, where he has been returning each day to make repairs. By his description, the crash was not as calamitous as it could have been, and the craft by no means permanently crippled. He told Lancaster and me in what proved to be a lengthy and altogether fascinating conversation (begun in his garret and continued on our trip to the Heath) that he believed with help he could have it once again 'cloudworthy' (his expression, and one I quite like) within half a day. He estimates that the journey to Iceland will take about thirty-six hours. It is longer than I had hoped, but so much shorter than any alternative that I am grateful.

He expressed some scepticism at our plan, but admitted cheerfully that 'I am but an inventor while you are a poet and an explorer.' This gratified Lancaster (he is a little vain, I find, and enjoys compliments), but made me rather nervous. Our plan really is a most tenuous one. We are pursuing it less because it is a good idea than because we haven't a better one.†

What horrifies me most is the possibility that we will arrive in Iceland in three days' time only to discover that the volcano is nothing more than a volcano, that there is no trace of the

---

*As do I. It is one of the few things Mr Savage and I agree upon.—HL.
†Both Mr Savage and Mr Lancaster often work in this way. It is why, together, they tend to be dangerous and unpredictable.—HL.

metaphysical about it, and that my wife is as distant to me as she was before.

We reach the barn at sunrise. (I say 'sunrise' because somewhere above the clouds, the sun is rising; all we can see, however, is a general brightening of the sky.) I am wracked with curiosity to view Kensington's machine.

The barn is much like any other. It is grey and wooden and large and commonplace. It stands on a rise above a field. The field is green and spotted with sheep. It is also commonplace. In the middle of it is an area of disturbed earth three yards wide and perhaps thirty long. Kensington identifies this as his crash site.

Lancaster and I help to open the barn door. What is inside takes my breath away. The machine is shaped like an enormous dragonfly. Its central hull (does one call it a hull on a flying machine?*) is about thirty feet long and maybe ten feet wide at its widest, and about the same in height and depth. (I should here state that, though I have been throwing estimates of size and distance about willy-nilly, I am in fact perfectly hopeless with spatial relations, and am very likely mistaken by no small amount.) Shingles covering the hull give the impression of scales. About a third of the way from the front (imagine again a dragonfly) are its four wings. They are made of canvas stretched over a wooden framework. They appear to be manipulated by a series of gears, levers, pistons, and other

---

*Yes. One does. I have checked with Mr Kensington—though I do not know why Mr Savage could not have done that himself.—HL.

such machinations, which are connected by means of dented metal pipes to what I believe is a steam engine.

The hull tapers somewhat toward the rear, and then abruptly splays like a hawk's tail. This at one time seems to have been covered similarly to the wings—but the only evidence of it now is a few muddy tatters hanging from tarnished tacks.

The front of the machine is nondescript—nothing to sug-

gest a captain's seat. As we draw nearer and I get a better view, I discover that the whole hull is open on top. My initial impression of a dragonfly was only partially correct; more apt would be to call it a longship with dragonfly wings and a tail. The scaled hull, which bulges at the middle to hold the engine, is built with the shallow draught of a Viking ship and narrows at the front to the same sharp prow.

On the underside of the hull are not wheels, as I would have supposed, but rather skids or skis. One of these is broken in a manner piteous to behold. The front of the craft is badly banged. The framework of one of the wings has snapped and is held together only by the canvas covering it. These injuries aside, however, the machine looks in much better shape than I had expected.

Lancaster is walking around and around it in wonderment. He keeps murmuring things under his breath, but all I can make out is, 'Brilliant . . . brilliant.' Kensington stands back a little, watching the two of us with apprehension. I believe he is nervous of our opinion.

He needn't be. It is the most incredible sight I have ever seen, and I tell him so. Lancaster is no less sparing in his praise. Kensington, though, is a humble creature and does not take compliments with the alacrity of, say, Lancaster; and he quickly begins speaking so that we can say no more.

'She's not looking her finest, of course,' he demurs. 'Better now than a week ago, but all the same, she took quite a beating. But I think we can have her up and about in no time, really.'

'What can we do to help?' asks Lancaster.

'Oh, well, I'm not sure. It's mostly tinkering which— Well, I don't mean to be— The fact is, there are certain things which I'm not sure anyone but myself will know how to do. If you'll pardon me.'

In any other man, such diffidence would strike me as unconscionably tiresome; but it does not bother me in Kensington. His confidence and kindness excuse his overzealous humility—and they show it to be not mere affectation, but a genuine desire to be gentlemanly. This I approve of, even if I cannot imagine it in myself. I am a coarser fellow than that.

'We quite understand,' Lancaster says kindly. 'We're rather advanced in our own fields, you know; Savage wouldn't have me write a poem, by Christ, nor I him lead an expedition. All the same, I know a thing or two about nautical maintenance, and I can't imagine an airship is so different than a boat. If you're willing to have another man tamper with her, I'm yours to command.'

'Oh, excellent!' says Kensington. 'Yes, I suppose that she must be similar to a sailing ship in many areas. In fact, we are I believe going to have to purchase some sailcloth to patch her tail.'

I leap at the opportunity to be something other than completely useless. 'I can do that!' I say. 'Shall I run back to town for it?'

Kensington looks like he's worried to put me out. 'Only if it isn't too much trouble,' he says dubiously.

His demeanour is finally beginning to grate. We haven't time for such scrupulous politeness. 'Look here, man,' I exclaim, '*you're* helping *me* to save my wife. My helping you fix your machine is only a means to my end—so don't concern yourself about any trouble you're causing me.'

'I'm so sorry, sir. You're quite right. As my sister once said—'

'Good God!' I cry. 'Lancaster, we've forgotten Lizzie!' In the excitement of our brief imprisonment and Kensington's aeronautical wonderments, it completely slipped my mind that we had promised to return for her.

The colour drains from Lancaster's face. He has not known Lizzie long, but he has apprehended enough of her character to know that we are in for a very stern talking-to and possibly some physical violence done upon our persons.

'Damn,' he says. 'Damn, damn, damn, damn, damn.'

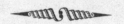

Twelve

In Which I Witness
Something I Wish I Hadn't.

I make it from Hampstead Heath to Pocklington Place in record time. My cabman thinks me mad, but it is no matter. We clatter through the morning streets at breakneck speed, hurtling past sleepy shopkeepers and bleary bakers, and I yell at him to go faster. As we plunge deeper into London the buildings loom and press together like the walls of a maze but our pace does not flag. We fly past the Museum and careen onto Oxford Street, where the cabman deftly wends his hansom through the morning traffic, already thick on this main artery of the city. We leave commerce behind us, and our speed increases in the sparsely peopled streets of the fashionable neighbourhood in which I live. He deposits me at the steps of my house, and I dash to the door and hurl myself inside. I run to my study, from whence I shall go upstairs and prostrate myself before Lizzie.

But what I find within my study brings me up quite short.

It is Simmons, standing stripped to the waist and fumbling with the buttons of his pants, apparently preparing to remove them as well. What is even worse than my butler playing Salome in the middle of my study is that my sister is watching the whole thing with an arch look on her face, and tapping her imperious little foot impatiently. She holds a paintbrush and one of those thin ovoid boards whose name I do not know but on which painters put paint,* and stands before a blank canvas on an easel. She spares me barely a glance and continues to regard the nudity being perpetrated. Simmons, by contrast, looks up at me in horror and throws himself behind the sofa.

'Oh, hello, Lionel,' says Lizzie casually. 'Simmons is being a dear and has agreed to pose for me.'

'What are you DOING?' I cry.

'I am learning about art, which is not necessarily what I would choose to be doing at the moment, but I was abandoned and at loose ends and so I took matters into my own hands. And now that I have explained myself, which is not a thing I was required to do but did only from some residual trace of the affection I once felt for you, you might return the favour and tell me where you've been all night.'

'Lizzie, for God's sake, display some propriety!'

'Alas, you have from a very early age bred into me nothing but contempt for propriety.'

I flail for a rebuttal, but in vain—Lizzie is in the right. She begins idly dabbing paint onto the canvas. I turn from her in

---

*It is of course called a palette.—HL.

exasperation and am confronted with Simmons lying half-naked behind the sofa, no doubt hoping to be forgotten.

'SIMMONS,' I say.

He is facedown on the floor, and I have never in my life seen him less dignified. But he summons all the dignity he can muster and says, 'Sir?'

'What in heaven's name are you *doing*?'

'I was to be her Homer, sir.'

'Her Homer?'

'Yes, sir. She cast about for a suitable artistic subject, and Homer came to mind. She asked me to pose as her Homer, and I saw no reason to deny her.' He has adopted a manner which suggests his actions to be the most natural in the world, and a fellow mad to think otherwise.

'YOU WERE GETTING NAKED!'

He pauses at that. 'Yes,' he finally admits. 'That is the case. I did not understand that nakedness was to be part of it when she first approached me.'

'Otherwise?' I prompt.

'Otherwise I never would have agreed, sir,' he says in a tone that is meant to be conciliatory but isn't, really. I do not know if he is lying or not. There is something of the gypsy buried deep within Simmons which reveals itself at very peculiar times—particularly in his nonchalance regarding certain aspects of the body.

The fault, then, is Lizzie's. 'Why,' I demand, 'did you ask Simmons to remove his clothes?'

'Homer didn't wear an English butler's suit from the reign

of Queen Victoria,' she says without looking up from her canvas.

'Nor did Adam and Eve wear fig leaves,' I snap back. 'But they are represented as doing so IN THE NAME OF DECENCY.'

'Don't talk to me of decency,' says Lizzie. 'You sold your wife to the Devil and then stayed out all night without so much as letting me know whether you were alive or dead. First I was angry and then I was hurt and then I was worried and then I felt the stirrings of ennui and so I found myself a diversion.'

'I'm sorry,' I say. 'But the evening turned out rather differently than we had anticipated. Now get dressed, we have to leave—Viv's time may be running out.'

'Differently? How so, differently?' she demands. 'An extra five minutes won't hurt your wife, and I'm going nowhere until you tell me what's happened and where you've been.'

'We were mistaken for government spies and imprisoned in a dungeon beneath Pall Mall.'

She drops her paintbrush and rounds on me. (We will never remove the paint from the carpet, I am certain.) 'Damn it!' she cries. 'You had an adventure with Ashley Lancaster and I missed it! Nellie, I shall never forgive you.'

'Forgive *me*? It was *you* who decided to come home!'

'Only because you wouldn't defend my honour! I wanted with every bone in my body to tackle that silly butler and dash into the club and join on the spot, but I couldn't because I'm small and probably wouldn't have been able to bring him down and just would have looked stupid, and because I'm a woman and being a woman in this horrid society of ours is awful, which you couldn't possibly know so don't presume to pass judgment!* So I did not tackle him: but then I saw that Lancaster was getting ready to hit him, and I really cannot have anyone doing violence on my behalf which I cannot do myself—it's not right. So what else was I to do, Nellie? It broke my heart, but I saw no alternative. And now you're yelling at me about it.'

I recognize how difficult it must have been for her not to be included, and I try to forgive her for being slatternly. Besides, we really do have to be going—and further argument will only prolong things. I take a breath and let it out. 'I'm sorry, Lizzie.'

The apology seems to mollify her. (I had of course apologised once already; perhaps she did not think it sincere.)†

'Well, I'm still dreadfully cast down,' she says. 'But I would consider forgiving you if you told me the entire story without leaving a single thing out. How did you escape?'

'If Simmons WILL PUT HIS CLOTHES BACK ON, I'll tell you.'

He does, and I do.

Lizzie is quite transported by the whole tale, and beside herself with excitement to meet the inventor and see his fly-

---

*There may be sense in what she says. I do not know, however, and I do not wish to court controversy and so shall not delve into the fraught question of feminism.—HL.

†Candidly, Mr Savage's first apologies rarely are sincere.—HL.

ing machine. Simmons is typically restrained, though something about his manner is queer—I chalk it up to his brush with nudity.

It is turning into a chilly, foggy November day. Simmons and Lizzie put on coats and we walk down the steps to the waiting hansom. The driver may think me lunatic, but he finds Lizzie beautiful and our money good. I dispatch them to the Heath, and go to locate a sailmaker.

Thirteen

In Which Repairs
Are Made.

Sailcloth, it turns out, is much heavier than I could have guessed.* My cabman lets me off at the edge of the Heath, and helps me to heave what cannot be less than several hundred pounds of canvas onto my back.† He looks concerned as I stagger under the load, and offers to help, but I decline. It doesn't seem wise to bring strangers to our air-wharf. One never knows who might alert the press. (Good heavens, I am beginning to sound like Lancaster—do adventuring and fear of publicity go hand in hand?)

My journey bearing the sail across the Heath will surely be immortalised in the annals of love. If it does not sound as glorious as swimming the Hellespont, it is because you have never walked a half-mile across a heath carrying sailcloth.

As I struggle with the weight I think of Viv. She has come

---

*I, too, can attest to this. I once sailed for an afternoon with Cousin Ashley upon the *Daydream*. I enjoyed it very much, but learned first-hand the weight of good sailcloth.—HL.
†This figure has been questioned.—HL.

to consume my thoughts. (I understand that this is one of the risks of falling in love.) At each dreadful step I see her face before me, and press on with renewed vigour. I recall how once of an evening I asked her what she was reading and she replied, 'A history of adventure,' and spoke no more. At the time I thought her manner cold. As I look back, however, it is clear that she was overflowing with love for me and I was simply too blind to notice.

I round the bend and see the barn before me. When I call out, Lancaster bounds down the hill to help me with my burden. He lifts the folded cloth off my back and says approvingly, 'This is rather heavy, Savage. We'll make a man of you yet, by Christ!' Then he puts it under one arm and trots back up the hill.

I follow, gasping for breath.

Though I was only gone a few hours, the flying machine looks much better. The broken wing is mended, the tail is stripped of its muddy tatters and is ready to be skinned, and the hull has been patched in several places. Simmons and Lizzie are here and appear quite at home. Simmons uses a rag to polish the dull metal of the engine to a gleaming brass, and Lizzie is bent down next to Kensington, who tinkers with knobs and dials on the bridge, recalibrating something or other.

They all look up as Lancaster and I enter. 'Look what I found!' announces Lancaster, dropping the bundle on the floor. He looks pleased to be quit of it, which makes me pleased.

'Oh look,' says Lizzie, still angry with me for forgetting her, 'it's a Lionel. How nice.'

'The machine looks better,' I say.

'Oh yes!' says Kensington. 'Yes, I daresay it does! Your family has been very helpful, Mr Savage. Miss Savage reminds me ever so much of Thomasina. When this is all over, you all must come to stay with us at Kellwick House.'

My previous frustration with him has vanished, and I have decided that I can live with his deferential demeanour if he can live with my callous one. 'Yes,' I say. 'That sounds— That sounds very nice. I would like that.' Friendship. What a peculiar thing.

Re-skinning the tail turns out to be difficult. The canvas has to be stretched tight as a drum or the craft will upset; so it is necessary first to cut the cloth precisely, then to stitch it together in a very specific pattern—all the while ensuring that it will fit over the existing frame, and that the stitching will not pull out even in extreme circum-

stances. (That is what happened when Kensington crashed.)

It is mid-afternoon by the time the tail is in working order. My fingers are bloody where I have pierced them with the needle, and my thumbs are bruised where I have smashed them with the hammer. (Tacking on the canvas was worse than sewing it together—I gained a new appreciation for upholsterers.) I have hit my head no fewer than three times walking under the wings and failing to duck properly, and one arm of my coat is ripped from catching it on a lever as I passed by.* But my heart is full, and I am happier than I can recall being in a very long time.

I may not have any native aptitude for it, but I believe I could learn to love the life of an adventurer. I mention something to that effect aloud, and Lizzie laughs at me and Simmons keeps a carefully straight face—but Kensington grins, and Lancaster claps me on the back, so I think I cannot be exclusively an object of mockery.

At around half past three Kensington announces that repairs are complete and it is time for a test flight. Together the five of us haul the flying machine out of the barn. This may sound simple, but it is not. The machine weighs several tonnes† and is very difficult to move. Here is how we do it. Kensington attaches a rope to the craft's prow (does one call the front of a flying machine a prow?)‡ and Lancaster ties the free end around his chest. We remaining four clap on to the rope behind him, and at his count we all pull together.

When the machine is out in the open it looks at once even grander and much smaller. The notion that we are going to fly it across the open ocean and into the mouth of a volcano becomes concerning to me in a manner I had not anticipated.

---

*Mr Savage wears this coat still. He refuses to have it mended. He says it is for sentimental reasons, but I believe it is so that when people point out the rip, he can tell the story.—HL.
†Doubtful.—HL.
‡Again, yes.—HL.

The bent wood of its wings, the sailcloth (so sturdy it seemed upon my back!), the little steam engine—they have a magisterial beauty when seen in the afternoon light of a misty moor, but it is the beauty of the miniature. They look too frail to withstand the stormy North Atlantic.

If the others share my dark thoughts, they do not show it—and Will Kensington, at least, is only enthusiasm. He dashes about readying his ship with indomitable good spirits, a model of boundless energy. He pulls a lever, and with a cough, a sputter, and a hiccough of smoke, the engine starts. Another lever, and the wings begin to move up and down slowly, as if the machine is waking from a long sleep. Kensington cries out triumphantly, and the rest of us applaud the young inventor.

Leaving the engine to warm up, he hops down from the ship. 'I believe it works,' he says with modest restraint.

'I hope so,' says Lizzie, 'because I'm coming with you!'

'On the test flight?' says Kensington. 'Oh, Miss Savage, I hope you do not think me impolite to refuse you—but it's entirely too dangerous.'

'*You're* going,' says Lizzie stubbornly.

'Well, yes,' says Kensington. 'Someone has to fly it. But in the event of a crash it would be very silly for more of us to be killed than is absolutely necessary.'

'Hm,' says Lizzie. 'Yes, that's true. Simmons, Ashley, Nellie—I regret to inform you that the three of you must remain on the ground, as your presence aboard is not absolutely necessary.'

'Lizzie,' I say.

'ARE YOU GOING TO ARGUE WITH ME, LIONEL SAVAGE?'

I see it is hopeless. 'No,' I say meekly.

'Captain Kensington,' says Lizzie, 'I declare myself your first mate.'

I shudder at the double entendre.

'Now hold on a minute,' objects jealous Lancaster. 'You can't just—'

'It would be a shame, Mr Lancaster,' says Lizzie stiffly, cutting him off, 'for our acquaintance to end scarcely before it has begun—would it not?' I have said already that Lizzie is more persuasive than a loaded gun.

'It would,' he concedes, and says no more.

Kensington looks to me for guidance, but it is obvious that we are all quite helpless before her. He shrugs and holds out a gallant hand, which she takes.

Before they can climb aboard the airship and disappear into the sky, however, something unexpected happens. Scotland Yard arrives, and we are all arrested for anarchists.

Fourteen

In Which Scotland Yard Makes a Mistake & I Am Glad to See Whitley Pendergast.

Lo! From the ground— Lo! Rising to the sky!
What is this thing which climbs upon the breeze—
Which rides the back of clouds like Arion
Upon his dolphin, ever higher, ever
More wonderful? My friends, I'll tell you straight—
'Tis nothing less than Progress manifest.

—From 'The Skyship,' by WHITLEY BARNABAS PENDERGAST*

M ore accurately, Scotland Yard arrives and *tries* to arrest us.

It happens like this. Lancaster is preparing to boost Lizzie into the machine when there is a shout and a

---

*I have taken the liberty of inserting this fragment, which was written by Mr Savage's comrade-in-words Whitley Pendergast—who was an eyewitness to the events recorded in this chapter, and who wrote voluminously of them. It seemed to me a fitting addition, and I thought the reader would benefit from a third-party perspective.—HL.

gunshot. We look east and see a dozen police officers swarming up the neighbouring rise. Now I must here state that, despite the questionable nature of my mental activity and pseudonymous writings, I have never in my life been chased by the police. I may say without shame that a thrill shoots through me, and I briefly consider how glorious it would be for us to make a heroic last stand here behind our buttress of ingenuity. But we do not. We haven't any weapons, firstly, and secondly Simmons counsels against it.*

When we first see the police, they are perhaps a quarter mile distant.

'Damn!' says Lancaster. 'What are they doing?'

'They can't possibly be here for *us*, can they?' asks Lizzie.

'I fear they are,' replies Kensington, his brow furrowed in annoyance. 'The police have harried inventors these past several years. They must have gotten wind of my machine.'

'My cabman!' I cry. 'The scoundrel informed on us! But what are we going to *do*? Simmons!'

The noise of our persecutors draws nearer. We can just make out their yells—the word 'anarchists' is repeated often, borne aloft on the afternoon breeze.

'It seems that Mr Kensington must flee,' says Simmons. 'If he is taken, his machine is likely to be confiscated.'

'I can't leave you!' protests Kensington. 'Come with me!'

'Yes,' adds Lizzie hastily, 'we'll go straight to Iceland!'

---

*There are times when I worry for the part of my family which lives at Pocklington Place. But then I remember that they have got Simmons, and my mind is eased.—HL.

It sounds like a most exciting proposition, and I consider it briefly. 'If we depart now,' I muse, 'we would be to Iceland sometime Wednesday morning—which, given that Wednesday is after all Odin's day, seems rather propitious. To arrive in the land of the pagan gods on the feast day of their chief strikes me as eminently sensible.'

'Doubtless, sir,' says Simmons, 'but we haven't any supplies or provisions. Surely we cannot be expected to storm the gates of Hell half-starved and weaponless.'

'He's right,' says Lancaster. 'It won't do, old boy.'

It is true; but all the same, Simmons's obvious lack of adventurous inclination is beginning to wear on me. He seems quite set on delaying the expedition, though I cannot for the life of me understand why.

The policemen meanwhile are thundering up the hill.

'Mr Kensington would really be very well served to depart immediately,' says Simmons.

'I'm afraid he's right again,' says Lancaster.

'But I can't just leave you!' says Kensington for a second time. 'It wouldn't be right at all! We're in this together now; it would be shameful to desert.'

'There's no shame in a strategic retreat,' says Lancaster. 'We can regroup later on, but if your machine gets taken then we're in quite a spot.'

'We'll all escape together!' cries Lizzie. 'We can land a few miles away and sneak back into the city at night!'

'I cannot help but point out,' says Simmons, 'that the machine has not yet been tested.'

Kensington nods. 'It's not safe.'

'So you're going to leave us for the police?' demands Lizzie, rounding on him. She fixes him with a glare that would have basilisked a basilisk; but somehow Will Kensington shrugs it off.

'I'm sorry, Miss Savage,' he says. 'But it wouldn't be right to take you aloft with the *Cirrus* in this state. There's no telling what might happen, and I would be villain indeed if I were responsible for your death.'

'Besides,' says Simmons, 'we can reason with the police. We've done nothing wrong, after all. Incidentally, they are quite close now.'

'What do you mean, "reason with them"?' says Lizzie. She is stubborn.

'If we all flee,' says Simmons, 'it will seem a tacit admission of our guilt. Our staying when we had means of escape will speak volumes in a court of law.* We must allow ourselves to be taken in order to clear Mr Kensington's name.'

'Oh, you don't have to bother about that—' begins Kensington; but he is cut off by the bellowing of a portly sergeant puffing his way up the hill.

'Simmons is right,' I say reluctantly. 'Best be off, Will Kensington.'

'I cannot in good conscience—'

Something whizzes by us and impacts on the hull of the machine. A split second later I hear the sharp crack of a rifle.

'Hold your fire, damn you!' thunders Lancaster.

---

*While I have the utmost respect for Mr Simmons, I am compelled as a solicitor to point out the shortcomings of his argument.—HL.

'Was that a *bullet*?' I ask in bewilderment. 'Are they *shooting* at us?' I've never been shot at before.

'Not very sporting of them,' says Lancaster disgustedly.

'I think,' says Simmons, 'that it is really time for Mr Kensington to be going.'

'But—'

Another shot rings out. We all throw ourselves facedown in the dirt, and Lancaster yells several things which make Simmons blush.

'It does seem,' says Kensington, 'that we should decide quite soon.'

'You should go, lad,' says Lancaster. He finds a large stone and, coming briefly to his knees, hurls it at our attackers. It seems a vain enterprise—they are still a hundred yards off—but his arm is like a cannon. The stone strikes one of the vanguard in the shoulder and he goes down. The others halt their advance to see to their companion, then draw up a line of battle.

'It's true,' I say. 'We'll sort things out here. Find somewhere to hide the machine, and contact us as soon as you're able.'

Kensington hesitates, then says, 'Very well. I feel a frightful ass, but I'll be off. I am so sorry, Miss Savage. I hope you won't think badly of me.'

'No, no,' sighs Lizzie. 'They're all quite right, of course. Off you go.'

'I will return as soon as—'

'Go, you idiot!' she says.

Kensington crawls on his belly to the front of the craft, then springs up and vaults over the gunwale. The sudden movement elicits several more shots from the police, none of which come near us. I hope there are no picnickers in the vicinity or their lives may be in serious jeopardy.* I cannot from my vantage see into the machine, but Kensington must have made his way to the engine; for the wings, which have been moving up and down lazily, begin to beat quicker. They move in alternation—first the back wing on both port and starboard (though I do not know which is left and which right),† then the front pair.

More shots, one of which murders an unsuspecting pigeon. Lancaster has been fumbling at his buttons for some moments; he now stands up, and I see that he has unbuttoned his upper body. He sheds coat and waistcoat and removes his shirt. I am less offended by his nudity than I was by Simmons's, partly because Lizzie is not staring at him and partly because he does not look entirely human. The muscles under his skin are not those of a man, but of a great beast in some foreign jungle. I was mistaken, Lizzie *is* staring at him. I am about to demand he make himself decent when he begins to wave his shirt over his head and I suddenly understand—it is a white flag of surrender.

The shots stop. We all clamber to our feet. The wings of Kensington's machine beat even quicker. The engine causes the ground to tremble.

Lancaster slips his shirt back on and raises his hands over

---

*There were none. I did learn, however, that one of these bullets prematurely ended a duel being fought nearby.—HL.
†I refuse to any longer be Mr Savage's research assistant. If you are curious, dear reader, look it up yourself: for I will not.—HL.

his head. Lizzie and Simmons and I do the same. We slowly advance toward the line of police. The portly sergeant barks something, and every gun is trained upon us. We continue toward them. They split into two groups and come at us cautiously from either side. Within a few moments we are roughly and impolitely handcuffed.

A small, thin man in plainclothes accompanies the portly sergeant. He seems the more sensible of the two. He says, 'My name is Detective Inspector Walter Dewhurst.* This is my colleague Sergeant Paisley. You are under arrest in the name of Her Majesty.'

'You can't arrest us, damn you,' says Lancaster. 'Do you know who I am?'

'No, sir, I do not. But we have it on good authority that you are all members of the'—he pulls out a notebook and checks something—'the Alec Rubeum, an anarchist circle intent upon the aerial bombardment of the Cities of Westminster and London.'

'That we're *what*?' I demand. 'Is this a joke, sir? I'm Lionel Savage the poet, and this is Ashley Lancaster!'

A murmur spreads through the ranks of police—my words have struck a nerve. I do not know if they know my name, but they certainly do Lancaster's. For a moment I think we have trumped them; but we have not. After brief deliberation they reject our story. I glance at my small party and at once see why. We are to a man covered from head to toe in mud and

---

*Inspector Dewhurst and I are acquainted. He is a good police officer and a good man. I am sorry that he is made to look foolish in these pages, for he is not so in life.—HL.

engine grease; our eyes are bleary and our hair wild; and Lancaster is but half-clothed.

'Don't think that's true,' shouts Paisley. I believe shouting is for him less a choice than a state of being. 'Look like anarchists to me!'

'I am compelled to concur with my deep-lunged colleague,' says Dewhurst. 'But we were told there were five of you.'

'Damn that cabman,' I mutter.

'Where is the fifth?' demands Dewhurst.

'There are only four of us!' says Lizzie.

'I heard otherwise.'

'No, sir,' says Simmons. 'There are but four.'

''E's lying!' cries one of the police. 'They both are! I seen 'im myself—'e went and got into that airship when we was dug in.'

'It's true!' puts in the fellow Lancaster hit with a rock. His collarbone seems to be broken and his arm is in an improvised sling. 'I seen 'im, too. There's five, guv'nor, ain't no doubt about it.'

I glance over my shoulder. The machine is still on the ground. Lancaster catches my eye and raises an eyebrow. He, too, is baffled. Why has Kensington not taken off? Were our repairs incomplete?

Dewhurst looks at us sharply. 'Is there a fifth in the airship?'

None of us say anything.*

Dewhurst orders Paisley to take the bulk of the force and

---

*Legally speaking, this was well done.—HL.

advance on the machine. He remains behind with three men to guard us.

'Why isn't he taking off?' hisses Lizzie.

'I'm not familiar with the Alec Rubeum,' says Dewhurst, taking out a pencil to go with his notebook. 'Are you an isolated splinter cell, or part of a larger organisation?'

'We're not anarchists, damn you!' says Lancaster.

I have a perverse impulse to offer no defence. If they want to brand us revolutionaries then let them do as they list. I have had quite enough of the rules of society. I am growing increasingly impatient with conventions which come between me and the reclamation of my wife. We haven't the time for this. Afterward I'll write a poem about it all, but at present what's called for is action.

Paisley's group closes in on the flying machine. He shouts an order and his men split into two pincers. He seems intent on encircling Kensington. The *Cirrus*'s wings are by now beating so quickly they are just a blur, and great quantities of steam pour from the engine—but still the craft sits squarely and firmly on the ground. There is a part of me which does not believe this enormous mass of wood, cloth, brass, and steel can possibly take flight.

'We've got you surrounded!' bellows Paisley. 'You have thirty seconds to surrender before we open fire!'

Kensington makes no reply. I have a sudden terror that perhaps one of the reckless shots from earlier struck him. I would be sorry indeed to lose the acquaintance of so poetical a person.

Lancaster appears to share my dark thoughts, for he says to our captors, 'If that boy's dead, you'll have the Devil to pay.' There's an alarming steel in his voice—which, taken in conjunction with his size and wild aspect, causes the policemen to take an involuntary step backward.

Only Dewhurst, who seems to suffer from the foolhardy courage peculiar to short men, holds his ground. He says, 'So you confess to a fifth?' and makes a note.

Lizzie says, 'You have no idea the inquest you're about to face.'

'You,' says Dewhurst primly to her, 'are guilty of lying to an officer of the law. That will be all, miss, if you please.'

'I don't please!' cries Lizzie. 'This is ridiculous! We're not anarchists, we're poets and explorers and artists! Under whose authority do you arrest us? Upon what charges? Seeking adventure? Pushing the limits of invention and ingenuity? Looking skyward when we dream?'

'No,' says the prosaic little man, 'you are arrested upon charges of treason, sedition, and anarchy, in the name of Her Majesty's government.'

'Twenty-eight!' shouts Paisley. 'Twenty-nine!'

We brace ourselves for the fusillade. But on the count of thirty, two things happen simultaneously—neither one of which has deadly consequences. The press arrives, and the flying machine begins to rise.

At first, the miracle happens almost imperceptibly. Where a moment before it pressed heavily into the damp earth, it now grows visibly lighter. It is as though it is made of paper— what looked heavy now looks nearly weightless. This eerie sight stops the command to fire in Paisley's throat. With an audible squelch the machine detaches from the earth. For ten seconds it simply hovers a foot off the ground. They are perhaps the best ten seconds of my existence. My entire world expands. It's as if my whole life I owned only a single volume of the *Encyclopaedia Britannica* which I believed to be the whole work, and that after twenty-two years of labouring under the impression that everything in the world worth knowing fell between the words 'Gouda' and 'Hippopotamus,' I am abruptly given the complete set.

This moment, I feel sure, will change the course of human existence.*

The noise of the engine increases in pitch and volume. The beating of the wings makes a sound like a gale in the treetops. Dewhurst's and Paisley's hats are blown off at the same moment, and neither man makes a move to reclaim them.

Time, which has stopped, resumes. Slowly at first, then with gathering speed, the craft propels itself skyward.

Behind me I hear the explosion of flash-lamps and the frenzied scribbling of pencils. To my left, Lancaster is staring, agape. On my right, Lizzie is grinning like a madwoman. The police have lowered their rifles and look on in wonder.

The machine is a dozen feet in the air and rising quickly when Kensington comes to the rail. He is smiling impishly. He

---

*This is so, and even now the ramifications may be seen. Already a new branch of government has been formed—the Aeronautical Office. Though at present it sits ignominiously in a single room in the basement of the Admiralty and is staffed only by a disgraced soldier named Perkins, there is little doubt that it will in the future become quite important.—HL.

raises his hand to his head and doffs an invisible hat, then bows to the police. 'Your pardon, gentlemen!' he calls. 'I have an appointment in Heaven!'

To us, he waves and yells, 'Please don't think me a deserter! I will see you all soon!' Then he throws a lever, and the machine shoots forward like a greyhound from its slip, gaining altitude with every moment. We watch dumbfounded as it flies off.

Dewhurst recovers first, but by the time he cries, 'Fire!' Kensington has disappeared into the fog. A few rifles crack, but with nothing to shoot at the gunmen soon break off.

When I rip my gaze away from where the airship vanished, I see that we have been joined by twenty or thirty members of the press. There are photographers, journalists, newsboys, sketch artists, and a handful of curious hangers-on. One of them says in a familiar voice, 'Good God, Savage, what have you done to your clothes?' and for the first time in my life I am pleased to see Whitley Pendergast. He has found me in a moment of glory, and I believe that my supremacy over him is forever sealed—for I am certain that the man has never in his strangest dreams dreamt of the adventure upon which he now finds me embarked.

'Pendergast!' I cry. 'How lovely to see you! You're looking unusually fresh this morning. As to the state of my clothes, I'm afraid I ruined them while escaping from a dungeon and building an airship and fighting off the police. You must come round for tea and I'll tell you all about it, if I'm not locked up in Newgate or off sailing the skies. By the way, you've got a bit of sticking plaster just under your nose.'

'Cut myself shaving, Savage, which is an act civilised men perform every morning—you ought to try it sometime. As for your exploits, I must say I'm impressed. Didn't think you had it in you, frankly. I'd shake your hand if you weren't covered in dirt.'

'And I'd shake yours, if you were any other man upon this earth.'

Before he can think of something witty to reply, a member of the press exclaims, 'By Jove, is that Ashley Lancaster?'

'Damn!' cries Lancaster. 'I haven't told Mummy I'm back! Savage, hide me!'

He tries to take cover behind me, but the disparity in our sizes makes it quite hopeless. My slight frame only calls attention to his distinctive height and breadth.

An excited ripple runs through the crowd. Dewhurst looks abruptly nervous. 'It is!' says someone else. 'It's Lancaster!'

'Ashley Lancaster's back in Britain!' cries a third.

The flash-lamps begin exploding all over again.

Fifteen

In Which Lizzie Commits an Indiscretion to Rival All the Rest, I Nearly Fight Another Duel, We Have Several Visitors, & Matters Come to a Head.

I t is morning. I am woken by birdsong, which is a drawback to living too near a park. I stare at the canopy of my bed, feeling claustrophobic. I have not slept well. I am perturbed. I am also excited. I am still I think thrilled by yesterday's commotion and the further prospect of imminent adventure. Which is peculiar. I had thought a night of sleep and reflection would cure me of this strange inclining. I am after all not an adventurer of the body: I am a wayfarer of the imagination. But still I find myself roused to the chase.

The remainder of yesterday was spent in a morass of bureaucracy and explanations. As soon as Lancaster and I were identified by Pendergast and the press (who have a keener eye than the police), all charges against us were dropped and profuse apologies were made. There still remained, however, many hours of explanation before Will Kensington's name was cleared. We had to explain the matter to several commissions, and it was made complicated by the fact that we of necessity had to gloss over a few significant details—for instance, the involvement of the Devil and Vivien's abduction. There are certain things one simply does not tell the government.*

By the time we made it back to Pocklington Place we were exhausted and discouraged. We had none of us slept in two days, and seemed no closer to launching our rescue expedition. We should have been famished but no one had much of an appetite, which offended Mrs Davis mightily. After a half-hearted attempt at conversation we collapsed into our respective beds.

Every time I began to feel the approach of sleep, however, Vivien's face drifted unbidden into my restless mind and I was plunged into a fresh whirl of remorse and concern. When at last I drifted off my dreams were troubled. As I stare at my canopy this morning, though, I do not feel tired. I wonder if today I will become a mariner of the air.

I rise and dress and make my way downstairs. As I descend I note that I have not shaved in days. I must do that, when there is time. It would be a shame to rescue my wife looking like a caveman. I think of Will Kensington. I have thought of

---

*This, also, was likely a wise omission. Even for a man as open-minded as I, there are parts of this (as I now know with certainty) entirely factual tale which were difficult to swallow at first blush.—HL.

him often since his ascension. I hope that he had no trouble either with bullets or engineering, and that he was able to put down safely somewhere. I wonder when we will see him again, and hope that it is soon. Yesterday's delay was unfortunate, and I am eager to be once more upon the trail.

There are muffled voices coming from my study. I open the door and collide with Lancaster, who is exiting hastily. He looks harried.

'Sorry, old boy,' I say, 'I was just—' Then I see Lizzie and break off.

She is standing in the middle of my study beside a full-length mirror, facing a canvas, holding a brush and that damned wooden board which holds paint, and wearing not a stitch of clothing.*

'LIZZIE!' I cry.

'Good morning, Nellie!' she says cheerfully, not looking up. 'Do you like my painting?'

She seems to be making a portrait of herself, by means of the mirror. She glances over her shoulder to observe her reflection, then turns and daubs a few strokes on the canvas.

'Put. On. Your. Clothes.'

'Alas, they are covered in paint. Besides, I'm not quite finished.'

From the look of it, she has barely begun. The canvas bears rough lines here and there, and the outline of an hourglass

---

*This is one of the instances I have alluded to, when Miss Savage's innocent acts of curiosity and exploration could be misconstrued as immoral.—HL.

which I am quite certain she made not from her own reflection but from the real thing resting on my desk. On the upper part of the outline are two circles I take to be crude breasts.

'Then for God's sake,' I cry, 'put on *something*. A rug, a lampshade, I don't care. Here.' I find a blanket on the arm of the sofa and throw it at her head. It tents over her neatly. She burrows out from under it and wraps it around herself, looking at me with deep reproach.

'Better?' she says scornfully. 'I find it astonishing that you call yourself modern men.'

Lancaster is hiding in a corner, facing the wall, hands over his eyes. The backs of his neck and ears are bright red, and he mutters something conciliatory to me which I do not catch and do not care to.

'Lizzie, you're a calamity,' I tell her. 'You're indecent.'

'You won't let me paint Simmons, you won't let me paint Ashley, God knows *you'd* never sit for me, so what am I supposed to do?' she fires back. 'I want to learn about painting. I want to learn why for two thousand years and more great artists have painted and sculpted the human body. What is it that they find so fascinating or beautiful or whatever it is they find it? I'm not indecent, Lionel, I'm curious. There's so much to know, and I want to know it all! Doesn't it bother you that we know nothing about art? But last night while you were feeling sorry for yourself and despairing over yesterday's setback, I was reading Tompkins's books of art history, and do you know what I discovered? I discovered that there was a painter— there have been *many* painters!—who don't just explain, but who actually *show you* how to get to Hell!'

'I believe I've mentioned as much,' says Lancaster, still facing the wall.

'Shut up!' I say to him. I cannot forgive him for seeing Lizzie in a state of undress.

'But it's true!' she says. 'You silly men don't understand the half of it! I believe that if we fly into the mouth of a volcano we'll be directly incinerated—but if we instead—'

'I've decided to kill myself,' I say abruptly, cutting her off. I am not interested in art. I am interested in the retrieval of my wife. I have been contemplating the matter all night.

'Lionel!' reprimands Lizzie—apparently angry not that I might die but that I have interrupted her.

'All things considered, it seems rather a poor time for it,' says Lancaster, taking the notion of my suicide in stride. 'Despair's fine and all that, but we've work to do.'

Neither of them seems to understand me. 'No,' I say, 'I mean, to find Viv. I've been thinking about it, and it seems the surest and most expedient manner.'

'Ah,' says Lancaster. 'Well now, that may be. But Lizzie said that she had ideas—'

'Lizzie stands naked with a paintbrush! I reject her ideas. Give me a bullet.'

Lizzie makes a face at me and flops down on the sofa. Wrapped in the blanket, she looks like a harem girl.

'You're serious,' Lancaster says with surprise and I think a little admiration. I have taken up one of the pistols from our duel and begin to hunt for a spare charge. 'You want to kill yourself in order to go to Hell to rescue my sister. Savage, that's a terrible plan!'

'It truly is,' says Lizzie.

'Don't be ridiculous,' I snap. 'Orpheus did it and it worked.'

'It didn't, actually,' she points out.

'It would have! I won't look back or do whatever else it is that I'm not supposed to do.'

Lancaster frowns. 'All of this is of course assuming you're going to Hell.'

I had anticipated this objection. It was one of my considerations during my sleepless pensing. 'Lancaster,' I say, 'I married for money and sold my wife to the Dev'l.'

'I retract my previous comment,' he says promptly. 'But still, Savage—'

'But nothing. It makes sense. And besides, I'm in love. Which means I'm lucky. So, quick, before Simmons comes in and throws a fit. I need a bullet for your pistol.'

I know Lizzie is upset with me, for she does not object. Lancaster, though, looks dubious. 'That'll necessitate an awful lot of clean-up, old boy. I'd really prefer—'

'Good God, man,' I cry, 'I'm talking about KILLING MYSELF for your sister and you're complaining about a little—'

I am cut off by the sound of my pernicious doorbell being rung vigorously and without cease.

'SHUT UP!' I bellow.

I hear the front door admit the bell ringer, and before I can say anything the door to my study is flung open and a funny-looking little man tiptoes in, carrying two fencing sabres.* We all swing to face him, and he cowers under our collective gaze.

---

*That is me.—HL.

'I'm so sorry,' he says.

He is short and slender and ginger-haired and beaked with the most magnificent nose I have ever seen. His dress is almost foppish, but somehow at the same time dull. His appearance is that of a boring dandy, which I had until this moment believed to be a contradiction in terms.*

'Oh look,' says Lancaster, sounding amused, 'it's Timely Hubert.' Who is Timely Hubert, and what is he doing in my house?

'Oh, hello Cousin Ashley, I heard you were back,' says the intruder. 'Your mother is quite determined to see you married, you know.'

'Who are you?' I demand.

'One moment, please,' says the little man, his attention still on Lancaster. 'She's frozen all your funds until you tie the knot, what?'

Lancaster looks poleaxed. 'Good God,' he says weakly, 'she's *what?*'

I don't care about Lancaster's funds, I care about my wife! 'Who *are* you?' I say again.

The interloper turns to me at last. 'I'm Hubert,' he says. I want to yell at him, Yes, I know you are Hubert, but *who are you?* But I hold my tongue, because I am well bred.† I must look blank, though, because he adds, 'Lancaster. Hubert Lancaster. Cousin Hubert. We met at your wedding.'

---

*I have resolved to take offence at nothing which Mr Savage says about my dress or my person. I have often been complimented, and by diverse acquaintances, on my taste in clothes and my fine figure.—HL.
†Be still, my pen.—HL.

I have no recollection of him. None at all. I recall my wedding, but not Hubert Lancaster. It's really a little alarming for an entire person to have been completely excised from my mind. I am about to ask Lizzie if she remembers him, but just in time it occurs to me that she was not at my wedding, which is still I suspect a source of annoyance to her. So I do not ask her. 'I was drunk,' I say to Hubert, which I was. 'What do you want?'

He looks uncertain. He takes out a handkerchief from his breast pocket and wipes the sweat from his brow. I believe he must have run all the way here from wherever it is he came.* He notices Lizzie's state of undress and the pistol in my hand, and looks perplexed. 'Is this a bad time?' he asks.

'It's a terrible time.'

'I'm so sorry. I don't mean to intrude. Well, I suppose I do—but I don't *wish* to intrude. But you see I'm agitated. Truth be told, I'm even a little angry, what? And I apologise profusely for the inconvenience, but I'm afraid I am, well, rather obligated to demand satisfaction.'

I stare at him. Lizzie stifles a laugh, but not very well, and adjusts her blanket. Lancaster is not attending.

As none of us say anything, Hubert continues awkwardly. 'For the wrongs committed by you against my family, and specifically my cousin Vivien, I find myself compelled to ask, I mean, *demand,* that you meet me on the field of honour.'

I fight the urge to laugh maniacally. 'You— You—' I cannot get the words out. 'You're challenging me to a *duel*?'

---

*I did. It was not less than a full mile, I might add.—HL.

'I'm so sorry,' he says, his eyes darting. 'But you really have behaved very badly toward my cousin, and . . . Well, if you wouldn't mind fighting a duel with me, I'd appreciate it.'

'You'd appreciate it?' I say incredulously.

Hubert nods meekly.* Lizzie's eyes are laughing. Lancaster stares vacantly into space.

The door opens and Simmons comes in, brought no doubt by the noise. 'Is everything alright, sir?'

'Perfectly,' I say. 'Cousin Hubert here is politely attempting to request a duel. I need some tea.'

'Very good, sir,' says he and leaves the room.

Lancaster has been standing in shock since Hubert's words to him, and he now finds his voice at last. 'Hubert,' he says, 'did you say Mummy's going to freeze my funds?'

'She already has, I'm afraid,' says Hubert.

'But that's illegal!'

'If handled by an expert solicitor,' he says, 'it isn't actually *quite* illegal.' Lancaster cocks his head, uncomprehending. Hubert looks uncomfortable and adds, 'Sadly, I *am* an expert solicitor.'†

'YOU froze my funds!' cries Lancaster, eyes blazing,

'No, no, your mother did!' says Hubert, his voice breaking.

---

*I must here say something. I am well aware that literary men take liberties with the facts, and represent things as being so which were not actually so. This is something with which we must all contend—so be it. But the way I am here painted by Mr Savage is I believe deliberately offensive. I am not so timid, or so short, or so bumbling, as he makes me out to be. (He does not overstate the grandeur of my nose, however.) I will say no more on the subject, but I had to say that.—HL.

†This, at least, did occur—though I certainly would not have said it unless pressed. I am not a boastful man.—HL.

Lancaster is at least a foot taller than him. 'I only made it possible. I'm so sorry.'

'Traitor,' spits Lancaster.

'But,' says Hubert brightly, 'she promises to release the money as soon as you're married!'

Lancaster's face, which has been pale, turns positively ashen. 'My God,' he says. 'I'm doomed. This is it. I'm actually doomed.' All things considered, I think he is taking a rather narrow view.

'I'm so sorry, Ashley,' says Hubert.

'Can we just pop back to me for a moment?' I say. 'You were challenging me to a duel?'

'Oh yes, I'm sorry,' says Hubert. 'A duel. For the wrongs you've committed against your cousin— I mean, wife— *My* cousin— Vivien.'

What is he talking about? Our marital discontent has certainly not been public—neither my sister nor my wife's brother had any notion. How is it that this strange person who calls himself my cousin is privy to information they are not? 'How on earth do you know about any wrongs I've committed against my wife?' I demand.

'Why, she told me,' he says with evident surprise.

'About what?'

'What?'

'What wrongs?' I am baffled. Have I unwittingly wronged Vivien in some way which is more generally known? I feel as though I am in a farce, challenged to duels left and right for unknown or unconscious slights. I say, 'You know, I have no idea what you're talking about. But that's alright. I'm not going to fight you.'

'You're— You're not?' he says, looking concerned. He dabs at his brow again.

'No,' I say. I have an idea in my head. 'But you're welcome to kill me.'

'Oh Lord,' says Lizzie.

'I don't understand,' says Hubert.

'I have an appointment in Hell,' I explain, 'but I am having some difficulty getting there. As such, it would be very helpful if you'd kill me.'

Lizzie covers her face with her hands and her blanket very nearly slips off.

'What do you mean?' asks Hubert stupidly, blinking several times.

'Don't ask questions,' I advise him. 'It's complicated to explain. Just kill me. Now, please.' I begin to unbutton the top of my shirt, so that his sword may enter my heart unimpeded.

'I can't kill an unarmed man!' says Hubert. 'It's not sporting.'

'Then hand me that sword, *then* kill me,' I say, reaching out for the second weapon.

'Very well,' says Hubert, and gives me the sabre. 'But why—'

'Don't ask questions, just do it.'

Lancaster has retreated to a wall, slid down it, and sits on the floor with his knees drawn up to his chest and his arms wrapped round his shins. His chin rests on his kneecaps and he looks absurdly like a small child. 'My life is over,' he moans.

'SOME PERSPECTIVE, PLEASE!' I shout.

He lapses into sullen silence.

'Very well, Cousin Hubert,' I say. 'I neither know nor care why it is you believe yourself my cousin, but I am ready when you are.'

He is looking about for means of escape. It irks me that he goes about challenging strangers to duels but hasn't the fortitude to run me through. He mumbles, 'I really don't think—'

'Hubert!' I say sternly.

'I'm sorry. I'm so sorry.' He gets hold of himself and raises the sabre. 'Where should I . . . ?'

I take his point and place it between the fourth and fifth ribs on my left side. 'Here,' I say solemnly. 'Steady now. Are you ready?'

'I'm a little nervous,' he says. 'Might I get my snuffbox before—'*

'HUBERT!'

'No, no, right, I'm sorry, what?' He refocuses. 'Right here?'

'Right there. And the sooner the better, if you please.'

'Lionel!' says Lizzie, apparently only just realising that I am serious in my intent. 'What do you think you're doing?'

'I'VE TOLD YOU FIFTEEN TIMES!' I say. 'I'm killing myself to get to Vivien!'

'To Vivien?' asks Hubert in befuddlement.

'Don't speak,' I say.

'Sorry,' says he.

---

*I did not say this, either.—HL.

'Nellie, I forbid it,' says Lizzie.

'Should I—' begins Hubert.

'Ignore her,' I say.

'If you ignore me—' says Lizzie.

'Plunge home, man!' I cry, alarmed. Once Lizzie has set her hook there is no disobeying her.

'But—' says he.

'Now, Hubert!'

Lizzie has picked up the pistol that I set down. She points it at Hubert. 'If you stab him, I'll shoot you,' she says calmly.

'It isn't loaded!' I protest.

'Isn't it?' says she.

'Is it?' wavers Hubert.

'No!' I say.

'Care to find out?' she says, her finger tightening on the trigger. Hubert visibly quails. I prepare to throw myself upon his sword point before he has a chance to lower it.

As I ready myself for the end, I hear the door open behind me. 'Ah, Simmons,' I say, 'just in time. Goodbye for now, old chap—I won't be needing that tea after all.'

'I'm not Simmons,' says a stammering voice which I have heard only once before but would recognise anywhere. 'Simmons is in the kitchen. What are you doing, my friend?'

It is the Gentleman. He is pushing a tea service. 'You!' I cry.

Hubert lowers his sword with relief. Lizzie lowers her gun.

'Hello!' says the Devil warmly. 'Been keeping well, I hope?'

'Lancaster!' I hiss. 'It's him!'

Lancaster is still slumped on the floor hugging himself. 'Him?' he says absently. 'Him who?'

'The— The—' Somehow it seems improper to say it. 'You know!'

'Oh,' he says, mildly interested.

'Oh goodness!' says Lizzie. 'Hello, sir, I'm Lizzie—'

'Don't speak to him, Lizzie!'

'I'll speak to whomever I please.'

'Then I hope you enjoy sleeping out of doors, for I am still master of this house and no sister of mine will have dealings with—that person!'

She stamps her foot in annoyance but says nothing. I turn back to the Gentleman, who wears a look of polite curiosity. 'I demand you return my wife to me at once!'

He frowns confusedly and says, 'Excuse me?'

'Vivien Savage,' I clarify, in case he makes a habit of this sort of thing and loses track. 'My wife. I know I accidentally sold her to you—'

(I overhear Hubert asking Lancaster, 'Who's that?' 'I believe it's the Devil,' he replies, to which Hubert says, 'My God!')

'—but I want her back,' I continue.

'I have no idea what you're talking about,' says the Gentleman. 'Tea?'

'NO I DON'T WANT TEA!' I shout. 'I want my wife!'

'Where is she?' he asks.

'Exactly!' I say.

'What?' says the Gentleman.

'Where?' I say.

'Who?' says the Gentleman.

'What have you done with her?'

'What have *I* done with *your* wife?'

I am losing my patience, and will do I know not what. Why is he playing dumb? I do not understand why he will not talk to me with gentlemanly frankness. If he does not want to return her, he need only say as much and I will then . . . challenge him to a duel? I laugh inwardly at the thought.

At that moment, the front door bangs open and a voice calls, 'Hubert! Hubert, where are you!' I know very well who the voice belongs to, but I cannot believe it. It does the most astonishing things (the voice, I mean) to my stomach, heart, lungs, and eyes. My knees weaken of their own accord and I put a hand on the desk to steady me.

A moment later my wife enters the room.

We must look a strange tableau before her. The Gentleman is trying to offer round tea, Lancaster is on the floor like a small child, Hubert and I are still holding our swords, and Lizzie is dressed only in a blanket, absently scratching her nose with the barrel of the duelling pistol.

'Oh God,' says Vivien, 'I'm too late. Lionel, I don't know what he's said but don't you dare fight him. He's trying to be gallant, but you'll just kill him and that won't get anyone anywhere. I forbid you to kill him.'

'I was about to kill *him*!' says Hubert, a little hurt.*

'Vivien,' says Lancaster, still on the floor, 'something dreadful has happened.'

Neither of them seem to grasp the obvious, extraordinary fact of her presence, but I do. 'You're alive!' is all I can say.

---

*I was not hurt. I was simply correcting an error.—HL.

'Hubert,' says Vivien sternly, ignoring me, 'put that sword down! Hello, Lizzie!'

'Hello, Vivien!' says Lizzie brightly. I think it terrible breeding of them both to be so informal upon their first meeting, but I do not say anything.

I round on the Gentleman. 'If you *ever* touch her again, I will drag you up from Hell and kill you with my bare hands.'

'But I *didn't* touch her,' says the Gentleman.

'Who's that?' Vivien asks no one in particular.

'You must be Mrs Savage,' says the Gentleman with polite interest.

'I'm Vivien,' says Vivien.

'It's such a pleasure to finally meet you,' he says, offering her his hand.

'Who are you?' asks Vivien.

'I'm— Well, I flatter myself that I'm a *friend* of your husband.'

I have been watching the scene in a reverie, which I abruptly pull myself out of. 'Don't talk to her!' I say, slapping the Gentleman's hand away from hers.

'Lionel!' says Vivien in a tone of remonstrance. 'That's no way to speak to your friends!'

'He's not my friend,' I declare firmly.

'I say!' says the Gentleman, looking hurt.

'Crumpets?' says Simmons, entering with a tray of them.

'Are you *really* the Devil?' asks Hubert.

There is a pause. 'Oh,' says Vivien eventually. 'Hello, Your Highness.'

'Hello,' says the Gentleman, looking a little embarrassed but also a little mollified.

'Hello, Mistress Vivien,' says Simmons.

'Hello, Simmons,' says Viv.

'You sold your wife to the Devil?' says Hubert, aghast.

'If it's any consolation,' says the Gentleman, 'I wasn't informed of it.'

Hubert still looks very confused. He says, 'But she couldn't have been with the Devil, she was with me.'

'I'll have a crumpet,' says Lizzie.

'Besides,' says the Gentleman, 'I am not in the habit of interfering with marital issues.'

'Then what are you doing here?' demands Lancaster.

'I'm bringing back a book I borrowed.'

Lancaster's brow furrows. 'What book?'

The Gentleman brightens immediately. 'Oh, it's a lovely thing called *The Idylls of the King*. It's by a great bear of a poet named Tennyson—'

Suddenly there is tremendous noise outside, and the whole house shakes upon its foundation.

'Good Christ, an earthquake!' cries Hubert, throwing himself upon the floor.*

In the silence that follows, we all look round cautiously. The house has ceased trembling as quickly as it began, and outside the window all is normal. I shrug off the anomaly as some supernatural phenomenon related to our visitor.

---

*I neither said nor did this.—HL.

Lancaster apparently does the same, for he recovers himself quickly and says, 'Vivien, I'm glad you're back, because I need your help. Mummy's forcing me to get married!'

'I know,' says Vivien, 'she's told me.'

'She's *told* you?' exclaims Lancaster. 'But I don't *want* to get married, by Christ! It sounds awful!'

I cannot help it—I begin to laugh hysterically. I believe I am become slightly unhinged. It is all too much. I haven't the slightest idea what is going on.

'Damn it, Savage, it isn't funny!' says Lancaster.*

I master myself with great difficulty. 'I'm sorry, old boy,' I gasp, 'but there is a certain undeniable irony to the whole thing.'

'It's entirely different, damn you!' he cries. 'You married for money, which is the same as prostitution only less honest. In my case, Mother wants me to wed in the hope that it will keep me closer to home. She wants to saddle me with a vapid young society wife who will throw dreadful parties and speak for hours on end about nothing whatever and rob from me my vitality and break my spirit and crush my will to live!'

'That sounds *awful*,' says the Gentleman. 'I'm so sorry.'

I had forgotten about him. 'Don't speak in my house!' I snap.

'I beg your pardon,' says he.

Vivien interjects. 'It's my house, too, and anyone may speak that has a mind to. Lionel, the fact that at this moment you look like a caveman doesn't give you license to act like one.'

---

*It is, though—a little bit.—HL.

I have forgotten to shave and now it is too late and I am entirely untroubled. This is the first time she has said my name since her return, and it makes the blood run hot in my veins.

('Yes, Lionel,' says Lizzie through a mouthful of crumpet. 'Listen to your wife; she's wonderful.')

'Thank you, Mrs Savage,' says the Gentleman, 'but I don't wish to cause trouble. I know I can be difficult, and he'—indicating me—'means well.'

'That's not strictly speaking always quite true, is it?' puts in Hubert, and I decide I like him.

'Oh, I believe it is!' says the Gentleman. 'Despite the short time I have known him, I feel an unexpected kinship with your husband, Mrs Savage. I think I understand him quite as well as he understands himself—'

'That's ridiculous!' I cry.

'—and I do not believe him ill-intentioned,' he finishes.

'That's very gracious of you,' says my wife.

'Not at all, not at all. In fact—'

'She TOLD you and you didn't tell me?' Lancaster has finally regained his feet, and looks pathetically at Vivien. It takes a moment for me to realise he is talking about his mother.

'When would I have told you?' asks Vivien.

'I SAW YOU TEN MINUTES AGO!' thunders Lancaster.

Something is not right. I blink. 'You saw whom?' I ask.

'Well, I'm sorry if I was focusing on my actual problems and not your hypothetical ones!' says Vivien hotly, ignoring me.

'When did you see her?' I demand.

'There's nothing hypothetical about a life in fetters!' he says.

'She couldn't tell you,' says Lizzie, 'because you kept blundering about with your eyes closed and wouldn't let anyone say anything.'

I begin to get an inkling of a conspiracy. 'You knew she wasn't in Hell?' I say to Lancaster.

'Not until this morning, old boy, but good Christ, Viv—'

Hubert cuts him off. 'You came here?' he asks Viv. 'That wasn't the plan!'*

'Neither was challenging my husband to a duel!' she retorts. 'And I had to see Simmons.'

'You ALL knew?' I cry, aghast and betrayed.

'Settle down, Nellie. Until this morning only Simmons knew.'

'Simmons!'

'I'm sorry, sir,' he says blandly, 'but you know that in matters of love I always hold my tongue.'

'Well damn it, how did the rest of you find out?' I demand.

---

*It was not. And though things may have turned out for the best, I wish very much that Vivien had consulted me before altering the plan. It is characteristic of her, though, that she did not. Both of my Lancaster cousins (I mean Vivien and Ashley) are strong-willed and fiercely independent. Though I love and admire them both very much, these traits can sometimes make them difficult. Once, for instance, Vivien climbed a tree at Garrick Hall and became stuck in the high branches. I offered to climb up and help her descend, but she refused. Instead, she tore up her petticoats and made from them a rope which she used to lower herself down. It very nearly worked, but the rope snapped suddenly and she fell to earth and broke her wrist. The next day, Ashley decided to prove that he could get down from the same perch with less difficulty. Well, he got stuck, too. I offered him assistance. He refused, and chose instead to jump. He broke an ankle and an arm.—HL.

'I dropped by to say hello,' says Viv. 'I met Lizzie and we became excellent friends and talked about art. I agreed to pose for her, and I'd managed to get about halfway out of my blasted corset when Ashley blundered into the room and had a fit, and then we heard you on the stairs and I threw my clothes back on and left in rather a hurry.'

'Good God,' I say. The earth reels beneath my feet. I want to ask a thousand questions, but the conversation is commandeered.

'Vivien, by Christ, what are we going to do?' wails Lancaster.

'About what?'

'About my funds!'*

Before she can answer there is a knock at the study door. Simmons opens it, but no one is there. After a moment we hear it again—but now that we are expecting it, it is quite plain the knocker is knocking at the old door to the library on the second storey. I look about in confusion. Everyone who should be knocking on a door from within the house is in this room.

'Are you expecting someone, Simmons?'

'I am not, sir. Shall I go and see—'

'Oh, never mind,' I say, and then I shout, 'Come in!'

The second-storey door creaks open and in walks Will

---

*This question has yet to be satisfactorily resolved. Mr Savage has declared his intention to finance the upcoming South American expedition—though given the fact that Mr Savage's money was originally Vivien's, and that it was obtained through marriage (which rite, or lack thereof, is of course the reason Ashley currently has none), there is some irony to this circular situation.—HL.

Kensington, his green eyes twinkling. He is soot-stained, wind-burned, covered in coal dust and engine grease, his hair is sticking straight up, his cheeks are ruddy, and his nose is running freely from the autumn chill—but he appears to be in perfect health and excellent spirits. A pair of driving goggles dangle from his neck. 'Good morning!' he says. 'I hope you don't mind, but I've landed on your roof.'

He descends the spiral staircase, his boots ringing merrily on the iron. I am remarkably glad to see him well, and it seems I am not alone in the sentiment—Lancaster meets him with a hearty embrace, and Lizzie throws her arms around his neck (about which I am not entirely pleased, for beneath her blanket she is still quite naked).* Even Simmons is demonstrative, and nearly smiles.

'Kensington!' I cry, pumping his hand. 'You're alive! How was your flight?'

'Excellent!' he says. 'The repairs worked beautifully. A stray bullet almost took out the engine, which was frightful because I didn't realise until I was at quite an altitude and then suddenly it coughed and sputtered and died completely, and we began to drop like a stone. It turned out to be a lucky thing I was so high up, because it gave me time to plug the hole with a bit of oilcloth and get the engine started again before we were dashed to bits. After that, I gained altitude until we were high enough to do some simple aerial tests. Satisfied that

---

*I hope the reader does not think me either pedantic or immoral for pointing out that beneath our clothes we are all of us quite naked.—HL.

we could survive the North Atlantic, I landed in a village just outside the city, visited a blacksmith to get a patch for the engine, borrowed a *Who's Who* to find your address, ate several gallons of stew at an inn, slept like a dead man for twelve hours, woke up, charted my course, and came directly here. I'm sorry for the delay, but I didn't trust myself to get us to Iceland without a meal and a good night's sleep. But everything's quite ready now, and standing by!'

The room is rather awed by his account. 'Kensington,' I say, 'I thought so before but now I am quite certain: you are the most poetical person I have ever met. Allow me to introduce my wife!'

'You found her?' he asks in bewilderment.

'I found him,' she says, extending her hand. 'Hello, Will Kensington. I've heard about you.'

'Madam,' says he, taking it and bowing. 'I have heard so much about you! I am very pleased to see you in so mundane a setting.'

'Thank you,' she says, smiling with amusement.

Kensington leans in and asks in a low, respectful voice, 'If you'll pardon the presumption, might I enquire what Hell was like?'

'Oh,' says Vivien airily, 'you mean being married to a man who doesn't love you?'

Poor Kensington is nonplussed.

'No,' I cry, 'I've had an epiphany! I do love you!'

'You have a remarkable way of showing it,' shoots back my wife.

'Yes, yes, yes,' says Lancaster, 'but what am *I* going to DO?'

'Ashley,' says Viv, 'we can make a plan to save you as soon as we finish the plan to save me.'

'Plan?' I demand. 'What plan?'

'I am afraid two circumstances have rather altered it,' she says, ignoring me.

'What plan!'

'The plan to make you fall in love with me.'

'But I *do* love you!'

'That is the first of the two altering circumstances I mentioned.'

'What's the second?'

'The second is that you sold me to the Devil.'

'Excuse me,' puts in Hubert almost inaudibly. 'I'm so sorry to interrupt, but I'm not quite clear on one point. What was the exchange?'

'Do you know,' says Lancaster morosely, 'I've been curious about the same thing.'

'Yes,' says Lizzie, 'your talk of selling suggests that something was given to you in exchange for Vivien.'

All eyes turn to the Gentleman, who holds up his hands palms outward in a gesture meant I suppose to absolve himself of any blame.* 'Please reflect upon the point that in fact there was no bargain whatever struck between my dear friend Mr Savage and myself,' he says. 'I had no knowledge that Mrs

---

*It is an amusing fact that the Devil in this instance truly was blameless. Can this be often said? I do not know anymore—as Mr Savage said, our perception of things has gone rather topsy-turvy.—HL.

Savage was anywhere other than here. She certainly never came home with me, as some of you seem to be suggesting.'

'Of course she didn't go to Hell,' says Hubert. 'She came home with *me*—as dictated by the plan.'

'WHAT PLAN?' I demand.

'Wait,' says Lancaster, 'we're not finished. Savage, what is the exchange you believed you had made?'

'I don't know!' I say. 'There wasn't one, clearly!'

'But you've been saying for days that you *sold* her to the Devil.'

'Yes,' says Viv, 'and I am quite curious—what exactly am I worth?'

I shrug uncomfortably. 'Well . . . Well, the truth is that I wasn't aware of any exchange having taken place. But it doesn't sound nearly the same to say that I *gave* my wife to the Devil, or that he *took* her—that makes me sound, well, rather passive. I suppose I may have exaggerated the situation for dramatic effect. And there was a possibility, I thought, that he would restore to me my poetic gift—which would have been a sort of transaction!'

They all look at me like I am a creature you might find living in a bog. Viv says, 'Lionel, you have before you a choice.'

The sound of her voice makes the breath catch in my chest. 'What is the choice?' I ask.

'You may face, for your crimes, trial by jury or by combat.'

'What crimes?' I ask.

They all look at me again with that flat look they are so fond of. Even Kensington does not seem eager to defend me. 'Oh,' I say. 'Those crimes.'

'Combat or jury?' Viv says again.

'I don't know!' I say. I don't want to stand trial. It is an absurd notion. 'Who is the jury?'

'They are before you.'

I glance at the faces of my friends. They are not soft. 'Well,' I say, 'that is clearly not an acceptable option. Whom must I fight?'

'You choose combat, then?' presses my tenacious wife. Was she always so? I do not know. The truth is, I know very little of her personality. I had thought she had none; apparently this is not the case.

'Wait a minute!' I say. 'I don't know! You didn't answer— who am I to fight? Because if it's Ashley, that's obviously not a good option either.'

'I require no champion,' says Vivien haughtily.

'You mean I'm to fight *you*? Very well, let us begin!'

Vivien is not a small woman; she is in fact very nearly as tall as I. But she is a woman all the same—and after all, I am become in the last two days quite a duellist.

'If you will, let it be so,' says she. A flash in her eyes makes me abruptly uncomfortable. It is what I have come to identify as the Lancaster Look—the same one her brother had when he stood over me pugilistically, and when he hurled the rock at the policeman. Hubert seems not to possess it.* 'Ashley, Lizzie, Simmons, Mr Kensington, Your Highness†—you will serve as our judges, and ensure that the combat is conducted

---

*Time will tell.—HL.

†I am at times forgotten by my family, but it does not bother me. I like to think it is because of my discretion.—HL.

honourably upon both sides. My husband fights to prove his love and remove the blemish from his name. If he falls, his love is false and his name besmirched forever.'

I try to laugh at her little speech, but it comes out chalky in my mouth. No one else laughs. Lizzie and Kensington and the Gentleman sit down side by side on the sofa. After a moment's deliberation, Hubert joins them. There is not room enough, and they sit with shoulders touching like sardines in a can. Lancaster leans against a bookshelf. Simmons stands at ease. They are prepared, it seems, for a spectacle. Their looks are intent and I feel awkward, uncertain what to do with my hands. I wonder if this is what it is like to appear upon a stage.

My wife removes her coat and hat. She hands them to Lizzie, then takes from Hubert his sword. I realise that I am still holding the other. So it is to be swords. I was not certain what she meant by trial by combat, but it now becomes clear. I prepare to fight my fourth duel in as many days. (Does my encounter with Hubert count as a duel?* Perhaps not. Nor I suppose does our run-in with the police. But they *felt* like duels, which is I believe the most important thing.)

Vivien tests the weight and balance of the sword with alarming professionalism. It had not occurred to me that perhaps she knows how to use it. Is such a thing possible? Surely not—I suppose she is simply repeating a procedure she has read in a novel.

Then she attacks, and I am proved quite wrong.

I defend myself as best as I am able, but I am no swords-

*I believe it does not. I do not count it as such, for myself.—HL.

man. I flail about wildly as she leaps and dances with the blade, flashing first this way then that, darting and lunging and displaying such skill as I have never witnessed. I should marvel at it, were I not doing my best to avoid being spitted.

As she presses her attack, she says, 'You married me for my—' (lunge) '—*money*. You never even—' (thrust) '—*tried*. You never even—' (swashing blow) '—*pretended* to like me. You never—' (another thrust) '—*spoke* to me. Never—' (slash) '—*looked* at me. And then, you sold me to the—' (riposte) '—*Devil*. You are the worst husband—' She disarms me. '*Ever*.' My weapon spins across the room, hits a bookshelf, knocks over a bust of Ovid, and falls to the thickly carpeted floor with a thud.

Her sword is at my throat. She is breathing heavily, her hair has come slightly undone, her cheeks are pink, her eyes are bright, and she is the most beautiful woman I have ever seen upon this earth.

'Where did you learn to do that?'

'I was a champion fencer at school. Which you'd know, if you'd ever bothered to talk to me.'

'I'm sorry.'

She does not reply. Nor does she lower her sword. She says instead, 'Verdict?'

'He doesn't love you and is a cad,' says Lizzie promptly.

'Seconded,' says Lancaster.

'Carried,' says Hubert.

'Now wait a moment,' I protest. 'That isn't true!'

'You chose trial by combat. You have lost the trial. It is proven,' says Vivien.

'That's not how it works!'

'That is precisely how it works,' says she. 'Only, if we were being quite proper I should run you through.'

'That's a terrible system!' I cry. 'It doesn't prove anything!'*

'If you loved me, you would have won.'

'But I do love you!'

'Apparently not.'

'I do!'

'Then pick up your sword and prove it.'

'No,' I say.

'Then leave.'

'Excuse me?'

'Either prove your love, or leave my house.'

'It's *my* house!'

On the couch, even Kensington puts his face in his hands. 'I mean,' I stammer, 'it's *our* house! You can't order me out.'

'Pick up your sword.'

'No.'

'Then you don't love me.'

'I do love you.'

'Then pick up your sword.'

I cross the room and pick it up. Who is this maddening woman? And what has she done with the snivelling creature who so plagued me for the last six months? I turn back toward her. She has not moved. She is standing tall, her bosom rising and falling from the exertion. The colour in her cheeks highlights the colour of her eyes, which is an impossible blue.

---

*I do myself favour the modern judicial system.—HL.

'You're a poet,' I say. I do not know why I say it.

'What?' she says, and I believe I have caught her off guard.

'You're a poet. You never told me that.'

'You never asked,' she counters, which is true.

'Lizzie found your poems. They're exquisite.'

She says nothing. Her sword is still raised and is pointing straight at me, but her breathing has quickened, and I wonder if I have scored a hit.

I do not know why I say what I say next—perhaps to press my imagined advantage?—and I do so against my better judgment; but after a moment of internal struggle I blurt, 'They have no structure.'

'Excuse me?' she says, eyebrows in her hair.

I try to stop, but I cannot. 'They have no metre. They don't rhyme. They have no *structure*.'

'Are you actually talking to me about the structure of my poems right now?' she demands, incredulous. She advances to within a blade's length of me.

'No, I'm not,' I say, 'that's my point—they *have* no structure.'

She strikes at my head. 'They don't NEED structure!'

I parry without thinking and cry, 'Everything needs structure!'

'Poetry doesn't,' she says, lunging.

I sweep her thrust to my left. 'That's absurd,' I say.

'You're absurd!' she cries, attacking with a flurry of overhead blows. 'Poetry is not precise! Poetry exists only to capture everything that CAN'T be captured. Putting it in blank verse doesn't make it any more capturable, it just makes it look pretty on a page.'

I manage somehow to come through the hailstorm unscathed, and say, 'You realise you're spitting in the face of five hundred years of genius.'

'No,' she says, sword raised but not attacking, 'I'm suggesting that for five hundred years people haven't considered that they might be missing something.'*

'You're impossible,' I say.

She looks at me. *'You're* calling *me* impossible?'

'YES!' I say. 'You put words together so beautifully, but you do so in a wilfully sloppy fashion.'

'IT'S NOT SLOPPY!'

'IT IS SLOPPY!' I surprise us both by attacking. It is an ungainly, lumbering sort of attack—but it is an attack all the same. She wards it off with no ado whatever and counters. For a few moments we advance and retreat in turns, in a reasonable facsimile of a fencing match.

I don't know why we're fighting. I forget why we're yelling at each other about poetry. All I want to do in the world is pick her up and spin her around and kiss her and tell her again and again how much I love her, and how sorry I am, and how foolish I've been, and how desperately I wish I could take back

---

*The fact is that both my cousins here were taking rather hard lines in an argument without any hard lines. Metrical modes have always fallen in and out of favour. I believe expending so much passion on such a diaphanous subject to be silly and misjudged. I should never have done so.—HL.

the last six months and return again to our wedding night and—

'When was the last time you wrote a poem?' she demands, breaking in upon my thoughts. I am thrown off and miss my guard and find her sword again at my throat.

'Don't change the subject,' I say.

'When?'

'Don't change the subject.'

'When?'

'The day before our wedding!'

'Why?' she asks.

'Because a poet can't live without love.'

A shadow passes over her face. Her sword point presses against my throat, in the hollow just above the intersection of my collarbones. 'Why didn't you love me?'

'Because you'd never love me.'

'BUT I DID LOVE YOU,' she cries, pressing harder.

'But you never told me,' I point out.

'I DID WHEN YOU ASKED ME TO MARRY YOU AND I SAID YES.' I feel a trickle of blood.

'Obliquely,' I mutter.

Vivien has regained her cool. She drops her arm to her side; the tip of her sword cuts a line in the carpet. 'There is nothing oblique about a proposal accepted.'

I cannot argue with the soundness of her reasoning, so I change tacks. 'Why did you tell your brother that you loved me?'

'Because I did.'

'Only at first.'

'No,' she says. 'I loved you.'

'Yes, I know, but then you stopped loving me.'

'No I didn't.'

My heart is beating very quickly. 'What do you mean?'

'What do you mean what do I mean?' she demands. 'I feel as though I'm being extraordinarily clear.'

'So—' I can hardly form the words. 'So you still love me.'

She does not say anything, but there is something in her face.

'You do!' I cry. 'You still love me!'

She again says nothing.

'I love you,' I say.

Still she does not speak. Her knuckles are white upon her sword hilt. I do not know if she is about to kiss me or skewer me.

'I'm serious,' I say. 'I love you. I think I've always loved you.'

'You've demonstrated it poorly,' she says.

'I know. I'm sorry. Please take me back.'

She stares at me, as if waiting for something. I stare back. Her eyes are—

'Is that it?' she says. She sounds angry. Her sword arm is rising.

'What do you mean?'

Her voice is withering. 'You. Sold me. To. The. *Devil*. And your apology consists of "I'm sorry, please take me back"?'

'Brevity is the soul of wit,' I suggest.

'DON'T QUOTE POLONIUS AT ME, YOU STUPID MAN.' She falls upon me with three overhead blows in rapid succession from her left side to my right. I counter them all, and she draws back like a serpent.

'Viv, look—'

'Don't call me Viv.'

'Mrs Savage,' I say, and she glares at me. 'Vivien! Please. Listen to me.'

She has no intention of doing so. Instead she raises her blade to her face, examining it minutely for damage, and asks, 'Is this about your pride? Did I wound it by not falling at your feet?'

'You wounded my pride by letting me marry you for your money.'

'That makes no sense,' she says, returning her attention from her sword to me. Her eyes are steely, I pun to myself.

'So why didn't you say no?'

'Because I loved you!'

'But you knew I was only after your money.'

'I DIDN'T KNOW THAT.'

'Well, you should have,' I say.

I can hear the rapid beating of my own heart. She says nothing more. 'Why did you marry me?' I ask at length. 'What were you thinking?'

'I was thinking that your favourite book is *The Idylls of the King,* and that maybe there was a reason for that. I was thinking that you love your little sister so much that I genuinely fear for the safety of her future husband, whomever he may be. I was thinking of the way your hand twitches when it's not holding a pen. And I was thinking of how if you stopped worrying so much about keeping the metre, which has never been your strong suit, you could be a truly great poet.'

'There will never be a great poet without structure.'

'Structure and blank verse aren't synonyms,' she says stubbornly.

'So I should use hexameter?' I demand. 'Spenserian stanzas? Alexandrine couplets?'

'Don't be daft.'

'I don't know what you're saying!' I say.

'Structure has nothing to do with metre.'

'It has everything to do with metre!'

'NO,' says my tempestuous wife. 'Structure is about the layout of ideas. Metre is just the arrangement of words in a line.'

'That's not true!'

'It is! You're being thick on purpose!'

'Poetry out of metre can be written by a child,' I protest.

'So can blank verse,' she counters.

'Not good blank verse.'

With the ghost of a smile she says, 'Unless it is an extraordinarily intelligent child.'

'Unless it is an extraordinarily intelligent child,' I concede.

'But it's the same with free verse!' she bursts out. 'Of course a child can write it, but unless the child is Mozart it won't be any good!'

'Mozart wrote poetry?' I ask. I hadn't been aware, but I ought to find some of it.*

---

*What is especially sad about this remark is that Mr Savage meant every word of it with an ingenuous sincerity quite unlike him. I am inclined to side with Miss Savage in the belief that he has in his pursuit of knowledge been rather lopsided.—HL.

'Oh for God's sake,' says Vivien. I do not understand. 'You could be good!' she cries.

'I *am* good,' I reply with wounded dignity.

'You could be great,' she says.*

'HOW?'

'By not being a STUPID, arrogant—' She regains her composure. 'By listening to me. By letting me help you. I want to help you.'

I do not say anything for a very long time. I am waging a war with my vanity. I at last conquer it, and say, 'Fine.'

'Fine what?'

In answer, I pull all the wretched scraps of poetry I've been labouring over off my desk and throw them into the fireplace. I drop my sword with a clatter on the hearthstones. 'I surrender,' I say. 'You win.'

Her jaw clenches and she raises her sword. 'Then you don't love me,' says the impossible creature.

'You,' I say, as my poems blaze, 'are infuriating.'

'You married me,' she points out.

'I married you,' I repeat. Saying the words aloud clarifies something in my mind. I pick up my sword. Very deliberately, I advance on her. I raise the blade to my lips in salute (it is something I have read), kneel before her, and lay it at her feet.

'Vivien,' I say. 'I am through fighting you. I am yours, body and soul. If ever I give you cause to doubt that again, bid me pick up this sword and I shall defend the assertion with my

---

*It is my own personal opinion that this is not true. I believe that Vivien has the genuine poetic spark, but that Mr Savage does not. I may perhaps be wrong in this. Time will tell.—HL.

life. In the meantime, let it be my pledge. If you will have me, I am yours.'*

I look into her shining eyes. I see myself reflected in them. She is silent a very long while.

'Simmons,' she says at last. 'Please hang these swords upon the wall. There they shall be kept until they are wanted.'

'Very good, ma'am,' says Simmons. 'I shall do so directly. Will there be anything else?'

Vivien glances at me. 'Yes,' she says. 'I need my things moved out of Lizzie's room. My husband and I have a poetical argument to finish, which I suspect will take several nights at least. It would be inconvenient to have to walk between bedrooms.'†

I may be dreaming it, but I am nearly sure that Simmons is smiling. 'Of course, ma'am,' he says, and leaves the room with his customary good grace.

---

*This was I believe well done.—HL.

†She said this with such an air that I almost thought there lay a less chaste sentiment beneath her words. Doubtless I was mistaken.—HL.

Sixteen

In Which the Adventurers Depart.

Well,' says the Gentleman. 'That was very informative. Well fought, my friend!'

I feel such an overpowering sense of goodwill that I do not even remember that I am angry with him. I bow to the couch, which applauds politely.

'Now will someone *please*,' I say, 'tell me what this "plan" was?'

'Oh,' says Vivien, 'it was nothing really—just a rather misguided attempt to make you fall in love with me.'

I smile and say, 'It worked, darling.'

'You forget yourself,' she says coldly, and my heart stops. 'You did not *pass* the trial, you *circumvented* it. We are still a long way from "darling."'

Lancaster laughs heartily and cries, 'Capital, by Christ!' Vivien cracks a smile, and my heart resumes its march. I have still to learn this peculiar woman.

'It really is a pity,' says Vivien. 'It was a splendid plan, and you quite ruined it. I had been building an imaginary lover almost since our marriage.'

'A *what*?' I say.

'An imaginary lover. To make you jealous. I began as soon as I realised the pit we had fallen into. I left signs everywhere.'

'Signs?'

'Yes—men's gloves, canes, hats, things like that. Love notes—I drafted them and had Simmons copy them out in a male hand. I had flowers and chocolates and sundry gifts sent to me from anonymous admirers. Surely you noticed the escalation in the last month? It was all driving toward a carefully orchestrated abscondtion which was to leave you in paroxysms of jealousy during which you would be struck with a thunderbolt—you loved me, and couldn't bear to see me in the arms of another man!'

I *am* thunderstruck. To suppose that this entire time, my wife has been a step ahead of me. There is only one peculiar thing—'I never noticed,' I say.*

'You never noticed what?'

'Anything. The gloves, the gifts, the notes. I was aware of them, but it never occurred to me that you could be unfaithful. I assumed the notes were from Simmons to Mrs Davis—' (Vivien shudders) '—and the gloves forgotten at parties.'

'But did the parties not tip you off?'

'What do you mean?'

---

*This is in many ways typical of Mr Savage. It is also the most amusing feature in a series of events which, in retrospect, was laced with some little amusement.—HL.

'You weren't suspicious that I should want to conceal my identity and dance with strange men on a weekly basis?'

'You— Do you mean— Are you telling me that you don't like society parties?'

She stares at me for a long moment. 'Who,' she says, 'do you think I am?'

'You don't! You don't actually like parties!'

'Of course I don't *like* parties.'*

'But, then, where *were* you these past days?'

'Hubert's, of course. I certainly wasn't going to take Mother into my confidence, or she'd never have forgiven you.'

'I'm so sorry,' says Hubert to me, concerned I suppose that I might hold ill will against him for his part in this plot.† But I am preoccupied with Vivien, and pay him no mind.

I sink down shakily into my desk chair. 'It was all an act,' I say, only beginning to comprehend the ramifications of what she is telling me.

'What was?'

'All of it! The parties, the frivolity, the flirting. That wasn't you at all?'

'Certainly not!' She sounds offended that I could ever have considered it. 'If I were a man I should accompany Ashley everywhere; but I am not, and so I cannot. I loathe society. It is a game which must be played, that is all.'

I forget that we have an audience until Lizzie says, 'Nellie,

---

*Vivien many times in the six months we were constructing and executing the plan complained to me of these parties. She quite loathed them.—HL.
†I was not, but he does.—HL.

you are in grave danger of being supplanted in my affections by your wife.'

I ignore her. 'But if— If you had just— Everything I hated about you wasn't actually . . . *you*! Why did you not simply appear to me as you are?'

'I did!' she cries. 'I did, and for the first fortnight of our marriage you ignored me entirely! I was a new bride, nervous and uncertain and in undiscovered country, and you locked yourself in this study and made it eminently clear you wanted nothing to do with me.'

'But that's because I was composing! I was finishing— I forget what I was finishing, but I couldn't be interrupted by *matrimony*! You're a poet, you must understand! I was composing. And when I emerged, I found you . . . vapid.'

'Where is it?'

'What?'

'What you were composing.'

'I forget what it was.'

'Liar.'

'It's in my desk.'

'Why is it not published?'

'Because I couldn't finish it.'

'Why?'

'I don't know. I became . . . stuck.'

'I COULD HAVE HELPED YOU GET UNSTUCK!'

With an exasperated sigh she throws herself down in an armchair. My head is spinning. There is a large part of me which is quite miserable, a larger one which is wracked with guilt, and a third and largest which feels as though I am the luckiest man upon the face of this earth.

'Well,' says Lizzie, 'in a sense the plan worked perfectly.'

'Yes,' says Kensington supportively. 'Mr Savage *did* realise his mistake, and through Mrs Savage's absence fell in love with her. I believe that everything is resolved.'

'Not everything!' cries Lancaster. 'I am still undone.'

Viv lifts her head and smiles at her brother mischievously. 'You know,' she says, 'I've been thinking it over—and I'm very near to hitting upon a plan for you! It will likely be rather dangerous, though.'

'Will it involve piracy?' he asks, perking up.

'It will.'

'And derring-do?'

'And rapscallionism.'

'And rakishness?'

'Rakishness, disguise, and swashbuckling.'

'God I've missed you!' exclaims Lancaster, and I can only agree with him. That I should ever have thought this woman anything but magnificent is and for the rest of my life will remain a source of deepest shame.*

'Or you could come with me,' says the Gentleman.

We all swing to face him. 'I could what?' says Lancaster.

'I mean, if you were so inclined—I am certainly not exercising any sort of metaphysical authority, let it be understood.

---

*As it should. There are very, very few women upon this earth who are like Vivien.—HL.

But if you were at all interested (I understand you are an explorer of sorts) you could certainly accompany me home.'

'Home—to Hell?'

The Gentleman winces. 'Oh,' he says, 'I do so hate that word.'

'Essex Grove,' I put in. 'Essex Grove is a much better name—it makes it sound more inviting.'

'Precisely!' cries the Gentleman, much gratified by my memory. He flashes me a shy smile.

'Well,' says Lancaster, 'that is interesting, by Christ. I considered stowing away on the four o'clock train to Paris, but I seem to have missed it. And so—'

'What time is it?' asks Hubert sharply.

Lancaster looks at his watch and says, 'Seven minutes past four.'

'Oh dear,' says Hubert in great agitation. 'I am so sorry. You must excuse me, what? Sorry!' And he flees from the room.*

'Do you know,' says Vivien thoughtfully as we stare after him in astonishment, 'Hubert is the first man in my life who has offered to fight for my honour.'†

Lancaster is about to protest, but the Gentleman speaks first. He points to the half-finished canvas (which is still upon the easel) and asks Lizzie, 'Did you paint that?'

---

*I was late for a rather delicate appointment, and to miss it altogether would have imperilled certain negotiations of international importance.—HL.

†This is to me a point of great pride. If you'll forgive a play on words which I would almost certainly deplore if Mr Savage committed it: I may have fought for her honour, but the honour was mine.—HL.

'I did,' she says.

I open my mouth to apologise for her impropriety, but the Gentleman says, 'I like it very much.'

'So do I!' says Lancaster like a puppy. He peers at it. 'What are those circles?'

'Nothing,' I hasten to reply before Lizzie can. But she pays Lancaster no attention. She is gazing at her handiwork.

She crinkles her nose. 'It's a terrible painting.'

'Oh, I don't think so,' says the Gentleman. 'It's the work of an inexperienced artist, certainly. But it's clear that you *under-stand* how to make a painting great, even if you do not yet have the skill.'

'Do you really think so?'

'Certainly. It's the understanding that counts. It's like music. Mrs Savage was speaking of Mozart—when you listen to Mozart, you of course hear his proficiency—you recognise, if you will, that he is good at his job. But what makes him great is his preternatural grasp of things you cannot even begin to comprehend. Surely you know what I mean?'

'No,' I say, even as Vivien and Lancaster answer as one in the affirmative. I sigh inwardly, knowing what is to come next.

'I am afraid I must plead ignorance,' says Lizzie with a venomous glance in my direction. (I was correct in my deduction.) 'Those responsible for my education have been found sorely wanting in certain areas. Ashley, are you really going with him?'

'Yes,' says Lancaster slowly, 'I believe I am. You see, the thing is, I've built my life around the explication of things that cannot be explained and the exploration of places that exist which everyone says don't. And now I have an opportunity, a very rare opportunity, to visit one. And I believe I once told Mummy I'd be damned before I got married, ha ha ha!'* His wonted good spirits seem to be returning by the moment.

'Good,' says Lizzie. 'I'm going with you.'

'Now see here,' says Lancaster, shocked, 'you can't just up and—'

'Are you telling me what I can and cannot do, Ashley Lancaster?' asks Lizzie sharply.

He looks appropriately cowed. After a moment, he says in a small voice, 'It will be nice to have some company.'

'It will indeed!' cries the Gentleman, beaming. 'I hope that while Mr Lancaster is off exploring the Elysian Fields you wouldn't be opposed to remaining behind in my cottage and drinking some tea and reading some books and perhaps even conversing a little? I do get most dreadfully lonely sometimes.'

'The pleasure would be all mine,' says Lizzie with a curtsy. 'And you can teach me all about art and music and things!'

'Lizzie,' I say, 'were you intending to ask my permission?'

'Certainly not,' she says with some surprise.

'You two could come!' says Lancaster.

'No,' says Viv, 'I don't think so. We have a very great deal to talk about. And,' she adds with a frank glance which makes me turn crimson, 'we have other unfinished business besides.'

'Oh good!' says Lizzie. 'I've been trying to tell Nellie that he really must—'

---

*Lady Lancaster, upon learning of this exchange and subsequent events, was deeply unamused.—HL.

Mercifully, she is interrupted by the Gentleman. 'Oh dear,' he says suddenly.

'What?' asks Lancaster, as eager to change the subject as I am.

'I've just thought of something. It's rather difficult for me to bring home guests in their corporal form. I quite forgot.'

Lancaster's face falls. 'But sir,' he says, 'there must be a way! Tell me that there's a way. I must leave England immediately.'

'There is a way,' says the Gentleman dubiously. 'But it will take some doing, and may not be achievable yet. It would be easiest with some form of aerial transport.'

Lancaster, Lizzie, Kensington, Viv, and I all begin to laugh at the same time.

'What is funny?' enquires the Gentleman.

'I think,' says Viv, 'that the trip will not be so difficult after all.'

'How do you know about the *Cirrus*?' I demand.

'Ashley and Simmons and Lizzie told me all about it when I was here this morning. It sounds very grand.'

'I— Oh.' In my state I cannot wrap my mind around everything. I give up.

'Am I to understand that you have access to a flying machine?' asks the Gentleman.

'Yes!' exclaims Lizzie, looking at Kensington proudly. 'Will invented one! It's what he landed on the roof.'

'But that's perfect!' says the Gentleman. 'Would he be amenable to . . . ?'

'There is nothing I should like more!' says Kensington, flushing at Lizzie's obvious pride in him.

The Gentleman claps his hands delightedly. 'Then it's decided! And I don't mean to rush you, but I am in fact on a bit of a schedule—would you be offended, Mrs Savage, if we didn't stay for tea?'

'Not in the least,' she replies.

'I need to dress,' says Lizzie. 'I'll meet you on the roof.' She hurries out of the room.

Lancaster does some hasty packing, I call for Simmons, and we make our way upstairs. The airship is perched elegantly between two chimneys. It has a few bullet holes, but somehow they only serve to increase the distinction of the craft. Vivien and the Gentleman are suitably impressed by it, and say as much. Kensington blushes, and in tearing spirits vaults onto the bridge and begins warming up the engine.

Lancaster arrives, changed into high boots, canvas trousers, and a sturdy-looking coat belted at the waist. He carries a rucksack and a rifle, and has rakishly tucked a machete in his belt. Lizzie emerges a moment later, fully clothed (for which I am immeasurably grateful) and vibrating with excitement.

She and Lancaster and the Gentleman face us for farewells.

Lancaster steps forward first. I extend my hand, but he ignores it and sweeps me up into a bone-crushing Krakatoan hug.* 'If you hurt my sister again,' he says in my ear, 'I will eat your heart.'

'And if you let mine into harm's way,' I say into his, 'I'll eat yours.'

He sets me down and grins at me warmly. I believe we are friends. He embraces Viv and says something to her, but I do not attend—for the Gentleman is pumping my hand enthusiastically and expressing his fervent wish that we meet often. I quite genuinely echo the sentiment.

While Lancaster helps the Gentleman into the machine, Lizzie steps forward. 'Vivien,' she says, 'I am sorry that we've

---

*See page 96.—HL.

had only such a short time to meet. But I promise you we'll be wonderful friends someday.'

'Oh, I am quite sure of it,' replies Viv, smiling.

Lizzie turns to me. 'Nellie,' she says sternly, 'when I return I expect my room to be vacated.' She hesitates. There is a glimmer in her eye, and she adds imperiously, 'And I want a violin!'* Then she smiles, flings her arms around my neck, and says, 'I love you.'

'And I love you,' I say, squeezing her for all I'm worth. 'Look after them—they need someone sensible.'

'So they do,' she says. I set her down. She kisses Vivien, kisses Simmons, and hurries to the machine. Lancaster boosts her up and Kensington helps her over the rail. I am gratified to see the solicitousness with which they both treat her.† Once she is aboard, Lancaster tosses in his rucksack and hauls himself up after it.

Kensington throws a lever and the wings accelerate into a blur. He appears again at the rail. He grins at us, bows slightly, and pulls on his goggles. Slowly, the machine begins to take on the appearance of weightlessness; then it rises. I am wonderstruck anew. I have learned by my acquaintance with the young inventor that there are two types of Progress in the world—and if one is deplorable the other is just the opposite. Lizzie, Lancaster, and the Gentleman are waving to us like

---

*Upon her return, her room was in fact vacated, and there was a violin lying in the middle of her bed. I know, because I purchased it. She has since become quite an accomplished musician.—HL.

†All men treat Miss Savage with much solicitousness. I have often noted and been amused by it. It often makes them look quite ridiculous.—HL.

madmen. Kensington does something to another lever, and the airship takes off like a shot.

It soars up over the rooftops of London, higher and higher until it is just a speck. Then the speck disappears into the fog.

Simmons and Viv and I stand in silence for what feels like a very long time, hands still raised in farewell. Eventually, I ask a question that has been on my mind: 'Simmons, was it you who alerted Scotland Yard?'

'I'm afraid so, sir,' he replies. 'I was worried that otherwise you would attempt to fly yourself into a volcano.'

'That was good of you, Simmons.'

'Thank you, sir.'

'I cannot, however, approve of "Alec Rubeum."* In the future, should you be called upon to invent anarchist splinter cells, I shall hold you to a higher standard.'

'Yes, sir. I fear I was in rather a hurry. I shall endeavour to do better next time.'

'I don't doubt it, Simmons. I have always said that you are a paragon, and I'm damned proud that you condescend to call Pocklington Place your home.'

'Thank you, sir. And sir, if I may say, I'm damned proud to call you my employer.'

I am so touched by that I fear I might cry. But I do not, for I am an Englishman. After a moment, Simmons discreetly removes himself, muttering something about mounting the swords upon the wall.

---

*The learned will note that the *rubeum allec* is a herring noted for its rosy flesh.—HL.

Viv and I are left alone.

'Well,' I say at last.

'Well,' she echoes.

'Does this mean,' I ask, thinking of Lizzie's emptying room, 'that you've forgiven me?'

'Lionel Savage,' says she, 'you ignored me for six months and then sold me to the Devil. I doubt very much if I shall ever forgive you.' My heart drops. 'But for better or worse,' she continues, and my spirit rises like Kensington's machine, 'I am your wife.'

My heart soars. She turns her face toward mine and looks solemnly into my eyes. We stare at one another, seeing before us a very long future filled with innumerable adventures.

Then she says with a dev'lish twinkle, 'Free verse isn't the *absence* of structure.'

And at last, I kiss her.

Acknowledgments

The bundle of pages in your left hand is, I fear, riddled with faults—anachronisms, inconsistencies, and infelicitous turns of phrase. The responsibility for these is mine alone. But I hope there are merits, too—and these are thanks to a bunch of really generous and brilliant people.

Mitchell Waters is the best agent a boy can have. Big thanks to him, Steven Salpeter, Anna Abreu, Holly Frederick, Jonathan Lyons, Sarah Perillo, and the whole Curtis Brown crew. Ed Park's deft, patient, and gentle editorial hand is a thing of beauty. I'm beholden to Annie Badman's tireless good humor, and to everyone at Penguin Press. Mahendra Singh's illustrations are basically everything I've ever wanted. Sarah Crichton's kind mentorship is Virgilian in its guidance. Olivia Birdsall suffered through more unfortunate pages of my writing than anyone should ever have to, and taught me a great deal.

This book began life as a play, and its first director was my dear friend Saheem Ali. Thanks to Pipeline Theatre Company for facilitating that first reading; Laura Braza, for astute direction of the subsequent workshop; the casts, for bringing it all to life; and Kristina Makowski, for shaping the world with her costumes. Special thanks to Tom Oppenheim, Libby Jensen, and the Stella Adler Studio of Acting for their exhaustive support.

Sophia, Isabella, and Molly Kensington have been very generous in allowing me access to their family papers. I owe them a great debt.

This book wouldn't and couldn't exist without the support of my family. Ma has been unstinting in her help and her encouragement. She's the smartest and the kindest person in the world. My big brothers are awesomeness personified, and I still want to be them when I grow up. Amanda and Kai gave me hope for the future and made sure I ate. Grandma Dee instilled in me an appreciation for art: it's thanks to her that I know the difference between Bosch and Breughel and can tell you with relative certainty who painted the ceiling of the Sistine Chapel.

Finally, thanks to Abigail—my partner in all things.